An

Michael stood over Jo like a statue, his lust-darkened eyes working over her, appreciating her nakedness. Jo suddenly felt like the cat he had described as her spirit. A vivid image sprang to her mind, of stretching and rolling on her back, pawing the air, allowing him to see glimpses of her hidden treasure. In the real world she reined in her instincts – only a tiny gesture of arousal getting past her defences as her thigh involuntarily slumped open a loose, provocative inch.

He saw it, licked his dry lips, and his mouth hung open for long seconds. He had caught another tantalising glimpse of her glistening seam, and his eyes locked upon it, hungry and wanting.

By the same author:

UNHALLOWED RITES

A FEAST FOR THE SENSES

Animal Passions

MARTINE MARQUAND

Black Lace novels contain sexual fantasies.
In real life, make sure you practise safe sex.

First published in 2000 by
Black Lace
Thames Wharf Studios,
Rainville Road, London W6 9HA

Copyright © Martine Marquand 2000

The right of Martine Marquand to be identified as the
Author of this Work has been asserted by her in
accordance with the Copyright, Designs and Patents Act
1988.

Typeset by SetSystems Ltd, Saffron Walden, Essex
Printed and bound by Mackays of Chatham PLC

ISBN 0 352 33499 1

Chapter One

'*All about you are the snares of temptation, traps to catch the unwary. Sins of the appetites, sins of the flesh . . .*'

Brother Colin was in full flow, his broad face flushing as he warmed to his favourite sermon theme. At the back of the mission hall, Jo wriggled along the hard pew, squeezing her leg against Graham's taut thigh. Graham looked like an angel; eyes clear as blue crystal fixed on the altar, skin flawless as a girls. But inside, he was a devil. If Brother Colin only knew just how much trouble Graham had restraining his newly ravenous appetites, he would probably have a coronary straight into the arms of his lectern.

'*For the road to salvation is narrow. The paths of destruction are broad and many. How tempting it is to stray off the path . . .*'

Graham shot her a warning glance – half frightened, half yearning – but stayed taut and still. Jo smiled back innocently – but casually picked up her jacket and flung it, apparently artlessly, across both their laps. She was going to have some fun with Graham –

1

pompous do-gooder that he was. And Brother Colin's sermon was the perfect backdrop to prove once and for all that golden-boy Graham was just as weak as the sinners whom they all publicly claimed they wanted to help – but so much despised in private.

Jo's hand began to snake under the hot fabric, finding the rough cotton of Graham's jeans.

'No,' he suddenly mouthed silently, frown lines creasing his teenage brow. But at seventeen years old, what boy could resist the temptation? Graham was a tight-packed bundle of testosterone and newly burgeoning flesh. Shoulders newly broadened, voice newly deep, the fuzzy hair that had started to grow on his chest, his chin and even his belly – all of this fascinated Jo. And as for his penis – much to Jo's amazement, that seemed to be growing bigger and fatter every week. She liked to keep a check on it, she told him. And when she checked its size, she liked to make sure it was all in fully functioning order. Now that really was fun.

He was shaking his head at her now, but trying not to attract the attention of John Elmore, one of the mission house's oldest members. He was sitting just the other side of Graham, listening attentively to the sermon, his pale, weepy eyes fixed on the sign written in huge crimson lettering across the bare white walls of the room: BE NOT AS THE BRUTE BEASTS THAT HAVE NO UNDERSTANDING.

Oh, if only we all could be, Jo sighed. Graham, despite all his missionary zeal, was a brute beast under the skin. It was the contradiction that really turned her on: all that outer purity barely covering the seething chaos of his teenage drives. She could feel it now, as a muscle twitched in anticipation along the length of his thigh. Slowly her fingertips drifted, like a dancing cranefly, up to his crotch. Ah, yes, his jeans had stretched pleasantly above a growing bulge. She could hear Graham's breathing accelerate – and then suddenly, as her fingers grazed the mound of his balls, his breathing stopped. Almost audible to the rest of the congregation, he sighed with pleasure.

As slowly as she could, she let her greedy fingers measure the tented breadth of his prick. In answer, a sharp jab of lust seemed to spear her own emerging clitoris. Wriggling a little closer to her prey, Jo began to stroke the thickness of his cock, pushing the tight cloth of his trousers even tighter around it, like a too-tight glove. Oh, he was restless now, leaning back against the pew, teeth gritted, a sheen of excitement glowing over his blond baby features. Just to tease him, she found the thick end and squeezed it, eliciting a murmured 'Jo!' that sounded more anguished than pleasurable.

John Elmore twisted noisily round and stared at them, his white eyebrows lowered in annoyance. Startled, Graham pretended to sneeze, then smiled and nodded pleasantly over to the old man. Oh, that angelic, pearly-toothed smile of his – it always worked miracles. Jo turned her face away, laughing to herself. He would be doing more than sneezing if she had her chance.

Nothing short of the Second Coming would stop Brother Colin, now that he was giving full vent to his bottled-up feelings. And that was what Jo thought they were; nothing but good old jealousy of anyone who had a healthy sex drive – and the opportunity to use it. Everyone knew his wife Enid had 'gone off' sex years ago, after the birth of their youngest child. So, all around him, Colin saw nothing but snares and traps, nubile girls in tight clothes, provocative advertisements, hidden innuendoes. The man must be like

3

a simmering volcano, she thought. After all, that was what she had discovered about Graham.

There was no way she would have guessed, up to those few weeks ago. After all, Graham was always polite to the verge of primness, the grown-ups' favourite with his sweet smile and angelic looks. When her mother had died, Jo had never for one moment expected to stay on with her father in Africa. He was too busy evangelising to bother with his one troublesome teenage daughter. So she had found herself here in the winter coldness at the Northford Mission House, with a whole new extended family. And of her new adoptive brothers and sisters, Graham had always lorded it over the rest as the most holy and untouchable of all. Sometimes he even took to the pulpit himself, speaking against all the sins of modern youth today. It had been enough to make you want to vomit, all that saccharine sweetness. Then came that one day when she had found out about the true Graham.

Slowly, her fingers reached for the metal tab of his zipper. The problem was, as she gradually unzipped the teeth, a quiet but distinctive rasping sound escaped from under the folds of her jacket. Guiltily, she looked up. John Elmore was staring over inquisitively. Graham helpfully feigned another sneezing fit. In a second she had his zip open – and there, as hot as hell itself, erupted his gorgeous cock. Luxuriously, she began to run her hand along its length, from the fat, knotty base where golden curls now flourished, to the swollen bulb-like end.

Suddenly she wondered how much time they had left. Brother Colin had got to the point in his diatribe where he compared the lust-crazed masses of the modern world to the inhabitants of Babylon. And what she really wanted was not just to hot Graham up

4

in the middle of this most sanctimonious congregation, but to – well, to make him lose that famous air of sanctity. Make him lose control. It had to be here, in this room soaked in the scent of wood polish, dying flowers and the sour breath of selfish prayers. What she really wanted was to crack that priggish mask with a spasm of uncontrolled lust. And the proof of that would come in uncontrollable dollops, all over the lining of her jacket.

The trouble was, even just thinking about it made Jo unbearably horny. She could feel the heat building up between her legs and every time her fingertips trailed across the increasingly damp end of Graham's cock her clitoris pulsed feverishly. Yet it had been him who had begun it all; prim, priggish Graham who had secretly revealed his sinful, uncontrollable self.

Jo had just taken a bath and, quite oblivious to her surroundings, she stepped out and began pampering herself in front of the mirror. There were no full-length mirrors at all at the Northford Mission but there, in the austere shared bathroom on the second landing, was the one mirror that allowed her to see her body from head to waist. For nineteen years old, she was maddeningly inexperienced. All her life, messages of purity and self-control had been rammed down her ears and into her brain. Sex was evil, boys were dangerous, her own body was a snare for sin. Publicly, she even half believed that crap. The other, braver part of her suspected that she was missing out on something pretty exciting.

As she stared at her pert, pretty breasts, she began to imagine someone reaching out to touch them. She hoped very much that the imaginary someone would know what to do, as she didn't have a clue. All she had were her instincts to follow. But after a slow start

5

in her teens, her instincts were really getting going this last year. She had crazy, sheet-twisting dreams in bed at night in which shadowy assailants did things to her. Things she resisted but secretly wanted all the more.

At times, it was impossible to sleep; she would have to get up, tiptoeing downstairs and silently sneaking out of the kitchen window. Once outside, she would simply walk; wandering down empty, colour-bleached streets, avoiding the yellow glare of the streetlamps. Restlessness drove her forward, until sometimes she would linger on the deserted motorway bridge, leaning on the icy rail to listen to the rolling thunder of all-night trucks disappearing into the darkness. The temptation sometimes hit her – to walk down the steep grass verge and stand on the sliproad with her thumb bravely high in the air. All kinds of adventures were possible, if only she had the nerve to take those few steps. But always she turned and took a steady course back to Northford, her only witnesses the stalking cats who either scurried out of her path or occasionally sat and watched her, their eyes shining like twin green lamps as they followed her lonely path.

And in the daytime, she felt all slowed down and juiced-up. She was aware of boys' eyes on her in the streets; she wished Colin would let her go out to clubs and bars like other girls, where boys could talk to her and even touch her. Sometimes she wanted that so much; her body felt stabs of desire when she passed a good-looking boy but she never, ever dared to speak to any of them.

In a mood of quiet experimentation she reached up in front of the bathroom mirror and began to rub both nipples simultaneously, feeling tingles of pleasure awaken her body. The nipples soon grew rubber-hard beneath her fingers and she began to try different strokes – rubbing, pinching, pulling, squeezing. Now they were so hard that they almost burned with pleasure.

Not only the physical feelings were enjoyable; there was the sight of herself in the mirror too. Shyly, she looked at herself. She was whitely pale, her cropped red hair cut feathery around a small, open face. Her green eyes were wide with wonder. It was like watching a private blue movie only, of course, she had never seen such a thing in her life. The girl in the mirror no longer looked like her – she looked odd, like a wild alter ego, stroking her cupped breasts, sliding her fingers down now, towards her tremulous stomach.

Sighing, she closed her eyes. Round and round her fingertips circled, massaging her sensitive nipples. Her other hand reached the sprinkling of reddish hair covering her pubis. For a moment she just let her fingers stray, caressing the curly hair. Then, with a little gasp, she slid her fingers into the slippery crimson gash. It felt as hot as melted butter, almost sucking her fingers deeper and deeper inside. Idly, she let her fingers push onwards, finding the circling grip of her inner passage, breaching it and penetrating herself with a sharp little cry. It felt like nothing else that she had ever known: overpoweringly sharp and delicious. Feeling giddy, she grasped the edge of the washbasin. She could see herself in the mirror as she had never seen herself before: her expanse of skin pallid, save for the deepening red of her stiffened nipples and a flush of crimson below her throat.

It was impossible to stop once she had started. Insistently, her fingers thrust further inside her, then jabbed back and forth, trying to find the perfect angle of friction. Suddenly she found it. With her two longest fingers fully stiffened and held slightly apart, she could fill her tightening hole as they pummelled back and forth, producing wave after wave of pleasure. Suddenly she felt dizzy, as if it was almost too much to bear. Reluctantly, she slid her fingers outside the clutch of her body and looked at the slick wetness covering her fingers. It glistened like Vaseline.

Restlessly, she began to wash her hands. At any moment someone might knock at the bathroom door. The thought made her stomach sink with horror. Then she remembered that most of the congregation had gone into the city to give out pamphlets. She might have another whole half-hour to herself. She could continue her wonderful explorations in complete, self-indulgent privacy.

This time, she raised one bare foot on to the adjacent bath rim. She could just, from this position, see her own long and luscious sex stretching from her pubic bone to the dark mysterious folds of her entrance and behind that to the even darker puckering of her back passage.

What she was doing felt obscene – surrendering to the lusts of the body. All her life she had been told that giving in to them was a sin. For a few moments, she made pretence of hastily washing herself, filling her cupped hand with water and rubbing it into the scarlet silkiness of her inner lips. But the spasms of pleasure were too seductive. Groaning out loud, she began to rub her swollen clit with the heel of her hand while sliding a few greedy fingers inside her entrance. Watching her reflection in the mirror only excited her more. The girl's hotly pointed nipples swung as she rocked herself. Her face was blank with lips parted in abandonment. And the sight of her hand ecstatically frigging herself drove her crazy. Losing control, she began to rub her left breast, feeling a dam of sensation build like a furnace inside her hips. The heat was centred on the pearly bud of her clitoris. A fiery pulse pulled her fingertips towards it; the sensations increased, then with a cry of delight she made contact. It was impossible to stay quiet. As her fingers eagerly massaged her clit, sharp yelps of pleasure erupted from her throat. Her hands were getting wetter and wetter. Warm juice was running out of her. Deep muscles gripped her fingers tighter and tighter. She was pushing now, harder and deeper, driving her body over the edge.

Almost there, she glanced into the mirror. Quiet, observant Jo had disappeared. Instead was reflected an incredible, sexual creature with lewdly parted thighs and panting lips. For a second she paused, appalled. No one must ever see her like this, she swore to herself. From childhood she had been trained to be modest, not flaunting her nakedness and never betraying any interest in boys or what she vaguely knew they could do to her. No, it would be better for this to be her secret, she decided. But what a secret – as her fingers dug greedily back inside her, she felt a fierce spasm of gratification unlike anything she had ever known. She felt alive, as if her body had finally, amazingly woken from childhood's sleep.

Abruptly, a noise broke her concentration. It took a few moments for her to identify the sound. A rasping sound like someone clearing their throat.

Guilt triggered her heart in a rapid hammer-blow. Her fingers stopped dead still, then slid with a shameful squelch from the inner folds of her body. Someone else was in the bathroom.

'Who's there?'

Looking round, all was still. Only silence answered.

The sound had come from the far edge of the room, where a row of toilet stalls stood with their doors emphatically closed. On bare feet, Jo wandered over to the first stall.

'Hello?'

The door swung open at her touch, revealing only the small toilet cubicle, a bottle of disinfectant and a loo brush. The same with the second stall. Maybe, she began to think, her guilty conscience was getting out of hand. Shame could play strange tricks on the mind. The third door swung open.

'Graham! What are you doing?'

Transfixed, she stared at him with wide eyes. There was no need to ask. His penis was hanging out of his jeans, looking huge and red, even as it began to wilt under her gaze.

'I – I'm sorry, Jo,' he muttered, trying not to look her in the eye.

Oh, no. He looked as if he was about to burst into tears, all burgeoning six foot two of him. Holier than holy Graham was having a surreptitious wank. It was so unbelievable. Jo just stood her ground, shaking her head.

'How long have you been here? I don't get it. Have you been here all the time?' The performance he must have been watching came back to her with an agonising jolt of memory.

'Oh, how could you –' she protested. It was so humiliating that she wanted to vanish into the ground and never come back for a thousand lifetimes.

But he was no longer even listening. He was staring down at her; eyes devouring her naked body. His tongue flicked across his lips like a serpent's as he weighed up the rosy tenderness of her breasts. Suddenly she saw his pale baby face contort, like a man in pain. He was in tortured, ball-bursting agony.

'Oh, Jo,' he moaned. 'Help me. It's too much for me to stand.'

Like a dying man he fell on her shoulders, pulling her tight against him. His hands clawed at her breasts as he flung her against the thin partition wall. She could feel the heat of his cock driving hard and damp against her bare stomach. He was sobbing, trying to find her mouth with his lips.

'Graham. For God's sake –'

His mouth made contact with hers and a tidal wave hit her senses. The thickness of his tongue forced its way inside her mouth, silencing her words, almost choking her. Graham's stubby hand slid fast over her stomach and into the wet welcome of her pussy. His fingers spread luxuriously, squeezing the heated folds of her sex. Unable to control her breathing, Jo began to pant with excitement.

'You're gorgeous, you're gorgeous,' he moaned, stooping to suck on the hard spike of her nipple.

'No, Graham. Stop. Anyone could come in.'

But despite the automatic response of her words, she was utterly lost. If he had stopped, she would have howled with disappointment. Her feet were almost lifted off the floor as he ground his fingers into her. Suddenly he knelt and kissed her navel. Then rapidly he spread her secret lips and dipped his head against her, pressing his face inside her. When his tongue began to lap at her, a long, throaty groan burst from her. It felt like pure delight. He was pushing her roughly against the partition wall, spreading her thighs so he could suck at her. Her juice was running into his hair; she loved it. All she could think of were the rasping strokes his tongue was tracing across her clitoris.

'Graham,' she gasped. 'No. Stop.' It was unbearable.

Underneath her, his strong arms lifted her buttocks, pulling her towards his face. As his fingers dug into the softness of her spread cheeks, she let her head drop backwards against the toilet wall. His tongue was moving faster now, flicking rapidly across her clit. With a cry like a pained animal, she felt the moment of no return. Then there was only bliss, as she seemed to swim in and out of consciousness. On and on his tongue rasped, keeping her hovering in a state of agonised excitement. Her climax ground on and on, surging in frantic, tongue-rasping waves. Finally, she had to push his head away with trembling hands. The pleasure of his tongue had turned to torment.

'My God,' she gasped. 'I don't believe this.'

Rising, he looked at her again with those desperate blue eyes. Compliantly, she let him lead her by the hand out of the cramped confines of the cubicle. Stumbling like a sleepwalker, Jo suddenly became aware once again of the door.

'Listen, they could be back any minute,' she entreated. 'You've got to stop.'

But it was no use protesting. Pulling her down on to an old bath mat spread across the cold stone floor, Graham stopped her mouth with kisses. Despite the power of her orgasm, she felt wonderfully sensual. As his naked cock jabbed between her thighs she became aware of his agony. He was trying to lay her on her back, desperate to penetrate her.

'No. We can't.'

His eyes were glassy with lust as he cradled her beneath him. The hot firmness of his cock nuzzled between her juice-smeared thighs. It would be so easy, she thought, to just let him slip inside her. Oh, just the thought of it, pushing and driving inside her, twisted her guts with excitement. She looked down at it. It was getting massively stiff and as Graham rolled above her it taunted her as the slippery head brushed her heated sex. She wanted it. But any minute now, their time would run out. Someone would knock at the door.

Then she heard it. The grumble and squeal of the van outside the window.

'Listen, Graham. It's the van. They're back.'

He gazed at her like a drunk. 'Oh, just let me –'

With a fierce jab, she felt the head of his cock slither along her inner folds. The pleasure was overwhelming.

'No. For God's sake.'

He was trying again. That cock of his had a life of its own, a questing need to bury itself. Desperately, Jo reached down and found it, circling it with her eager hand. The effect on Graham was at least to keep him still. Lying prone beside her, he let her explore him, moving her fingers up and down his thick shaft until she felt him twitch and buck. It felt so good inside her hot hand that Jo wanted to do all kinds of things to it – kiss it, squeeze it, lick it, suck it.

But there was no time. Downstairs, she could hear the front door opening and a flurry of footsteps in the hall. Instinctively, she began to squeeze his shaft, pulling back and forth. In reply Graham cried out loudly, thrusting his hips in the air. He was on another planet now, his need so great it had to be released. To Jo's horror, he began to grunt rhythmically as her fingers sped up and down his cock. It was loud and very, very obvious.

'Shut up!'

He was close, she could tell, but whether seconds or minutes from a climax, she had no idea. For a second, she paused. Footsteps rang out even closer on the stairs.

'Do it, do it,' he groaned.

'Keep your mouth shut,' she hissed.

'I can't stand it. I'm nearly there.'

13

And, looking at him, she could see what he meant. His cock was dripping into her palm with excitement and his testicles were fat and purple. He was rolling on the floor in agony.

'Shut up,' she hissed. 'There's someone coming.'

A knock at the bathroom door. The echo rang out in the silence, freezing them both to the spot. In anguish she looked into Graham's face as she answered.

'Just a minute.' Jo's voice sounded strangled with guilt. 'I'm in the bath. Give me ten minutes, will you?'

'Who is that?'

My God. Had she changed so much? Did she even sound different?

'It's Jo. Just me, Jo.'

'Very well, Jo.'

Shit, it was Colin himself. If only he could see through walls, he would not have sounded so calm. 'Just don't be all day. People want to get ready for dinner.'

'I know.'

'Five minutes and I'll be waiting.'

'OK.'

But it was not OK. She just had to do something about Graham. He had lost his senses, rubbing himself against her like a dog trying to mount his mistress's leg. Decisively, she swung out from beneath him and knelt over him, straddling his narrow white hips. His eyes gazed hungrily at her swinging breasts and moved greedily down to the parted seam of her pussy. With quick efficiency she grasped his cock and began to pull on it, aiming the head at her scarlet lips glistening just above it.

Again, Graham began to groan loudly, his eyelids drooping ecstatically across his glazed eyes.

'Shut up, Graham,' she demanded.

But it was too much for him. Each pull on his cock

was sending him closer and closer to the best orgasm of his life. Volcanic groans were erupting from his thrashing throat.

'Quiet down,' she hissed. Then she reached forward and slapped her empty hand over Graham's contorted lips. Beneath her restraining palm she could feel his teeth grinding in excitement. On and on she worked at his cock, faster and faster. The sense of power gave her a thrill that glowed inside her belly. Raising his head, he watched hypnotically as she jerked at his cock, pulling it ever closer to the gorgeous wet seam of her cunt. It was only inches away when he twisted beneath her. She had to lean forward with all her weight to keep her hand clasped over his frantic mouth. But still she managed to keep her aim true. When the muscle in his prick jerked free she was still stretched above him, tantalisingly close. And his eyes took it in, before he convulsed in ecstasy; the amazing sight of Jo's open sex receiving jet after jet of spunk spurting from his tormented cock. It looked beautiful and sticky. A weaker spurt flung out, raining softly against the petals of her pussy lips. Still Jo worked at his cock, hypnotised by its gorgeous convulsions.

'Jo!' Colin's voice thundered through the thin door. 'Get a move on. I won't stand for this kind of selfishness!'

Although she still squeezed his shaft as hard as her hand could hold it, only a tiny dribble of come emerged. He was emptied. Reluctantly, Jo let go of him and squeezed a spasm out of her own excited pussy. Graham rolled his lust-drunk eyeballs up to heaven. She had released his mouth and he was slack-lipped and breathless. Jo had to stifle a giggle.

'Honestly, Colin. I'll only be a minute,' she shouted, trying to keep the laughter out of her voice. 'I'm not

15

being selfish, honestly. Quite the opposite. I just need to finish cleaning up.'

Smirking, Graham shook his head. Jo could see the pulse still throbbing at his neck. The long red tube of his cock still twitched spasmodically.

'Oh, yeah, Brother Colin, she's not selfish,' he whispered conspiratorially to Jo, as he ran his hands appreciatively over her smooth waist and hips. 'Not selfish at all. In fact, she just performed a minor miracle. In fact, give this girl a sainthood for her charity to others.'

'For lust creepeth among them, like a beast stalking in the night. And he stalks you also, even you who laugh while he plots to devour your flesh . . .'

Just as Brother Colin reached the climax of his sermon, the stimulation became more than Graham could bear. Twisting towards her, he thrust his hand beneath the camouflage of her draped jacket and slid his hand up her thigh. Thrusting her skirt up, he drove towards the heated mound beneath her panties. Impatiently he pulled the gusset aside to reach the wet chasm of her sex; it was a trial of strength for Jo not to scream with pleasure. Stubby fingers found her entrance and dug hard inside it. In reply, she squeezed her hand around his penis as tight as a vice, tugging in short, sharp, unobtrusive movements. But when she looked at his face, it was contorted by suppressed emotion. He was biting his lip as suppressed pants of pleasure threatened to burst from his labouring lungs. Beneath the jacket, his thighs tensed as they swung open around his swollen genitals. Jo's wrist worked back and forth in tiny, vibrating movements, feeling the warm pre-come deliciously moisten her hand as she masturbated him into a state of delirium.

Quickly glancing over at John Elmore, she felt a wave of relief. Thank God the old man had nodded off to sleep. And Colin himself had entered some kind of mesmeric state, eyes fixed upwards on heaven – or was it some kind of juicily fabulous vision of hell he was fixated on? Jo no longer cared.

As Graham's orgasm approached, his need to feel her grew more and more desperate. Luxuriously, his hand tugged her pubic hair, grinding against her sex. Then he forced his fingers deeper and deeper inside her. Turning her face to one side, Jo closed her eyes in a kind of agony. His hands began to claw in spasms, almost hurting her with his brutality. She knew these grabbing movements; they were a sure sign of his imminent ejaculation.

'Be as sheep in the fold, not turning each to your own devices. For the obedient flock is a happy one; the unruly sheep falls prey like a lamb to the slaughter. For always the beast is in watch and waits . . .'

Jo recognised the phrase: the beast. It was nearly the end of the sermon. The beast that allegedly stalked them had given her nightmares as a child. But now she knew big, hairy beasts didn't really prowl down the corridors of the night. Maybe the beast was something else, after all – something big and hairy you sometimes wanted to seek you out and climb into your bed at night.

She could hear the main double doors opening behind her. Just a few seconds more – only a few seconds now and he would be there. No – they both would be there. It was the thought of Graham losing control here, in the middle of this pious congregation that made her insides melt. If she could send him into that wild paroxysm here, in this temple of hypocrisy, the effect would be incredible. Her own muscles were already tightening and pulsing around Graham's big, rough fingers. All she needed now was to feel the

17

involuntary spasms of his cock and the fast rain of come spattering on her coat.

The long wooden pew creaked as someone else sat down on it. With lust-heavy lids, Jo glanced up in the direction of the sound. Thank goodness it was only Jo's room-mate, Emmi. Because whoever it might have been, she could not have stopped now. Graham was so close to orgasm that warm fluid was making him slick along his whole length.

Almost out of her senses, Jo glanced over at Emmi. For God's sake, she was watching them; eyes round with amazement as they furtively masturbated under the extended jacket. What a time for her to come back. Her timing was unbelievable.

Unbelievable. The word froze in Jo's brain. The violence with which Graham's cock jerked made it almost fly out of her hand. Hot come was flying upwards, spattering the lining of her jacket, soaking her hand with lovely, gooey spunk. Like a trigger, the sensation made her mash her pubis on to Graham's hand. He felt so thick inside her; all she had to do was lean forwards and *grind*.

Her eyes squeezed tight and her mouth opened wordlessly. A blast of pleasure sparked in her clitoris and raged through her neural paths like dynamite. All she was aware of was Graham's fingers pushing hard inside her, triggering spasm after spasm of delight. Her head suddenly slumped backwards, knocking against the hard wood of the pew.

People were shuffling and muttering around them. Coming back to her senses, Jo hastily adjusted her skirt, covering juice-smeared thighs that she hoped no one would notice. She could feel Graham trying to mop up beneath the jacket and hurriedly zipping up his flies.

She felt exhilarated; floaty and light-headed. Her

body was tingling in waves from her centre to the extremities of fingertips and toes. And no one had even noticed them. Golden-boy Graham had been wanked off in their midst. It was hilarious and delightfully wicked, both at the same time.

But of course, one person had noticed them, after all. Emmi. She was glaring at Jo like a mother who finds her child washing teacups in the toilet. Jo folded up the semen-stained jacket carefully and slid along the smooth pew towards her. It wasn't as if she had any right to stop Jo from enjoying herself. If she didn't like it, it was just tough.

'Hi. Good to see you,' Jo said sweetly, though a little short of breath.

It had been three long weeks since Emmi had gone off to her aunt's in the north. Three long weeks without even a phone call. And Jo guessed she was now supposed to be overjoyed at her return. Well, to be honest, Emmi had caused her some pain and grief, going off like that. They were supposed to be best mates. It should be of no surprise to her friend that she had found other ... distractions to keep her occupied.

'Yeah, sure,' was all Emmi said, still burning holes of fire with her eyes. 'Are you coming upstairs?'

'Sure.' Jo turned round. Graham was hanging back behind her like a lost sheep.

'All right, Graham. That's it. I need to talk to Emmi. Alone.'

Dismissed, he wandered off.

Suddenly Emmi's face lit up with something more than disgust.

'Hey, listen. Have I got so much to tell you. There's this place, Jo. I've been staying there. It's like paradise. Like heaven just landed on earth. And I'm going back. Come on up and I'll tell you all about it.'

19

Chapter Two

'What exactly are you up to, Jo?'

Emmi flung herself down on the threadbare bedspread and waited for an answer. It was strange to see her back again. She looked too bright and vital against the institutional yellow emulsion illuminated by a nasty mobcap light.

'You mean Graham?' Suddenly it was hard to explain. After all, before Emmi had left, Graham and his religious fervour had been the butt of many a joke between the pair of them. They had even gleefully imagined what sort of drippy, evangelising girlfriend he would go for. So Jo tried her best to sound sophisticated.

'I was bored. He was available. It's fun teasing Graham. He's a lot more fun with his pants off.'

'Yeah, well that wouldn't be difficult. He's hardly Robbie Williams with them on.' Emmi's voice was heavy with sarcasm. 'He's a religious nut, Jo. Don't say you let him fuck you?'

Jo blushed. Never in her life had she heard Emmi talk like this. The interrogation was getting painful.

'No. He wants to, though. He says we could just practice. You know, for when we get older.'

Emmi's face was a picture of disbelief.

'Jesus Christ! What century are you people living in? I suppose he wants you to bear him nine kids and trail around the world carrying his Bible?' Emmi sat up, eyes flaming. 'Wake up, Jo. There's more to life than trying to grab a bit of furtive sex under a raincoat. At Fenris Gate there's complete freedom to be who you want or what you want. Everything can change. Your whole identity can change.'

Jo sat down on her own bed, opposite Emmi, and took a good look at her. There was something more than attitude that had changed since her absence: she glowed with vitality, with a dusky, honeyed tan across her heart-shaped face and pale sun streaks glinting in her fair hair. Against the drab paintwork and faded posters of their room, Emmi glowed like a golden sun-worshipper.

'Well, what's all that supposed to mean? You've changed. I can see it. But don't talk in riddles. What does it all mean?'

Flinging herself back down on her bed, Emmi stretched luxuriously, raising her arms high above her head. She even moved differently, Jo noted. She was aware of her body; slower and more self-regarding.

'Oh, I can't just rush into that. Let me tell you how I got there. Do you remember how my Aunt Belle was always nagging me? Well, now she's even worse. Rent-a-nag. Went on and on, just because I spoke to some lads down in the village. Well, I stood it three days and couldn't take any more. I took off on the road. Started hitching and got a couple of good lifts in trucks. Going well, then I was dropped at some garage in the middle of nowhere and got stranded, hanging around on the roadside. Shit, I nearly rang

Aunt Belle and asked for my bus fare back. Well, thank God I didn't bother. It was already dark when a van stopped. A couple of guys and some girls in it, going back to Fenris Gate after a trip to the town. They asked if I wanted a bed for the night and that's how it started.'

'So, go on – what's so great about it all?'

Emmi rolled over on her stomach and stared at her friend, her face cupped thoughtfully in her hand.

'I don't know where to start. It's just like a collection of brilliant images – sunshine in the forest, the beautiful animals they keep, the love and respect everyone has for each other. And Michael – it's his farm they all live on – he's so deep and wild, Jo. He's like a father to us all.

Coming back here, I can see how all the rules control you. Colin's sermon tonight – I mean, how can anyone take that garbage seriously? Listen, I'm not getting at Christianity; Christ was okay. It's just the way people like Colin turn that stuff around and kind of twist it all into chains. He wants you all to be sheep under his control. What he's preaching is that nature is evil and dangerous. He means your true nature, your natural self. I heard it properly for the first time tonight. But nature is a good force, Jo. Nature and our natural instincts are what Michael says we are put on earth to enjoy.'

'This Michael. Do you fancy him, then?'

Emmi laughed. 'Course I do. But so does everyone else. He's a beautiful man with amazing gifts. When you hear Michael speak, it's like you can suddenly see the whole world clearly. And he can do things. Incredible, magical things. I can hardly believe some of the things I've seen.'

They were silent for a while until Jo suddenly asked, 'Do you let this Michael fuck you, then?'

It was hard even saying the word, but she wanted Emmi to know that she alone didn't have a patent on bad language.

Emmi shook her head dismissively. 'You really don't get it, do you? All this monogamy, this pairing off like Noah's ark is just the brainwashing going on round here. It's social control. It's keeping men in charge and you stuffed with babies. If sometimes it feels right with Michael and we want to express ourselves with our bodies, that's fine. That's what I'm saying. It's natural. Without society's rules and regulations.'

'It sounds weird to me. Like you wouldn't know where you stand.'

'Exactly.' Emmi smiled, looking approving for the first time since her return. 'At Fenris Gate you never know where you stand. That's what is so exciting.'

Emmi began to pack all her worldly belongings in preparation for an early start. Jo watched, feeling the wrench of sadness, as if the world would never feel stable again. They had been room-mates for two years now and were undeniably best friends. If she had family, sisters or even aunts, her feelings might not have run so deep. But day after day of conversation and laughter, the sharing of dreams and doubts and silly jokes, had made Emmi the closest person in the world to Jo. Emmi's caustic view of Graham had unnerved her too. She had wanted to sound cool and knowing but, beneath the veneer, Emmi was absolutely right. Graham was a hypocrite just like the rest – the only difference was that she and Graham had found a temporary but satisfactory use for each other.

Betrayal and abandonment seemed to suck the air out of the room. Jo sulked, struggled with a growing deep hostility towards Fenris Gate and its sudden conversion of Emmi. As Emmi's half of the wardrobe emptied and her backpack grew full, Jo half-heartedly washed and undressed for bed. She was huddled under her blanket, turning over the morbid thought that this would be their last night spent together, by the time Emmi finished washing and slipped on her baggy T-shirt. But instead of climbing into her own bed, Emmi came over and sat on the edge of Jo's mattress.

'What is it?' Jo snapped. She could no longer be bothered stifling her resentment.

'Listen. I don't want to part bad friends.'

'Well that's easy. Just don't go then.' She was surprised to hear herself being so honest. A moment earlier she had had no intention of letting her true feelings out.

'I have to go. I can't stay here.'

Emmi dropped her arms around Jo's shoulders. The pain of their parting was so sharp that Jo had to look away from her friend's piercing eyes for fear of crying. Suddenly Emmi leaned forward and kissed her quickly with affection. Unable to draw back, Jo slumped against her, sliding her arms around her friend's neck. Closing her eyes tight she allowed herself a long moment to enjoy the warmth of Emmi's body. Again, Emmi's mouth sought out her lips. This time, her mouth seemed to linger. It felt pleasant to be kissed by the girl but, as soon as a vaguely sensual flutter started up in her veins, Jo pulled back. Yet she could see from Emmi's soft and yearning face that she had wanted to continue. Puzzled, Jo wriggled back from her.

'Look at this,' Emmi said, suddenly breaking the tension of the moment. Rapidly she pulled aside the neck of her T-shirt and slid it over her bare shoulder.

There, emblazoned on the back of her shoulder was a small tattoo.

'A deer?'

'It's a fallow deer. A doe. It's a picture of my animal spirit. Michael says we all have a spiritual identity, a part of our soul that always runs free. I've seen her, Jo. She's beautiful, with a soft grey hide. She's a part of me and I of her.'

Jo gazed at the tiny representation of a soft-eyed doe. And somehow, the rounded curves of the creature's limbs, its arching neck and gentle face reminded her of Emmi.

'Do you identify with an animal?'

That was easy. Jo had loved one animal above all others since she was a young child. 'If I could choose to be an animal, it would be a cat. Green eyes, red glossy coat, long slinky tail. There's something about the way they love pleasure – but also love to hunt.' She smiled. Just imagining herself prowling low across the ground made her want to purr with pleasure. Or roll over on her back and catch her tail with her paws.

'I can see that,' laughed Emmi. 'A bit solitary too. Watching the world with those big green eyes of yours. Independent, except when mating. Cats are really wild when they get together in a group. The queens are really hot.'

'Oh yeah? And nocturnal too. Padding through the night with all my senses switched on full. I'd love that. When everyone's asleep and the world's all mine. I'd simply love it.'

'Listen,' Emmi said with sudden earnestness. 'When I say Michael is deep and powerful, I mean he can show you another side to yourself. If you wanted to, he might be able to help you explore yourself. Why not come with me?'

'Forget it.' Really, these people had taken Emmi in

too far. 'I don't need your help, or this Michael, thank you. I'm staying here. Really, the people here aren't so bad, you know. And it's where my father expects me to stay. I can't just run off on a whim. It's my home.'

Taking her hand, Emmi slid it over the densely coloured image of the fallow deer. It felt raised and slightly warm. Jo let her fingertips work across it slowly.

'I can visualise you bearing the image of a cat on your shoulder.' Emmi was very close, speaking more intensely than Jo had ever heard her. 'I feel I should save you from this place. From yourself.'

Again, Emmi tipped her head and kissed Jo's lips. Again she lingered, dry lips against dry lips. This time Jo did not back off. She and Graham sometimes kissed, but then it was with hard, jaw-aching need as climaxes approached. This was different. Emmi pulled back and began to kiss her face in sweet little pecks across her cheeks and chin. She was smiling into her eyes. Then she lowered her head again and this time kissed her on the mouth once more, applying deeper pressure. When Jo drew back to breathe, Emmi slipped her tongue between her parted lips. A frisson of pleasure shot through Jo's body. Like a scalded cat, she pulled back against the wall.

'Don't.'

'Why not?' Emmi was gazing at her sweetly.

'You know,' Jo frowned. Couldn't Emmi even guess that a bit of friendly kissing was going to turn her on? Because, for sure, it was doing. Playing around with Graham had already left her as hot as simmering treacle. If she had been alone, she would definitely have had a lazy evening playing with herself, pushing a pillow under her backside and letting her fingers caress herself to peak after peak of pleasure.

'Kissing like that. It could turn me on or something,' Jo tried to explain.

'And is that so bad?' Emmi asked, reaching up to stroke Jo's cheek. 'All these gender rules. They don't matter either. I want to show you something. I need to, Jo.'

Dumbfounded, Jo found herself once more on the receiving end of the girl's kisses. Her head tumbled with protests but Emmi sealed her lips. Again Emmi's stiff little tongue made a foray into her mouth. Unwillingly, Jo began to respond; returning a little pressure, allowing her jaw to grow lax and greedy.

After a few minutes of sweet and sensual kissing, Jo pulled back again with a gasp.

'I don't think this is right,' she whispered. Emmi was awakening her too fiercely. Deep under the bedclothes she could feel her already hot sex grow wet with freely flowing juices. Whatever her brain thought of Emmi as a loving, affectionate friend, her body recognised only a lover. It wasn't right. She felt ashamed of herself getting so excited by the girl's kisses. She dreaded Emmi reaching down and finding out she was so juicy hot and horny.

'I do,' replied Emmi, sliding her hands down the neckline of Jo's nightshift to find her naked shoulders. 'You mustn't be frightened. I've learned things. Things we need to share.'

The touch of Emmi's fingertips on her bare flesh made Jo shiver and weakly drop forward to suck again at the girl's lips. Now, when she closed her eyes, Jo felt herself sink into a dark whirlwind of need. All she could think of was her body and its craving to be touched. Despite all her inhibitions, she found herself lasciviously thrusting her tongue into Emmi's hot mouth, running it around her sharp white teeth and plunging it towards the heat of her throat. It was as if,

27

with her eyes shut tight, she could forget that this was a girl and just concentrate on the need that was flooding her body.

She became aware that she had slipped backwards a little and Emmi was pressing above her as they embraced mouth to mouth. The girl was stroking her arms, running her long nails up and down the soft inner flesh from armpit to wrist. Involuntarily, Jo felt her spine arch provocatively as their bodies began to slide together. She was desperately trying to ignore the wild signals coming from her overheated sex. Compared to this long, lazy exploration, Graham was always rushing and urgent, desperate to relieve his explosive cock. A slow build-up was worse, Jo hazily realised. It was impossible to play it cool. Or maybe better, if you absolutely didn't care that your lover could see you were completely juiced-up and out of control.

With a gentle movement, Emmi slid her hand from Jo's arm to the soft folds of her nightshirt. Gradually she moved her fingers from her shoulder to the small swelling of Jo's left breast. The sensation was overwhelming. As the girl's finger and thumb closed over the hardness of her nipple, Jo gasped out loud.

'I'm sorry,' she apologised, embarrassed by the noise she was making. 'I can't stay quiet.'

'Don't be.' Emmi was smiling at her, her face suffused with yearning. 'No one can hear us.'

Jo tried to push reality out of her mind. She had never even thought about sex with another girl in all her life. She had never for once guessed that her body could respond so wildly. But all she wanted now was for Emmi to go on and on – deeper and further into her, exploring what she was slowly realising was the most luscious possibility for pleasure.

As Emmi continued rubbing her nipple through the

cloth Jo slumped back on the pillow, breathing fast. There could be no denying now that she was madly turned on. Decisively, Emmi began to unbutton Jo's nightshirt, pausing between the buttons to drop her head and kiss her hot throat and the shallow valley between her breasts. When she finally dropped her head and began to suck lazily on the hardened spikes of Jo's nipples, Emmi's pleasure also became clear. She too was lost in the sensual enjoyment of Jo's breasts. Licking and nuzzling, she took the entire crimson circle of her aureola inside her softly feminine lips. The feeling made Jo weak. Reaching out to Emmi she wanted to touch her but didn't know how. Frantically, her hands began to grab at Emmi's shoulders, pulling her down. Oh God, she thought. I don't even know how girls do it. Somehow she has got to show me. I'm so hot I'm going to explode.

'Slow down,' Emmi whispered, breaking off for an anguished moment from her attentions to Jo's breasts. 'Do you want me to get in bed with you?'

Jo nodded. She could feel the girl's saliva drying on her hardened nipples. Somehow she had to get some relief from her torment. But when Emmi kneeled up above her to pull her T-shirt off over her head, Jo felt embarrassed and confused again.

Emmi's body was lovely but strange. She had seen her undress every day with only the most casual attention. But now she eyed her with a new and greedy intentness. Her breasts were small and full with two pink and hardened nipples tilting up into the air. She looked soft and smooth with the golden tan glowing across all her body. But it was her blonde curling pubis that both fascinated and repelled Jo. She had only just got used to Graham and his incredibly different genitals. Emmi's pussy was so much like her own pleasure-seeking parts, and yet so different. Jo

29

was not even sure if she could bring herself to touch the other girl.

In a moment Emmi had joined her in bed and Jo felt the breath-stopping luxury of naked skin wrapping naked skin. Suddenly the sex of her lover no longer mattered. She could feel Emmi's own pretty breasts rubbing against her own and she reached down to cup them, luxuriating in the sensation of rubbing twin nipples against each other. Emmi was above her, still kissing her, stroking her hair and sliding gradually into the space between Jo's laxly parting thighs. With a gasp she felt the heat of Emmi's sex rubbing against her leg. It was softly slippery, generating more heat than she could ever have imagined. It began to excite her now, the nearness of this strange, lubricious organ.

'Isn't it good to be naked,' Emmi whispered, 'to cast off human clothes?'

She began to squeeze hard on both Jo's nipples at once. It was painful but madly exciting too. 'Animals take their pleasures without guilt,' she murmured into Jo's ear. 'Do you want me to show you?'

Jo was dizzy now, her pulses racing, her veins on fire.

'Yes,' she moaned, rolling beneath the girl, feeling her ribs rise and fall as her lungs fought for air. 'I can't take much more.'

Emmi worked her way downwards and looked intently at Jo's supine body.

'In the animal world,' she murmured, 'creatures explore and lick without human guilt.'

In illustration, her head bent low and she unrolled her tongue across the sensitive skin of Jo's stomach. It triggered an almost unbearable fluttering between Jo's legs. She began to cry out, raking Emmi's blonde hair, urging her to move to her aching pubis but fearful too, of how it would feel to have a girl touch her there.

The downward movement was inexorable. Soon Emmi's head slipped down over her stomach, across the mound of her pubis and sank into the briny parting of her sex. Jo felt herself begin to tremble in anticipation. She could not believe she was having sex with another girl and that it felt so incredible and yet so right.

Like an explosion of pleasure, Emmi's tongue gently brushed over the swollen bud of Jo's clit. Unable to stop herself, Jo cried out hoarsely. Again the tongue made contact, stiffened and lapped to and fro. All Jo could think about was that tiny centimetre of flesh. Never had she felt such burning delight. Eagerly, she began to thrust upward, pushing into Emmi's face, lost now to any pointless sense of decorum.

For a few moments Emmi indulged her, licking and tasting, even taking the whole of that exquisite bead of pleasure inside her soft lips and slapping her warm tongue against it again and again. Jo began to grab at the sheets, her legs wide open, feeling a monumental release start up in her muscles. But then Emmi stopped, as if sensing the girl could only bear so much direct stimulation.

'Get on your hands and knees,' Emmi said. Jo was dazed, craving just those two or three more strokes that would send her over the edge. She barely knew what to do. Her brain was scorched and giddy. Guiding her, Emmi pulled her up.

'I want you to feel your body like an animal,' Emmi crooned. 'Like a wildcat, standing on four strong legs.'

Shakily, Jo descended on to her hands and knees. She immediately felt madly sexed-up. The position felt crazily exhibitionistic. Emmi was kneeling behind her rear end, her open palm reaching down to cradle the spread lips of her sex.

'Oh, your scent is driving me crazy,' she whispered.

As she did so, she began nuzzling with her nose and lips against the parted cheeks of Jo's buttocks. With her head buried in the pillow, Jo began to sob. Her body was on fire. Somehow, something had to satisfy her soon.

Never before had anyone touched Jo's body in such an uninhibited way. Emmi sniffed and licked her anus, sending lightening bolts of excitation sparking up her spinal column. For a few moments, she struggled with mental reproaches of disgust and dirtiness, until the pleasure built up so powerfully that Jo simply buried her head in the pillow and let herself go. She imagined herself to be an animal; balancing on her toes with neck long and buttocks pushed back at the top of her hindlegs. Emmi's tongue was exploring her, nuzzling downwards now, to the dew-heavy opening that felt swollen and puffy between her legs.

Emmi's hands joined in the exploration. Long, probing fingers parted her cheeks and then slid into what now felt to Jo like a wide, gaping chasm. With a sharp intake of breath, Jo felt herself being breached. Skilfully, Emmi began to finger-fuck her, at the same time as her tongue once again rimmed the tantalising flower of her anus.

Jo wanted to howl. She was close to orgasm, but her body was too tense, it was almost locked up. Frantically, she tried to back on to Emmi's fingers, wild for the fast thrusts of them frigging deep inside her. Slowly, Emmi slid her mouth downwards, until her tongue reached the outer edge of Jo's entrance. Then, suddenly thinking better of it, she withdrew her fingers and dropped on to her back before sliding beneath the arch of Jo's thighs.

'Get down on my face,' she whispered hoarsely. 'You're so juicy I've got to lick it up.'

Shaking with excitement, Jo lowered her sex on to

the softness of Emmi's face. Like an electric shock, her clit came into contact with Emmi's bristling tongue. At the same time, Emmi's hard, insistent fingers dug inside her. Jo began to howl into the pillow, biting the cloth between her teeth.

On and on the girl's tongue slapped against her, searching around the protrusion of her clitoris, rubbing hard and fast. Faster too were the jabbing thrusts of Emmi's fingers, driving deeper and deeper into her insistently grabbing muscles. More and more juice seemed to flow out of Jo; she could hear her body squish with pleasure. She was almost creaming with delight as the sensations built higher and higher. Emmi's probing little tongue gave her no rest. Faster than Graham could ever drive his cock, the splayed fingers fucked her until all she could feel was molten, quickening ecstasy.

'Oh God,' she moaned into the pillow. 'Don't stop. I'm there.'

The thrusts burned inside her like vicious spears of delight. She was on the edge for a second, hovering. Then, with a scream of utter surrender, Jo's orgasm erupted. At the same time, Emmi pulled the whole of her swollen clitoris into her mouth and sucked hard.

Jo thought she was going to die. Pleasure hit her in battering spasms, sending her to some other place of darkness and brutal force. Each time her ecstasy was about to ebb, Emmi started it up again, sucking her clit and driving hard into the pulpy wetness of her sex. Never before had she known a climax could be drawn out beyond the snatching of a few pleasurable seconds. As pleasure built and discharged again and again in her spasming pelvis, Jo began to feel weak and delirious. Finally, she had to pull away from Emmi and her maddening, delicious tongue and topple over on her side to rest. Her heart was pounding in her ears. Between her legs, her cunt burned and tingled; she could feel her deep internal muscles pulsing rapidly as they recovered from Emmi's onslaught.

'Oh, I thought I was going to pass out,' she whispered. 'Did I make a lot of noise?'

Emmi only giggled, pulling her under the blanket.

'If anyone asks, you'll have to say it was me,' she laughed. 'Groaning with misery at the thought of leaving here.'

'Or me groaning at the thought of staying, more like,' Jo added.

'Well, we've still got tonight together.' Emmi snuggled up, wrapping her slender arms around Jo's shoulders. It felt blissful. Jo shut her eyes, never wanting it to end. Her fear of losing something if she and Emmi had sex evaporated. What they had now seemed stronger and much more beautiful.

But soon it became clear that Emmi was far from sleepy. She started talking about Fenris Gate, while sliding her legs comfortably around Jo's hips.

'It will be May Day soon. Michael says the Beltane festival is one of the most important moments of the year. You see, as the earth comes back to life we celebrate her fertility. There are all the animals to care for and all the crops to tend. It's so different, Jo. It really means something, not like city life.'

Jo was drifting off in a post-orgasmic daze, illuminated by visions of golden crops and nodding herds. Sheep, cows, horses – and deer?

'That deer you saw,' she asked suddenly. 'Are there wild deer around the farm, then?'

'Kind of,' Emmi said slowly. 'Not all the time but, yes, when Michael calls them. And lots of other animals too. Even kittens like you,' she teased, dragging her nails in a playful claw along Jo's shoulder. 'Or are you a full-grown cat?'

34

'Oh, at the moment just a sleepy little kitten', she yawned. 'Happily curled up in my warm bed.'

But there was something more than comfy about Emmi's tantalising claws. There was something subtly arousing in the slow trail of her nails. The gentle scratching made Jo's flesh stand up in goosebumps.

'Do you want to suck then, little kitten?'

Emmi slid up beside her and offered her sweet little breast. With only a second's hesitation, Jo sank down and began to lick, tentatively at first, at the pretty nipple. It felt more pleasant than she might ever have imagined. With her lips puckered around the sweet flesh, she closed her eyes and drifted.

'That's right, little kitten. You can lick as long as you like.'

She imagined them both to be as warm as only fur can make you. Drifting halfway into sleep, she suddenly recollected that as a girl in Africa she had once taken in a stray cat. She was a thin, pointy-faced little thing who had nevertheless grown trustful over patient weeks, until in the end her nervous wildness had been quelled and she had gladly taken scraps from Jo's hand. Mother and father, on the other hand, hated the mangy creature and gave orders for it to be shooed away whenever it appeared in the garden. Her superstitious old nanny, too, had cursed the creature, making the secret sign to ward off the evil eye.

'That cat has the look of a wandering spirit,' she had said, shaking her grey old head. 'You keep that creature out of here or its gonna look into your eyes and take a bite out of your soul.'

Jo's old-fashioned bedroom had been way off limits to the little stray but, one night, she had smuggled her inside in her satchel. There, as the light of the oil lamp cast shadows of moving branches against the wall, she had released the cat on to her bed. Whiskers bristling with curiosity, the slender cat had investigated her new environment; treading her claws into the sinking hillocks of the quilt and sniffing delicately at the leather Bible on her pillow. Tenderly, Jo had stroked her fine-boned face, watching in fascination as the small creature batted the muslin mosquito nets with her paw and then finally slumped down sleepily against Jo's shoulder. All night the little cat had stayed close, sighing as she changed position, her tiny heart thumping through ragged fur.

In the dawn light, Jo had been woken by the tickle of the cat's rough tongue drawing gently across her face. For a long time she had lain still on her back, listening to the whooping sound of birds waking in the garden beyond. The sensation of the coarse tongue rippling over her skin was quite lovely, like a promise of long, tender kisses to come. Blinking slowly, the cat had stared deep and long into her eyes, opening the black slits of her pupils wide. Soon after that night, the cat had disappeared, strolling off into the jungle. But Jo had never forgotten the tender little exchanges of that night.

Now, as she drifted off to sleep in Emmi's arms, visions and fancies tumbled around her head. Half dozing, she felt her and Emmi to be two lazy kittens slumbering in their nest. As Emmi had said, animals know no shame, only instinct. Fancying herself free of her human shape, she could follow the pleasurable lead of her instincts, to sniff and taste and snuffle in the warm folds of Emmi's body. Without the curse of thought, she followed the taste on her tongue down, down, from Emmi's sweet nipple to her smooth stomach. Then, with only the smallest hesitation in her mind, she sank into the wet fur between her legs, licking like a pussycat, until Emmi pushed her away with a satisfied sigh.

Chapter Three

'*A* nd what do you think, Jo?'

Brother Colin's eyes did their best to skewer inside her brain. Jumping in her seat, Jo looked at the others collected around the table, searching for a clue. What the hell was she being asked?

Because if he *really* wanted to know what she thought about, in the privacy of her own head, Colin was in for a shock. Since Emmi had tiptoed off down the stairs to Fenris Gate that bright spring morning exactly one week ago, Jo had thought about nothing else but sex, sex, sex. It had been bad enough when she had started getting physical with Graham; her concentration had been blown apart. But the sheer power of her encounter with Emmi had left her obsessed. The way she looked at it, before this, all her fantasies and needs had been kept in a nice safe bubble, to be visited in the privacy of her own bed, and preferably in the dark. Graham had done his best to pierce that bubble, but in the end she had never let him get through the protective film. But Emmi – gorgeous, sweet-fleshed Emmi – she had burst through the protective walls like a hammer hitting a soap bubble. And, at last, tonight was the night of her promised phone call.

'You think Emmi's gone for good, don't you, Jo?'

Graham was prompting her, trying his best to help her out.

'Oh, Emmi.' Jo tried to get a grip on the conversation. 'Yeah, I think she's gone for good. Definitely.'

Every week they had this meeting – the Friday meeting – for all the younger people to talk out issues with Colin. When she first arrived, Jo had thought it was great to have a say in how they ran the place. But soon it had become perfectly clear that it always ended in Colin laying down the law, usually with some kind of tract or religious quote to back himself up.

Emmi's running off was a big, big issue to Colin. It was a loss of credibility; a potential loss of power.

'So where do you think she's gone, Jo? No. Don't answer straight away.' The smile from his facial expression category named 'reassurance' was enough to make her heave. 'Just remember the loyalty you bear to your friend's safety,' he coaxed with grating sincerity. 'You young people don't realise – the wider world is a dangerous and wicked place. I'm sure you wouldn't want to feel responsible for any mishap that might befall your friend. If you tell us where she is, we can help her. Tell the truth now.'

Jo hesitated for only a second.

'I just don't know.' She could feel a mask of red flushing across her cheeks. Everyone seemed to be staring at her with disapproving expressions.

'And if you did know,' added Colin, eyeballing her with full intensity, 'would you tell us?'

'Of course,' Jo snapped back, her voice pitched high with the effort of lying. Then she caught sight of Graham, eyeing her sardonically. He waited until

Colin had lain off her then, secretly and conspiratorially, gave her a knowing wink.

The meeting drifted on to other issues: responsibility for upkeep of the house; volunteers to design some new leaflets; fund-raising to send people abroad. It was hot in the dusty back room plastered with faded posters and mouldy books. Someone had opened the sash window overlooking the street, but the breeze hardly shifted the grubby net curtains.

Jo settled back down into her daydreams. To her, everyone else around the table – the two dopey girls and Graham's younger brother Pete – appeared only half-alive. She, however, felt too alive to even sleep. This morning she had risen well before dawn and stood for almost an hour by the metal parapet of the motorway bridge. Her head spun with visions of intimate flesh-parts and piercing replays of pleasures so sharp that her heart seemed to skip a beat, even in memory. Something was quickening inside her; her body no longer felt completely her own.

As if at a prompt, something brushed against her leg, breaking her reverie. Irritated, she tucked her legs further back beneath her chair. But a moment later, she felt it again. A feather touch, sliding up her knee towards the raised hem of her skirt. Anxiously, she looked round.

Graham.

Still, she had to give him credit for being helpful since Emmi had left. Although she had told him not to get her alone, today was not the first time he had done his best to defend her against Colin's inquisitions. Now he was pretending to read the notes in front of him but was secretly staring at her with those yearning blue eyes of his. And brushing the top of her thigh with his fingertips. As his lips parted a little, she could see the lust making his face slack and glassy.

All she had to do was move away. But there was something seductive in Graham's teenage sex angst. His fingers were drawing a pattern on the outer muscle of her thigh, a delicate figure of eight that grew imperceptibly longer each time he traced it. Indirectly, he was slowly making his way towards the edge of her hem, high up towards her hipbone. And when she looked at his face, the expression of need written across it was so raw that it made her clit pulse with desire.

Jesus, sex was confusing. She had already decided she didn't like Graham. But at this moment, every cell in her body wanted him. And in a strange way, she even blamed Emmi for leaving her like this – so hot and ready, like a runner on the blocks, all primed to start a marathon of sex. There was nothing else for it, she decided. She was going to have to escape to her room and relieve herself of some of this tension.

Concrete-heavy minutes ticked by on the wall clock. At last it was nearly six, leaving only one more hour before Emmi's call. Colin drew the meeting to an end. So it was with a wave of irritation that she heard Colin asking herself and Graham to hang back. Sheepishly, she looked up at Graham as they both stood, waiting for Colin's pronouncement.

'We've got to find Emmi,' Colin started. 'I think it would be a good thing if you both put your heads together. Get some leaflets out with her picture on them. Brainstorm some ideas, print something up and get out and about to youth clubs and cafes to distribute them and chat to any likely kids. She won't have gone far.'

'Yeah, that's great.' Graham smirked, genuinely pleased.

'Jo?'

The whole thing was making her sick. 'I don't

know,' she faltered. 'Maybe if Emmi's gone she should just be allowed some freedom. It's like – forcing her or something. Invading her privacy.'

'Jo, do you have a problem with community responsibility? Do you want to talk it through?'

No. She just wanted to get out of here. Colin's big, red-faced presence was irking her. 'No, Colin. Honest. No problem. Anything you say.'

Upstairs, Jo slumped on her bed in a bad mood. No problem. What a joke. But then again, it wasn't as if she even knew where Emmi had actually gone. All she knew about Fenris Gate was that Emmi had been picked up as a hitchhiker on the edge of the North York Moors. It was all just too much. It was as if Graham and Colin were tightening invisible bonds around her life and strangling everything young and hopeful inside her.

Maybe, she thought, if she was less full of tension her mind might clear. After all, she was wound up like a mechanical alarm clock. Absent-mindedly, she began to pull up her skirt and touch her leg, just where Graham had stroked it. Closing her eyes, she traced the same pattern on her leg with the tips of her fingernails. Imagining herself through Graham's eyes, she enjoyed the silky texture of her skin and the way the muscle swelled slightly and then curved inwards before reaching the prominence of her pelvis. In the darkness behind her eyelids, she conjured Graham's delight at the feel of her skin and the sharp anticipation as his fingers brushed the cotton frill of her knickers.

What would he want to do next? Ah, yes – slide a finger inquisitively beneath the edge of her knickers, exploring the previously unsullied softness of flesh. Maybe lift the edge of the fabric a little and slide a

41

couple more tentative fingers inside the warm pocket between flesh and fabric. Unable to resist further, she hooked her thumb inside the gusset of her panties and began to stroke the lips of her pussy through the cloth. Wetness. Gorgeous, warm, syrupy wetness. For a few minutes, she simply massaged the cloth with her fingers, feeling it getting wetter and wetter. Her head filled with dark and shapeless visions. Of Graham and his unbearable need. Of her own white and slender body. But mostly her mind lingered on the memory of Emmi's skilled and knowing fingers and the way they had teased and tormented her until she had wanted to open her legs as wide as her thigh bones could stretch.

Eagerly, she lifted her T-shirt and began to rub at her breasts with her free hand. The nipples were already hard to her touch. Feverishly, her other hand massaged her clitoris, breaking off each few moments to slide into the hot well of her cunt. It was wonderful. All of Northford Mission's rules faded away to no more than background chatter in her brain. Her body was ripe and bursting for pleasure. She intended to linger there, enjoying her magical responses, sating herself with all the burning orgasms she could stand.

A knock at the door. Jo moaned distractedly, then decided to ignore it.

A second knock. Louder and more insistent.

'Jo!'

No. It was Graham.

'Are you in there?'

Longingly, she squeezed the circle of her inner muscles around her fingers, feeling their hard wetness grip like a handshake. Surely, if she ignored him, he would go away. Lazily, she glanced at the door to check the key was turned.

The key was not even in the door.

'No, no, no,' she whispered to herself, trying to

42

scramble up and wipe juice-smeared fingers across her bedspread at the same time.

It was too late. The door slowly swung open. Graham came in just as she managed to swing her legs over the side of the bed. Glancing down in panic, she could see her white knickers discarded in a tight bundle on the floor. Her T-shirt was halfway up her chest and her skirt was a wrinkled concertina scrunched around her hips.

Graham took it all in within a second. Carefully, he closed the door behind him and crossed over to her, eyes bright with excitement.

'Oh, Jo,' he moaned, dropping on his knees beside her. 'Just let me see you.'

His nearness made her wet with excitement. Yet she hated herself for it too. Maybe, like Emmi had said, her nature was totally contradictory. What was it again? Cool and independent, except when hot to mate.

'Get lost,' she tried ineffectually. She was sitting on the bed with her bare feet hanging over the edge. Graham grabbed one of her feet and began to stroke it. It tickled.

'Get out of my room, will you,' she hissed, kicking her foot free. 'You get on my nerves.'

'You make me feel incredible,' he replied, suddenly pressing his forehead to her bare knee. 'I can't stand this. I can't. If you just let me touch you, I'll go away.'

He was kissing her in small dry pecks across her knees. The kisses seemed to flutter like a flock of excited butterflies, churning up her lust-heavy abdomen.

'No. Go away now.' But in her mind, she realised how easy it would be to just let him carry on. Oh my God, his mouth was lapping upwards now, above her knees. To her horror, she found her legs beginning to

43

tremble with excitement. It was terrible to feel so completely out of control.

'Get off me!' she cried, kicking out against him before he could notice his effect on her. 'Graham, I do not want you. It was a mistake. Just leave me alone.'

'All right, all right,' he whispered. 'If I can't touch you, at least let me see you. It's been days, Jo. I'm in agony. I don't want to sin either, but I can't stand it.' His face was a picture of torture. It really did pain her to see anyone like this.

'Just let me see,' he begged, gently parting her tightly pressed knees apart. It was the look on his face that did it. Sheer, desperate lust. The total loss of dignity.

Her thighs widened. 'Ah, yes,' he moaned, as he craned to see. Jo knew her pussy lips were swollen and slick with juice without looking down. It was Graham's face that she wanted to watch. A dull light gleamed in his eyes. His cheeks visibly flushed with excitement.

'You are so gorgeous.' His eyes feasted on the purplish seam and darker, glistening entrance. Instinctively, his hand worked down to the bulge of his cock and rubbed against it rhythmically.

Dipping his head, he leaned forward to kiss her inner thigh.

'No. I said don't touch.' Something was kicking into gear now, in Jo's head. That was it – the sheer power of the situation. Graham on his knees, drooling like a pet dog. It almost made her wet herself with enjoyment. Grabbing his hair, she held him back, although he started to rub his nose and cheeks against the flesh of her inner thigh.

'All right. I won't touch you,' he breathed raggedly. 'But why not show me what you were doing just now. Go on. I won't touch you. I won't even try.'

'Why should I?'

Graham was so hot for it now that his hand was stuck to his crotch. Angelic, stupid Graham was rubbing the swelling of his cock in long, yearning strokes. All the old fire rapidly ignited in Jo's guts.

'Just let me lie next to you on the bed. Just so I can see, Jo. It's not even a sin, not even any contact. I tell you what – we can forget all that rubbish about looking for Emmi. What do you say? We can just tell Colin we did it and nothing came up.'

Tempting, she thought. Maybe he wasn't so stupid after all.

'And that's the end of it, then,' she pressed. 'No more barging into my room. No more sneaking up my leg. Agreed?'

'Oh, yeah.'

In a second he was up on the bed. He curled up affectionately beside her, with his chin propped up on his hand so he could see her outstretched body.

'Do you . . . you know, masturbate a lot?'

'Sometimes.' She was suddenly frozen by a paroxysm of embarrassment. Maybe this really was getting a bit too intimate. But to help her, Graham suddenly lifted her floppy hand and dropped it gently into her warm and squishy sex.

'Show me,' he whispered. 'I'll never forget that time I first saw you; I thought I was going to die. It was like a dream come true. Every fantasy I've ever had, only better. I couldn't stop myself watching. When you touched your breasts I had to get my dick out. But when you started to drive your fingers inside – God. I can't explain. I thought my insides were going to burst. Only now I want to see it, up close. Please, Jo. Please.'

Tentatively, he rocked her hand across the dewy petals between her legs.

'Oh God, if it's the last thing you do for me . . . show me. Do you use anything? Or do you just use your fingers?'

As he rocked her fingers, she felt a burning resurgence of the flames that had been licking her close to a climax. Closing her eyes, she began to rub her index finger gently around the soft bulge of her clit. Everything felt deliciously wet. Only a few strokes returned her to a state of swollen expectancy. Excitedly, she began to massage her sensitive entrance with her other hand, feeling it tighten as delicious sensations flooded into her passage. Then, deliberately to excite her spectator, she performed her new party piece. Arching hips into the air, she reached backwards with her juice-sodden fingers to find the tight, rosy hole of her anus. Then, sliding the lubricated end of her little finger inside it, she twisted her wrist so the two longest fingers of her hand could also dabble pleasurably in the hot pool of her sex. Meanwhile, her other hand could lazily circle her clit, controlling the rate of her approach to orgasm.

The effect on Graham was hypnotic. She could hear him rustling and rearranging his clothes and then gently shuffling up between her legs. Opening her eyes from this bliss she looked up to see him kneeling between her thighs, his glorious cock red and jutting tautly above her open sex. Involuntary reflexes tightened inside Jo's body – just to watch Graham pulling so quickly on his shaft, driving his fist up and down, gave her senses a seismic jolt. His need was so raw that it made her crotch convulse with excitement.

'Show me,' he panted, his face flushing. 'Show me how much you want it.'

It wasn't hard to do. Splaying her two fingers, she began to pump them inside her wetness.

'Do you need my cock inside you?' he crooned, his

46

hand moving so fast up and down his cock that it was almost a blur. His other hand was cradling his balls, rubbing them slowly. 'It wants to get in there.'

'Yes,' she moaned, twisting her head to one side. 'But you can't. Just look,' she gasped. She felt gorgeously vulnerable, her body stretched and long with her knees up high on either side of Graham. She could just see the hard spikiness of her nipples below her eyeline as they jutted fiercely into the air. She knew the show she was putting on was mega-erotic. What was it he had said? Like all his dreams come true. The thought thrilled her, making her lift her pelvis even higher, offering him a prime view of her slippery seam, only inches from his staring eyes.

Maybe that was the reason her orgasm halted reluctantly in her congested nerves. Because it was a show. Because, instead of the lazy, self-indulgent frigging she had been enjoying before, all she could respond to now was Graham's frenzied jerking off.

She tried circling her clit more slowly, starting up little frissons of sheer pleasure that made her groan. Above her, Graham's movements were becoming jerky and frantic, as long, low grunts erupted from his throat. His cock was a deep crimson, the wet head bursting like purple fruit. She longed for more time – yet at the same time wanted him to lose control violently all over her.

'I want to fuck you,' Graham was muttering. 'Push it in you and give you a good hard fuck. Go on, fuck yourself. Do it harder.'

Beginning to ride towards the crest of her climax, Jo pummelled harder inside herself, offering Graham the view of her twin fingers working quickly in and out of her encircling entrance.

'Let me in you,' he growled. 'Let me fuck you. You need it. Look at you. You need my cock.'

For a wild second, that truly was all Jo wanted – to feel the hard meat of his cock driving so much faster and deeper than her own fingers could. The thought of it made her liquefy. Eagerly, she lifted her legs and wrapped them around his narrow hips. Gripping him with her bare ankles, she pulled him towards her, all the time panting with excitement.

'Jo,' he grunted. 'Oh, I can't – oh, let me come on you. Oh, oh –'

Too late. Graham's twitching cock had taken as much of a beating as it could stand. A long jet of come erupted from him, then another. Ecstatically, Jo felt it fall hotly on her thighs and cunt. Deliriously, she rubbed it into her skin, trying to scale the last few metres of the dizzy height of her climax. Closing her eyes tight, she concentrated on the glutinous texture sliding over her thighs. With both hands she massaged it into her skin and kneaded it into the naked prominence of her clit.

It was no good. Graham was sheepishly offering her a tissue. Finally, feeling a little foolish, she stopped and curled her knees back together.

'Nearly dinner time.'

What was it about Graham that made him so … mundane? Bad temperedly, Jo hobbled over to the sink and began washing herself. Good God, she was frothy with juices. It felt uncomfortable now, like cooling jam. Oh, if only she had come. Her pelvic muscles ached with need. If only Graham had driven into her – oh, just the thought of it made her even weaker. She could almost feel the heady mix of pain and pressure soaring up her clutching passage. Oh, if only.

'Didn't you want to do something before dinner?' he continued artlessly as he waited beside her to use the sink. Really, they were like an old couple or something. It was driving her crazy. And what was it he was chattering on about?

Dinnertime.

Seven o'clock.

'What time is it?' she shrieked.

In seeming slow motion, he lifted his arm, squinted at his watch and delivered the verdict.

'Ten past seven.'

'Shit! Shit! Graham, get out of here, will you.'

Not bothering to dress, Jo jerked down her skirt and T-shirt and scurried off down the stairs. But when she got to the mission hallway, the payphone on the wall hung still and silent in recrimination.

John Elmore shuffled past, on the way to dinner. Jo stood to one side, suddenly conscious of her bare feet and tousled appearance.

'Mr Elmore, do you know if there's been a call for me? A friend said she'd ring at seven and I think I've missed it.'

But the old man simply shook his head and shrugged.

For long minutes, Jo hunched on the wooden bench in the hall, shivering without her shoes, wondering how she could have been so stupid as to let Graham distract her from the most important phone call of her life. All seemed hopeless, the future a black canvass stretching as far as she could see, when suddenly the phone rang out, shrill and vibrant.

'Hello.'

'Hi. At last. I rang earlier and someone else, maybe Jean Pickering, picked it up. So I put it down fast.'

A thick blast of warmth spread through Jo's limbs as she heard Emmi's voice down the line.

'Sorry. Anyway, it's great to hear from you. Oh, I'm so glad you rang back. It's hell here. I can't stand it without you. How are you?'

Emmi's voice sounded slightly distorted, but otherwise it was hard to believe she was hundreds of miles away. The sound of her voice suddenly made Jo want to reach out and touch her. A burning lump rose in her throat.

'Oh, it's just amazing here. Today the sun came out and we went up to an old pool in the forest. And tonight Michael's leading this – I don't know, ritual, I suppose. He's chosen me to take a special part in it. I'm excited, but things can be a bit scary too. How are things with that bastard Graham? I hope he's managing to keep it inside his pants.'

'Oh, Emmi,' she began, before hearing her voice crack. 'I don't think I can handle it.'

There was silence, then Emmi's snarl. 'Just tell him to fuck off.'

'And Colin expects me to get out there and do things with Graham all of a sudden. He's so heavy, you know.'

'Honest, Jo. I am sorry. Listen, if it really does get too much, come up here. The nearest village is Thorsby. Got it? Thorsby on the edge of Moerland Forest.'

'Oh, I don't know,' said Jo, recovering a little. 'It's not that bad. Maybe I can sort it all out. But since, you know, our night together, well, I can't think straight. I want to be with you.'

She waited to hear what her friend would make of this.

'I know. It's the same with me. Oh, Jo, you need to come here. I do want you with me. You can't stay in that Victorian dump all your life. We'd have the most amazing time. Things are happening so fast here. I could talk to you properly about all this.'

Just listening to Emmi made Jo feel weird. Aching need seemed to grab inside her.

'I feel so frustrated,' she blurted. 'I can't stop thinking about what you did.'

'Me too.' Emmi's voice had turned a bit breathless too. 'The way you responded. It makes me so horny just thinking about it.'

'I know. Oh God.'

'What are you wearing?' Emmi suddenly enquired.

'You're not going to believe this. That black skirt and my red T-shirt. Nothing else.'

A long silence.

'Wow. Why nothing else?'

'To be honest, I was upstairs playing with myself. Thinking about you.'

There was no need, she instantly decided, to mention Graham's part in it. After all, what she was saying was true. Economical, but true.

'Listen. I'm in the phone box at Thorsby. There's no one else around. My pussy's getting wet just talking to you. I've just opened my shorts. God, I'm soaking. Do you want to hear what I want to do when we meet up again?'

The sound that came out of Jo's mouth was barely a croak. 'Yeah.'

'Then go into the mission hall. Get one of the candles off the shelf.'

'What?'

'You know. A nice thick one.'

'I can't.'

'You can.'

Jo found that she could; that indeed she wanted to very much, despite any protestations. Although her walk to the mission hall was rather unsteady, she soon returned cradling a thick white candle in the crook of her arm.

'Hi. I've got it,' she confessed into the phone.

'Then get your hand up your skirt.'

51

'I can't. I'm in the hallway. People are walking past every few minutes.'

'Get your jacket off the stand. Go on.'

Feeling dizzy with excitement, Jo tottered over to the coat stand and pulled her jacket down. Then she draped it casually over her knees and picked up the phone again.

'Right. I'm ready.'

'OK. Close your eyes. Imagine this. It's dark. We're sitting in one of the big barns. I'm sitting there next to you. It's a hot summer's day but we've just come into the shadows to get cool. But there's a strange scent in the barn – really wild and vital. You notice they've been using this place to mate the animals. You can hear a muffled groaning from behind the animal stalls. And the sound of animal hide slapping on hide. The air is salty with sex. All you can see is the thrusting and bucking of shadows against the wall, but it turns you on. It makes your skin tingle with excitement. All that wild fucking in the darkness.

You can reach out and touch the hot flanks of a large animal lunging fast, so fast that the rough hide burns your outstretched palm. All that hard power, driving deeper and deeper. You wonder what that much power must feel like. You want to share it. You press gently against the rough flank of the rutting creature until it tickles your stomach. Your nipples get hard from the friction, rubbing up and down, back and forth. You press harder. The lips of your pussy part against the creature's flank. Its rubbing you faster than you can stand. OK? What are you doing?'

Jo swallowed, trying to lubricate her parched mouth.

'I'm wanking myself off.' Her hand was so wet the juice was right up in the cracks between her fingers.

'OK. I've got my pants down round my knees. I'm

leaning against the glass of the phone box. I'm imagining the pad of my finger is the tip of your tongue, lapping over my clit. Are you nearly there?'

The front door opened. Jo looked up, red faced. It was only Graham's brother Pete, running into dinner. Quickly he scampered past.

'Yeah. Really close.'

She had to hold her fingers motionless just to speak. Otherwise, she realised, nothing but strangled moans would have come out of her mouth.

'When you get there, say "I'm coming", will you?'

'Sure.'

'Now push that candle inside you.'

'Now?'

'Yeah, while I tell you what happens next.'

The long hard cylinder of wax was getting warm beneath Jo's jacket. Tentatively, she ran her fingers along its length. It was much too long, but a nice, solid width. A little shakily, she explored the tapered end and found the little tuft of wick. Then, parting her legs wide beneath the jacket, she aimed the pointed end at her wet opening. When the hard wax made contact, she gasped down the phone.

'What is it?'

'It's really hard.' Carefully, she slid an inch inside herself. 'As hard as rock.'

'Now ease it backwards and forwards. Gently at first.'

Jo obeyed the voice down the phone. As the candle tip pushed her hotly clinging walls apart, deeply thrilling sensations began to build in her abdomen.

'How does it feel?'

'Like I can't get enough,' Jo gasped. 'Like I want it never to stop.' Clutching the phone to her ear, she began to thrust the candle in a steady rhythm, feeling her thighs fall open weakly. 'Am I still in the barn?'

'Yes. I'm behind you now. Pressing you hard against the creature. It's fucking away, thrusting its huge cock inside its mate, really slapping into her. You can smell it, the briny scent of come beginning to stream out of it. It's like all nature is fucking; the primeval force is so strong that you can taste the juices on the air.

I push you even closer, squeezing your lovely, hard little tits, pushing your wet pussy into fur and bristly skin. And now you can see it. A huge leathery animal cock, grinding away. And it's so big it makes you feel dizzy just to see it. And you know what you think, don't you? You wish it was inside you, don't you? That you were there underneath it, bent over naked in the straw. That this huge phallus, the source of it all, pummelling away like the strokes of time itself, was fucking you. So I push you closer, so close that you can feel the hard wet base of the shaft squeezing against fur and flesh. And you touch it. It's like touching the core of nature itself. It pulses with life, slippery with potent seed. It's dripping already, getting closer and closer to explosion point.' Emmi paused for breath and said, 'God, I can't go on much longer. Is it pushed deep inside you?'

'Yeah.' It was a hoarse whisper. 'Almost there.'

With eyes closed shut, Jo was lost in a landscape of darkness. All her senses were focussed on the long, hard object pounding inside her. Gingerly, she grasped the end and turned her hand so the heel of her palm just brushed her clitoris.

'Almost there,' she breathed again.

'So I pull you down on the ground and hold you there. I push my hand into your pussy and it's wet; so wet and ready. And you want it, that primal cock; you want it forcing its way inside you. It's so big that you want to scream. It's jamming into your tight little

54

entrance. But it's the most fantastic sensation, like connecting with something ancient and strong. It's so big that you don't know if you can take it, even just into the entrance, but I hold you tight, stopping you from collapsing forward. And it's so wet, like a long slippery pole, that it slides inside you and starts working back and forward, almost lifting you off the ground.'

The candle was burning inside her, stoking up that incandescent spot, far inside, near her cervix.

'Emmi,' she cried out. Her hand was pushing the hard rod of wax as deep as she could inside her, all the time grinding the heel of her hand against the pulpy wetness of her pussy.

'OK. He starts to come. Gushing hotness inside you. You struggle to get away now, because the feeling is so powerful. But I hold you there tight, gripping your waist, making you take it. It makes you shake with pleasure. You hold him tight like a vice but he thrusts faster and faster. All you can feel is that hot rain, bursting in waves inside you. It's incredible. He's filling you up. Oh God, I'd love to see –'

'I'm coming. Oh – now, yes –'

The hardness filled her. Her mind swam with wild images – of being overcome by the relentless animal phallus, of its overwhelming stabbing force. In her imagination she felt the hot gush of seed scalding her most sensitive skin. A wave of liquid fire seemed to rise and then explode from the centre of her body. For a long drawn-out moment, Jo pushed the candle as deep as she could stand it. Then it began to ebb. She was aware of her bare feet flexing against the cold floor. She opened her eyes. Shakily, she lifted the phone to her ear.

'Emmi?' she croaked. 'Did you get there too?'

'Oh yeah. Yeah, I'm just trying to recover. A car just

drove past. God, I think the driver saw me going into overdrive with my foot jammed up against the door. He definitely slowed down. I think I'd better get going before he decides to turn round for a replay.'

'Jo, what's going on? Dinner's almost over.' It was Colin, of all people. Glowering at her from the main doors, with a smear of gravy staining his white shirt.

'Sorry, Colin. I'll only be a sec. I'll just say bye.'

'If you are cold,' he continued, glaring at the jacket across her knees, 'you should wear your shoes like everyone else.'

Thank God; he then turned on his heels and was gone.

'I heard that,' laughed Emmi down the phone. 'I'll ring again next week. Seven next Friday.'

'Yeah, you do that. I'll be thinking of you. Take care, won't you?'

'Take care yourself. And make sure you don't let Colin get hold of that candle.'

Jo laughed. 'This candle's mine now. It's pretty well melted away. Though it sounds like nothing compared to whatever you're getting over at Fenris Gate.'

'You are right there. This place is something else, Jo. I never knew anywhere could be like this. The whole place is amazing. It's sheer fucking magic.'

Chapter Four

There was something going on in the barn. Jo could hear it – a gigantic, pounding heartbeat, pulsing out into the night air. It was not a pleasant sound. It was relentless and machine-like, as if some horrible experiment was being taken to its most dangerous limits and beyond. Quivering in the cold darkness, she shrank back into the shadows.

What made it worse was that she could hear everything so acutely: the grinding of flesh, the feverish panting, the dangerous creak as the wooden building rocked on its foundations. Ears twitching with pain, she began to shiver. At some time soon, she knew she had to enter the dark precincts of the barn. It made her heart shudder with terror. She could feel all her hair rise at the roots and stand upright.

A snap of a twig behind her. Licking the dry corners of her mouth, she turned and tried to pierce the black night with her powerful vision.

A dark shape was shuffling towards her. Instinctively, she tried to shrink down to the ground, compressing herself into as small an object as she could.

At the same time she listened sharply, trying to detect the source of the movement across the yard. It was almost impossible to track the shape while the pounding rhythm of nature built to a crescendo inside the barn. No – she could not tell where the intruder now was. But she knew the dark shape was watching her. It was waiting for the chance to pounce.

Trapped between the cacophony inside the barn and the stalking darkness of the shape in the yard, a terrible tremor began in her bones as she crouched down low in the dirt. She wanted to be somewhere else. She wanted to be anywhere but here.

The dark shape grabbed her arm. Hissing and spitting, she tried to wriggle free. It would not let go. It was holding her. She cried out, her heart exploding with fear. It was as dark as shadow but the hand that held her was tight as steel. She could feel cool, metallic claws puncture her skin, drawing precious blood.

Opening her mouth to the night air, she howled with terror.

'Jo! Jo! For God's sake keep quiet.'

Through sleep-drugged eyes, Jo struggled to identify the huge shape hovering above her. Viciously, she struck at it, trying to dislodge the iron grip of talons from her arm.

'OK, it's OK. Calm down, will you.'

At last the sensation of being held ceased. Panting, she looked about herself, trying to distinguish dream from reality. She was hot with sweat but simultaneously cold from fear. At last the wisps of her dream floated off to reveal an even starker reality.

'Graham. What the hell are you doing here?'

She was furious. Sitting up she did her best to get a grip on the situation. 'What time is it? Are you crazy?'

'You ask me that? You're the one acting like a

complete maniac. I thought you were going to draw blood just then.'

He was rubbing his arm angrily, though no doubt she had barely scratched him. Jo's head was clearing. How typical of Graham's upside-down logic. Oh yeah, of course she was crazy for striking out at an intruder in her own private room in the middle of the night. Just like it was always her fault for provoking him to his sexual outbursts with her supposed flagrant behaviour. Oh no, it had nothing to do with him at all.

'I was dreaming,' she spat. 'Now would you please get out of here and let me get back to sleep.'

'But, Jo –' He lowered himself down on to the edge of her bed and laid a hand on her arm.

'Will you get off me!' Curling away from him on to her side, she decided to stonewall him. The Graham situation was getting out of control, she decided. Tomorrow she was definitely going to have to give it some serious thought.

His hand remained like a dead weight on her back.

'I need to talk to you,' he whispered in a low tone, no doubt intended to ingratiate. 'I've only come to tell you it's all OK. There's nothing to worry about. We can do what we want.'

Cryptic bloody riddles, she thought, sighing loudly and pulling her sheet up under her chin.

'What are you talking about?' she asked flatly.

The dead hand began to rub her back in an attempt to console.

'Come on, Jo. You know. What we both want to do. Look. I've got some.'

With a very bad feeling in the pit of her stomach, Jo rolled over and squinted up into the gloom. Graham was holding out a small packet that she guessed could only contain condoms. She did not speak.

'Honest, Jo. It's all sorted. We don't even need to worry about Colin. He's quite happy about it, so long as we use these. After all, like Colin says, its better we express ourselves in a meaningful relationship that God will sanction than go off with anyone else outside the Mission. He was incredibly reasonable about it, actually.'

At last Jo broke the silence, trying to strip all emotion out of her voice. 'And why exactly did you tell him? Explain. What was going on in your brain?'

She couldn't see Graham's face, but reckoned that even he must be looking sheepish at this point. But no, when he spoke he was completely without insight.

'Oh, he was asking me about you. He's really concerned. Thinks you might go off the rails like Emmi. So when I told him we already have a thing going on together, he said it was just what you needed – that it would settle you down. In fact, he said it was best for us to make a commitment and get married – you know, as soon as we can. And in the meantime, you know – sex is OK.' He was waiting for an answer; for the first time his speech faltered. 'So here I am,' he added with a nervous laugh.

'Sex is OK,' Jo said slowly. 'Oh, I see. It's OK with Colin. And of course it's OK with you, Graham. So that's fine. Only you forget someone else.'

'Huh?'

Jo was already getting up, groping around for the key to her bedroom. Finding the piece of cold metal, she slipped out of bed and went to the door.

'Come here, will you.' Dutifully, Graham followed her until he stood on the threshold. At last she let out a hiss of anger, as scalding as a jet of hot steam from an over-pressurised engine.

'There's something you forgot, Graham,' she spat, jabbing him out of the door with her finger. 'You and my so-called Brother Colin, my supposed protector. You forget to ask me, that's what! How dare you talk about me, like – like a piece of nothing that can't decide for herself what to do? Well, I've decided a lot of things over the last two minutes. And one of them is that I never want to feel your creepy hands on me again in my life!'

With a hard push he was out of the door, his face dumbstruck, his limbs soft with shock. Then the key turned in the lock and Jo leaned her head against the hard door. For the time being at least, she had what she wanted. She had a little time before the inquiries of the morning to make her escape.

Sheer, raging anger sped Jo down as far as the motorway bridge. With a jumbled collection of her possessions shoved into a shoulder bag, she tiptoed down the backstairs and let herself out as usual at the sash window in the kitchen. All the way along the grey, moonlit pavements she raged: at the pair of males talking about her, deciding her life, foisting their chauvinistic prejudices on her. It made her want to scream.

It was only on the thin arch of the bridge that she first took any real account of her surroundings. Until then the streets had been deserted, echoing to the lonely beat of her footsteps. Every pair of curtains was drawn and all doors were locked securely. She felt like a complete outsider – orphaned, enraged, betrayed. But before she could sink too low in a well of self-pity, she noticed a small white creature blocking her path across the motorway bridge.

It was only a cat. A sleek, well-tended cat sitting upright on the ground with her tail frisking gently from side to side. But it stopped Jo in her tracks as it lifted its pointed little chin and regarded her coolly with eyes alight like two green orbs of electricity.

61

'Who are you?' she whispered into the night.

The cat only sniffed with proud disdain and batted her tail against the ground. Was it a sign? Jo wondered crazily. Was she supposed to turn back? Or was the cat some kind of magical symbol of her own catlike identity? For in that moment, her interrupted dream returned to her vividly. When she had dreamed herself to be shivering outside the barn, a part of her fear had stemmed from being so small and vulnerable. Her senses had been so heightened because she had believed herself to be something other than she was – she had convinced herself in her dream that she really was a cat.

Yawning, the white cat showed a set of pearly sharp teeth and then snapped her jaws back together with a soft click. Turning, she whipped her tail around and padded silently down the pathway to the motorway sliproad. Hesitantly, Jo followed. As she descended the dark ravine she could just see the small white blur of the cat slinking on ahead. But when she reached the wide expanse of whitely lit tarmac, the creature had disappeared.

There was nothing for it, Jo realised, than to hold out her thumb and wait. A few trucks thundered past, headlamps careering across the landscape. She started to get cold and stamped her feet impatiently. Maybe, she thought, I should just turn round and have a long think about this in the morning – after a good night's sleep in a warm bed.

But up above her on the motorway parapet was a white shape. It could have been an empty paper bag blown by the wind and trapped against the metal grille. Or maybe, Jo thought, it was the strange white cat placidly watching over her.

Jo kept her thumb up as a sleek saloon car slowed down a few metres ahead of her. Peering inside the green illuminated interior she found Maurice, a balding, middle-aged salesman on his way to a breakfast meeting in York. Once inside, the car was warm and comfortable. And it felt good to be moving, with the glittering motorway Catseyes disappearing beneath the wheels like a moving chain of diamonds. All Maurice wanted was some company to stop him falling asleep. Yawning, Jo listened to his talk of sales targets, goals and pensions. It was a small price to pay. At last she was speeding on her way to Fenris Gate.

By the time Maurice dropped her off on the bridge outside York, Jo was sick of his aftershave that smelled like it had been processed from chemicals and his increasingly probing questions about her destination. And above all, she was dog-tired. Now that shops were opening in the cobbled streets of York and the bells of the towering Minster were ringing nine o'clock, Jo's exhaustion was dissolving away her new confidence. Traipsing through the city to the main route running east, she began to wonder at her rashness – if she had not lost her temper, she could have been getting up to a normal day with a normal breakfast. Her eyes were heavy from lack of sleep and she was beginning to feel sick with hunger.

Finally, she stopped in one of the old squares of the city beneath the medieval walls. She had a few pounds in her purse, which she knew she really should keep for emergencies. Still, she considered, her good spirits were the most important thing. So, after finding a cheap cafe she ordered a huge breakfast of toast, eggs, bacon, tomatoes, sausage and tea. The warmth from her stomach soon spread to her limbs. Her brain began to wake up as the sun shone in through the smeary cafe window. It was a newly confident Jo that set off again at ten thirty to stand on the gritty kerbside, where most drivers guiltily turned their eyes away from her and roared on ahead.

The first car to stop contained two young lads on their way to Newcastle. On a gut instinct, Jo refused the lift, avoiding their leery eyes. But when, after another long hour, the next driver said he was heading for Middlesborough but had never heard of Thorsby, Jo started to get worried. Even worse, she began to think about chocolate bars and mugs of hot coffee. More than anything, she wished she could just lie down somewhere and have a long nap. Her back and legs were aching from standing and despite the thin sunshine she was getting cold. Then, at last, a beat-up old landrover pulled up. Desperate now, Jo looked inside. Brilliant – a woman.

'I'm trying to get to the North York Moors,' she gabbled through the lowered window. 'Thorsby, to be exact. You going anywhere nearby?'

'Sure. Hop in. I can get you about six miles from Thorsby. Throw your bag in the back.'

Jo barely had time to notice that Bridgit, as she introduced herself, was a youngish, Celtic looking woman with bright red, hennaed hair. Then, like a veil falling over her, Jo slumped back into the seat and off into a long, dreamless sleep.

It was afternoon when she woke. The landrover was circling a vast expanse of empty scrubland with not another car or building in sight. Above hung a bright, jewel-blue sky dotted with a few skimming birds. All around them was brown and purplish vegetation as far as the hazy horizon.

'Wow. The moors?'

'Yes indeed. One of the last great open spaces in Britain. That's why we live up here. It's good to get into York every month or so, but really me and Dan just want to enjoy the world as it was meant to be.'

Yawning, Jo wriggled upright. 'But what do you do? There's no work out here I guess.'

Bridgit turned the vehicle off down a single-track lane covered in rutted potholes that bounced the tyres up and down. Jo rubbed her eyes and took in the white lines of drystone walls and a few hardy looking sheep.

'Why don't you come and see? You've missed the one bus to Thorsby village ages ago. There's plenty of room at our place to put you up for the night. And I can show you what we're into. What about it?'

She already liked Bridgit. There was something open and easy about her manner. She was so unlike the judgmental types at the mission. And her leather jacket and hippy-style clothes were pretty cool.

'Sure.'

After all, Jo had nowhere else to go.

Dan and Bridgit's place was a squat, tumbledown farmhouse built of ancient, mossy stone. Around the back were sheds and outbuildings where Dan and Bridgit kept a small collection of livestock and a pond for a flock of squawking geese. Jo thought it was incredible; a kind of fairytale retreat set miles and miles from civilisation.

A long-coated border collie sprang up to Bridgit, smothering her with doggie kisses.

'Yeah, yeah, Kit. And where's Dan? Is he in the studio?'

Circled by the exuberant collie, Bridgit and Jo crossed the cobbles to the largest outbuilding. It was an ancient timbered barn in which large, velux windows had been set high into the roof. Inside, the whitewashed space was filled with light that illuminated a series of vast canvasses propped against the walls. Dan was working on a painting and draped in a grubby, paint-spattered shirt. Black hair straggled to his collar but his face was warm and sensitive as he noticed Jo. She fancied an intense, artistic light burned in his dark eyes but as Bridgit introduced her, she felt him relax as he welcomed her.

'So, you're an artist? I've never met an artist.' Jo glanced at the painting he was working on. It was a dramatic series of lines, like a cave painting showing strange creatures rearing one against the other.

'No, I'm just a dauber.' He smiled, showing neat, polished teeth. 'Bridgit's the artist. Didn't she say she was in York finalising arrangements for a major exhibition? That's one of her pieces, there.'

Dan pointed to a bizarre sculpture that filled one corner of the studio. At first glance it was like one of the huge stuffed animals Jo had seen in museums, but there was something odd about it. It was neither a bear nor a buffalo but suggested both. Part of the ribcage was exposed to reveal a ticking clock. Its feet were reptilian claws; its eyes, luminous jewels.

'It's a mythical creation,' Dan explained. 'A kind of tribute to extinct species. But Bridgit's exhibition is mostly around the theme of wolves. They are just tremendous.'

'I'll show you.' Bridgit smiled. 'But let's leave Dan in peace and check up on the real animals first.'

Outside, spring sunshine filled the yard. A flock of clucking hens scurried out of their way as they approached a wide barn door.

'We prefer to live out here with our animals,' Bridgit explained as she swung the double doors back. 'The winters are hard but it's magical too. We couldn't live in the city anymore. It's madness. No one can create there. Duke's my pony. He's a real beauty.'

It was gloomy inside, but Jo heard a scuffle and welcoming snort as a large creature moved towards them across his stall. Then she saw him; a lovely chestnut pony who whinnied pleasurably at the sight of Bridgit. Gently, he snuffled his velvety nose into his mistress's palm.

'But I thought Dan said you modelled wolves. Surely you don't keep them here too?'

'No. You're right.' Bridgit was stroking Duke's ears, pulling on them playfully. 'In the end you just have to let your imagination take off and work from that. But all my animals are my models in spirit. The idea is that they live quite unselfconsciously. They represent the untamed spirit in my art. So even Duke, who is beautifully domesticated, is still wonderfully wild at heart. You see, he doesn't think self-consciously in the way we do. If he licks my hand, it's not an attempt to charm me or even, as some stupid people think, to lick essential minerals off my skin. It's just pure, pleasurable affection. Animal instincts are not perverted like ours. With my art I want people to remember what that feels like – to have pure, unadulterated instinct. What do you think, Jo?'

Duke was tentatively sniffing Jo's hand now. She was a stranger to him but she clearly intrigued him, judging by the way that he was extending his huge tongue to delicately lap at the crevices between her fingers. It tickled.

Jo had been listening hard, growing more and more interested in what Bridgit was saying.

'I feel like what I want has been distorted all my life,' Jo admitted dreamily. 'I've been taught that only humans have reason and that gives us choice. But really, I guess it just loads us up with guilt. I wish I could be like Duke. Just follow my instincts and express myself. You know, sometimes I feel like there are two sides to me. Do you know what I mean? The goody-goody who wants to please everybody and then another part. She's not bad – only a bit dangerous.'

Bridgit laughed and slid her hand through Jo's arm. It was hard not to warm to the older woman; she seemed so accepting and non-judgmental.

'So you think you're a bit dangerous, Jo?' She smiled. 'Well, maybe Fenris Gate is the place to find that out.'

'You know it? Tell me. Go on.'

'I know Michael Ruthen.' Bridgit's face glowed momentarily as she recalled him. 'He's quite a famous shaman. That is, he works with magic and spirits, rediscovering old techniques. That's why I went to see him last year. In some ways his ideas are similar to mine; in other ways they're not. You'll certainly be impressed. And he'll do his best to wipe out the goody-goody in you.'

'I don't understand.'

'Oh, Michael's pretty charismatic. Seductive, I suppose. But I resisted.'

'Why? Because of Dan?'

Again, Bridgit's face broke out in that coolly amused smile.

'Maybe. Though Dan and I are pretty open about not letting our relationship shut us off from new experiences. No, there is also something about Michael Ruthen that might have upset my equilibrium – my karma, let's say. I wanted to get my exhibition work ready and at a time like that it's important to stay in control. That's always important, Jo. Stay in control of what happens to you.'

'But if you give in to your instincts, like you say, aren't you going to lose control of yourself?'

'That's the trick, I suppose. Use your reason to check out what you are getting yourself into. Make sure you are safe and secure. Then let yourself go. Let sheer instinct overtake you.'

'I'd like to do that,' Jo said with a fierce intensity. 'I want to go way beyond what other people think is OK.'

'Oh, Jo.' Bridgit smiled ruefully. 'I think you're going to have a wild time at Fenris Gate. But just promise me – keep a bit of yourself back from Michael. Don't let him overwhelm you.'

'Of course not. Well, I haven't even met him yet,' she added.

Disengaging her arm, Bridgit sauntered over to an even darker part of the old barn.

'And then there's Seth. He's one of my favourite models.'

The pure white creature looked at them from his strange, slitted eyes. Seth was a long-haired, amber-eyed goat. Jo held back warily.

'I don't know if I like him,' she confided to Bridgit. 'Goats are symbols of the devil. Aren't they used in black magic?'

Bridgit laughed, stroking Seth's long, curling horns.

'Exactly. They have become a symbol of all that human beings seek to repress. Symbols of the dark side and orgiastic sex. But is that evil, Jo? Or is it a kind of evil to hold down our instincts so tightly that we fear them? I think it is. Actually, Seth is a complete scamp. He ate one of my favourite T-shirts off the washing line last week. But he looks really fierce as a model. Anyway, let's go in and get some dinner ready. It's a change for me and Dan to have a guest.'

Bridgit was as creative a cook as she was an artist. That evening, the three sat down around the dining table to a vegetarian feast of spicy, raisin-studded pilaff, cashew nut roast and a spread of crunchy, primary-coloured salads. Dan poured rich, burgundy wine into deep, gilded goblets. Jo had never tasted food like it. In Africa her parents had preferred their cook to recreate bland European food. And the food at the Northford Mission had been plain and poor, bought in bulk from the cut-price warehouse. Listening to Dan and Bridgit talk about art and people she didn't know, Jo let herself get lost in the pleasure of new flavours and textures as Dan politely kept her wineglass full of smooth, velvety wine.

Dessert was a succulent Moroccan cake of almonds and dried fruit. Dan produced another smaller glass of sweet white wine to accompany it.

'That was just – amazing,' Jo managed, after helping herself to the last slice of cake.

'I'm glad you enjoyed it. Because I want to ask a favour.' Bridgit's smile suddenly looked a little less confident. 'But you know, if you don't want to do it – just say.'

'No, no problem. Anything. Honest. You've been brilliant. Putting me up and everything.'

'Well.' The older woman pushed her wineglass away and looked momentarily over to Dan for support. 'I'd really love you to model for me before you go. All afternoon, I've had this idea. It's a bit complicated, but it's about your spirit, Jo. I want you to model with the wolves.'

'Brilliant. No problem.' Then Jo thought for a second. 'You mean sit still while you draw me?'

'No. I'm not a painter like Dan. My work is more experimental – I'll be putting the wolves in a dark space, with a soundtrack. I'm thinking about maybe a video loop projected on the wall. I want to film you.'

'OK.' Jo was less sure now. 'Do I have to do anything? I mean, I can't act or anything.'

'It doesn't matter. Listen, why don't we have a go

now? Dan's going to clear up, anyway. I was thinking of using candlelight. The light will be perfect now.'

'OK.'

Bridgit's studio was far, far different from Dan's. If she had not known the room belonged to an artist, Jo might have thought the place was a hunter's trophy-room or a weird, paralysed zoo. But it was not fear that ran through Jo's slightly drunken mind. Instead, a wave of excitement and wonder moved her through the maze of spellbound creatures. With outstretched hands she stroked the rough fur of gigantic, wide-jawed wolves as they silently bayed to an absent moon. Some of the creatures she noticed were very strange indeed; bizarre morphs of humans and animals of exaggerated or mixed sex. One half-woman, half-jackal reared to show a row of many-nippled breasts. An extraordinary looking werewolf posed gymnastically, bent backwards on hands and feet, like a pastiche of the naked woman made into a coffee table Jo had seen in a magazine. But he had a large, erect penis protruding upwards from his groin. Other creatures appeared to be hermaphrodite, showing both male and female parts.

'What do you think?'

Bridgit was lighting a scattering of flickering candles along the walls of the room while Jo moved through the creatures as if through a magic land.

'Like nothing I've ever seen before in my life. Except maybe in dreams – or nightmares.'

Deep within her, the animals seemed to start up echoes of ancient fears and beliefs. Myths and legends sprang to the surface of her mind; of the half-bull, half-man Minotaur, of the shapeshifting werewolf and the ancient animal gods of Egypt. She understood now that Bridgit had an amazing talent.

'They are inspired by pagan art – ancient myths and

peasant ritual. I want people who see my art to feel like they are entering a dark chamber of their mind. One they rarely visit, but one that is always there – a part of their unconscious mind. Here, Jo, want another drink while I set up the camera?'

Bridgit produced another bottle of wine and a couple of glasses. Despite her head already being light and woozy, Jo reached for another glass. Whatever it was Bridgit wanted her to do, it was apparent she might do it better if she was relaxed, she told herself. And there was also the strange, conspiratorial closeness that was developing between herself and Bridgit. Jo was pleasurably intrigued. She very much wanted to please Bridgit, but also to learn from her cool and assured manner.

Bridgit raised the lightweight camera to her shoulder and did a quick light check.

'OK. I'm all set.'

'What do you want me to do?' Looking into the blind eye of the camera, Jo felt a sudden embarrassment. All this equipment – and all these deep ideas – she was sure to blow it somehow.

Putting down the camera, Bridgit suddenly walked over to her and took both her hands.

'Remember when we talked this afternoon about instinct.' Her fingers tightened around Jo's palms, making her suddenly look into the golden intensity of the artist's eyes. 'You said that sometimes you want that to overwhelm you? Well, look around you. These are figurative representations of instincts inspired by dreams and stories. Cast off your inhibitions for a short time. Take off your clothes if you want. I want to see you as a human being exploring these instincts. Just be yourself wandering through my exhibition – curious and maybe a little bit scared. OK?'

Looking up into Bridgit's candlelit face, she wondered momentarily what the older woman would think if she knew about her encounter with Emmi. Would she be shocked? she wondered. Bridgit was so outspoken, but often, Jo guessed, people only lived in a world of ideas. Would the fact that Jo found Bridgit physically attractive be too much of an unwelcome reality? After all, she clearly had a wonderful relationship with Dan.

'OK. I'll try.'

'Just forget the camera's here. In fact, forget I'm here too. Pretend you've just wandered in here and you can do what you want without anyone ever knowing.'

Rather shakily, Jo began to wander through the labyrinth of creatures, feeling stupid and self-conscious as Bridgit followed her with the blank eye of the camera trained upon her. Tentatively, she began to reach out to the creatures. Avoiding the more extreme sculptures, she wandered up and down the aisles of strange statues, reaching out and stroking them, or just stopping to stare in awe. Soon she stopped in her tracks to concentrate on a fairly realistic black bear that crouched by the far wall.

'He's beautiful,' she murmured, as her fingers ran through the thick pelt running along his back.

'Why not ride him?' came a whispered response from Bridgit, from behind the camera.

Still feeling graceless, Jo dropped to her knees beside the sculpture and began to explore the ruff-like fur around his head and razor-like jaw. How scary, she thought, if such an animal had the power to suddenly bound back to life. Her hands ran over his short curling tail as a strange yearning ran through her veins. The pressure on her to perform for the camera was growing. Maybe that was it, she wondered drunkenly. Maybe she should ride him for the film.

She had changed into her only skirt for dinner and now, when she tried to climb on to the creature's broad back, it restricted her legs. No longer quite as self-conscious, she hitched up her skirt and let her legs grip the wide animal torso. The thick fur tickled the inside of her thighs pleasurably and suddenly Jo wished she really were alone here. She imagined that in a very few minutes it would be possible to rub herself to orgasm against the ticklish hide. Then, remembering Bridgit's filming, she did her best to put such crazy ideas out of her brain.

Leaning forward to caress the bear's thick neck, she became aware of the eyes of the surrounding creatures twinkling in the candlelight. Bridgit was right. If only she could do it justice, this would make a stunning piece of film. In her mind's eye, she could see herself as the one, luminously living creature among this strange, statuesque zoo.

'Undress.'

Jo almost had to ask Bridgit to repeat herself. Of course, she realised: artistically, it would look incredible to see a naked girl among these animals. Jo told herself that Bridgit was simply trying to create an atmosphere that had nothing to do with sex itself. After all, her sculptures were only artificial pieces of fibreglass and fake fur. Any suggestion of sexuality was all coming from Jo's overheated imagination. The wine was helping that mood too, she told herself, as she began to unbutton her top.

She could just see the impassive black orb of the camera lens following her movements. It made her want to perform; she wanted to seduce it and her as yet unseen audience. Sliding her cotton top off from her shoulders she was aware of the contrast of her smooth creamy flesh against the thick fibrous fur of the bear.

Digging her heels around its belly, she felt a warm surge of arousal spread between her legs. The back of the creature was broad – so broad that it stretched her passage vulnerably. Quickly, she unbuttoned her bra and felt her small breasts nuzzle free. Now the camera's touch felt almost tangible, as if the recording it made was indeed a kind of caress. As the dark eye of the lens passed over her white breasts she felt her nipples rise hard into the air. The equipment obscured Bridgit's face. Jo was thankful for that.

The rough tickling between her legs was aggravating her now. If she had been alone, she would certainly have begun to rub against that deliciously bristly pelt. So, Jo reluctantly slid off the bear's back and began to wander along the shadowy aisles of creatures. Whether it was the wine relaxing her mind or the magic of the candlelight dancing over strange and dreamlike bodies, she could not tell, but her mind felt utterly at one with the performance she was giving. Yesterday or tomorrow no longer seemed important. She wanted to explore her instincts and be filmed as she did so.

Moving from one phantasmogorical creature to the next, she caressed them and pressed herself hard against skin and fur. Some were scaly against her naked breasts, others coldly smooth. Approaching the strangely endowed werewolf, her mind again raced back between her legs. If only, she thought yearningly, I could explore that oddly positioned phallus which rose so strikingly from his pelt. It was quite well proportioned, she realised. About the size of a man's cock but made of a gorgeously hard material that would never, ever go soft.

Coming back to herself, Jo realised she had been standing for quite some time, staring at the long hard cock with her mouth lasciviously open.

'Ride him,' came the whisper from Bridgit.

Jo licked her lips nervously. If she kept her back to the camera, no one would ever know that it was her in the film. Whatever instinct she indulged would be an utterly anonymous gratification. Very slowly and gracefully, she stepped forward and began to caress the creature's wild, ecstatic face.

She was aware of the camera burning against the naked flesh of her back. Leaning forward, she began to caress his ears and neck and then ran her fingers along the wiry fur of his stomach. With a little jolt to her heart, her fingers reached the hard protuberance of the false penis. It was shiny and hard and felt cold after the deep pile of fur. Gently, she slid the arc of her fingers around it, as if it were a man's cock she wanted to measure in her hands. In a kind of sympathetic response, she felt the muscles of her vagina grip on emptiness as it longed to be filled.

As she leaned across the creature, she was aware of the camera probing her body from behind. She guessed that the eye of the camera could not see what she was doing to the phallus standing up from the creature's body. Nevertheless, the suggestion of action just beyond the camera's reach would in itself be disturbing and maybe arousing. She was naked from the waist up, and her skirt was still concertinaed up around her hips as she leaned across the sculpture. In her mind, she could picture her legs slightly parted as she leaned forward over the creature and the skirt rising so high that the most tantalising glimpse of her white panties would appear just beneath the hem of her dress. Imagining herself on film like this made her pussy wince with excitement.

'Ride him,' came the whispered voice again.

Obediently, Jo walked to the creature's side and slid across its narrow waist just above the massy protuberance of the hard cock. She felt like a child on a bizarrely adult merry-go-round. In front of her parted thighs she could feel the violently hard phallus pressing against her pubis. If only she was alone, she thought bitterly. It looked perfectly shaped to just slide deep inside her. She could imagine herself pressed down hard on it, experiencing wave after wave of orgasmic release. Instead, she tried to calm herself by pressing the damp front of her knickers against it, hoping that both Bridgit and the camera could not tell that the strange protuberance excited her so much.

'Do you want some help?' came the voice from behind the camera.

Jo looked up in anguish. Bridgit could mean only one thing. In answer, she felt her clitoris pulse in greedy anticipation. She was aware of the camera being placed carefully down on a plinth in front of her. Then, in the space of a hammerblow of heartbeats, Bridgit moved out of the shadows and stood beside her.

As soon as the older woman slid her warm arm around her naked shoulder, Jo knew it would be just wonderful. Closing her eyes, Jo felt the woman's fingers run gently down her back and then tentatively run up across her breasts. The sensation of Bridgit's hands cupping her erectly sensitive nipples drove her wild. Overcome by excitement, Jo clung to her, pressing her mouth to her bare arms. Finally, Bridgit reached down and kissed the top of her head affectionately.

'Do you want to follow your instincts all the way?' she whispered.

Jo clung to her. 'Yes.'

'Do you want me and Dan to help you?'

Looking up quickly, Jo saw Dan standing in the shadows, his shirt open and long hair framing his sensitive face. Her heart seemed to gallop even faster than before. Both Dan and Bridgit together – her head swam at the thought of it. She had not seen him arrive, but somehow his presence seemed so right.

'Oh, yes,' she breathed passionately, staring up into Bridgit's gold-flecked eyes. 'Oh, yes. Just show me what to do. I want to go all the way; as far as I can go.'

Chapter Five

*D*an and Bridgit. Together. Jo's head reeled dizzily at the thought of it.

Bridgit was behind her, winding her bare arms around Jo's naked chest, kissing the top of her head gently. Whenever her warm fingers brushed against Jo's soft breasts, Jo's breath caught excitedly as her nipples sprang hot and hard against the woman's touch. She was melting in a pool of hot juices all over the rough-pelted sculpture of the wolf-man on which she sat. Anxiously, she looked over to where Dan stood in the shadows. Would he be shocked to see Bridgit touching her?

Dan's sardonic smile reassured her.

'I feel a bit left out. Do you mind if I carry on filming?' he asked softly.

'No.' Even to her own, blood-pounding ears, Jo's voice sounded like a hoarse gasp.

Like a sleepwalker, Dan crossed the darkness towards the discarded video camera. He had slipped his shirt off but his jeans clung to his narrow hips with the elegant assistance of a buckled leather belt. Jo suddenly acknowledged to herself just how strong the pull of attraction was towards him. She had barely glimpsed him earlier, but had quietly envied Bridgit. Yet at the same time, her desire for Bridgit had been slowly mounting all afternoon as well. What was it Emmi had said? Animals take pleasure naturally, without guilt. So this was it. No guilt, no shame. She could have it all.

When Dan ambled over to her and his hands slid down her naked spine, she groaned out loud. She could feel the pleasure in his fingertips as he tenderly rubbed her smooth skin. Then he hesitantly began to reach round to her breasts. Jo swung her head to one side in a kind of torment, so great was her pleasure; she wanted him so much to touch her.

But, with a teasing click of his tongue, he pulled back. Hoisting the camera to his shoulder, he watched her and Bridgit through it, the lens seeming to stroke her with its fascinated stare.

Behind Jo, she could feel his partner pressing yearningly against her.

'You are so lovely,' Bridgit sighed, turning her attention to Jo's naked legs. Almost out of her mind with excitement, Jo felt the woman's hands run from her knees to the tops of her legs, pulling the crumpled layer of her skirt even higher.

'Here. Let me take it off.' In a moment the skirt was unbuttoned and only Jo's white panties covered her nakedness.

Closing her eyes tight, Jo could vividly imagine the shot Dan would be taking. From his viewpoint in front of her, he would see Bridgit's excited exploration of her thighs and the way she could now barely stop herself rubbing forward against the thick shaft of the sculpted phallus. Without looking down, she knew she was as wet as she had ever been, the whole of her centre clenching with the fierce ache of need. The instinct to perform for the camera washed over her again; stretching upwards she felt her breasts rise on her ribcage, felt her throat stretch backwards. She could only guess what effect the images through the lens were having on Dan.

Bridgit's fingers began to play with the lace trim of Jo's panties, sending thrills of excitement pulsing rapidly along her nerves. While Bridgit pulled off her own clothes, Jo clung to her. Finally, Bridgit slid behind her so that Jo's back pressed against the warm bounciness of her breasts. At last they pressed smooth flesh against smooth flesh and the artist began to kiss the nape of her neck with small, mind-blowing kisses.

'Do you want it?' she whispered, so quietly that Dan would not be able to hear. 'Do you want to try my invention? I can help you.'

Jo couldn't speak. She just nodded her head quickly. In response, Bridgit slid her hand inside the wide parting of the younger girl's panties. The heat and lubricious wetness made her sigh pleasurably. Jo simply sat back, cradled against her female lover while she peeled back her panties to reveal the fuzz of pale-red hair surrounding her glistening pink labia.

'You really are lovely.'

Her fingers expertly teased the burning bud of Jo's clitoris, making her pant rapidly as a bucking orgasm approached.

'Shh, not so fast,' murmured Bridgit. Her tantalising fingers moved downwards now, towards the open well of Jo's entrance.

As two slender fingers pierced her, Jo felt her body shudder and jolt. Looking up with misty eyes, she could see Dan training the camera on her, following her every movement. It was almost killing her with excitement.

'In many cultures there is a secret initiation among the women into the mysteries of sex. Different fetishes – like our wolf friend's phallus – give a girl her first pleasure. Do you want to try it?' came the whispered voice.

'Yes,' she gasped.

'Then let me raise you.'

Raising Jo by her shoulders, Bridgit started to pull her above the artificial penis but a sudden fear struck the younger girl as the hardness of it brushed her thigh.

'Don't let go,' she gasped, struggling to hold Bridgit's arm so she would not suddenly drop her on to that fierce-looking appendage.

'Here. Let me help.' Dan quickly put down the camera and came towards her. Jo was aware of him grasping her, as her legs scrabbled helplessly against the side of the sculpture.

The next few moments of Jo's life seemed to be an exploding firebomb of sensation. Dan's bare chest was against her face. She could smell his sweat. Her mouth was pressed into muscle and a tangle of dark body hair. Behind her, she could feel Bridgit lifting her groin, parting her lips until the rounded end of the phallus forced its way inside her. It knocked the breath from her lungs. All of her mind was concentrated on the gripping waves of pleasure as an inch and then two inches of solidity seared inside her overheated body.

Dan was in front of her, holding her tight beneath her arms. Meanwhile, Bridgit held her thighs so she would not drop too suddenly. Jo hung like a rag doll, swinging deliciously above the phallus that was the focus of all her nerve-raging bliss.

Moaning into the darkness, she felt them lower her – very, very slowly. With each downward movement her entrance stretched wider than it had ever spread before. The phallus was hard and resistant but thankfully she was slick and wet. As inch after inch squeezed inside her, Jo felt it embed deep within her – quite still and irresistible but as hard as a hammer forcing apart the softness of her body.

'Do you want more?' whispered Bridgit, reaching round to feel the hard stalk of the shaft pushing inside her wet entrance. 'Can you take it?'

Oh, she wanted more. She wanted it all. Nodding her head, she panted a reply.

'It gets thicker towards the base,' murmured Dan. 'Say if it hurts.'

It already hurt. But the pain was not something she feared. It was a pain that scorched her, driving heat through her veins and filling her mind with pounding blood.

Very gently, Bridgit let her drop another inch. She felt impaled on it, her feet flailing against the hairy sides of the sculpture. Instinctively, she leaned forward into Dan's body, pressing her face into his hard belly. He was excited too. She could feel his hard-on flexing against her stomach. That turned her on even more. She found herself scrabbling for it, trembling fingers struggling with the intricacy of belt and buckle.

'Yes, yes, feel it,' he mumbled, as he helped her with a few expert movements of his hands. The rubbery length of his cock sprang out of his jeans, jutting against Jo's nakedness. Greedily, she reached for it, hands clawing at hair and skin and wetness. Inside her gripping hands, his cock jerked wonderfully, probing hotly against her stomach and breasts.

For what seemed like hours – but was barely seconds – Jo felt her orgasm rise up and up on a slow-motion roll. The artificial phallus was almost completely inside her – a piercing hardness inflaming

83

all the nerves of her abdomen. Bridgit was massaging her entrance, teasing her engorged clitoris with maddening, juice-heavy fingers. And Dan – Dan was suddenly going wild, his cock driving hard against her ribs, leaving smears of wet pre-come on her hot skin.

They were all breathing fast. Bridgit's fingers were doing magical things in the wetness of her centre. Dan began to lift and drop her shoulders, making her slide up and down on the rigid cock. Jo started to wail. There was no turning back. A fire was erupting in her belly. Suddenly Dan grabbed his cock and began to masturbate himself, giving long, tight-fisted tugs aimed at Jo's jolting breasts. It was all a crazy frenzy of body parts.

'I'm going to come,' Jo managed to groan. 'I'm, I'm –'

Dan's cock-end was a crimson bulb beneath her drooping face. His hand was a frantic blur. It drove her over the edge.

As Bridgit's fingers squeezed her clitoris, Jo's body stretched in a first almighty spasm. Dan's cock was erupting too; warm dribbles of come pulsed against her body. Still Bridgit's fingers kneaded her. Deep inside her body, Jo felt all her muscles grind around the hardness of the sculpture. It was so hard and long that she could feel the very top of her channel burn incandescently as it gripped like a vice, squeezing wave after wave of ecstasy through her nervous system.

'No,' she moaned at last, as the pleasure in her body turned to white-hot pain. 'Stop, stop. I can't stand it.'

Thankfully, at last, Bridgit stilled her hand. Struggling momentarily, they lifted Jo up and off the weird sculpture. As she slithered to rest on the floor, she could see the sculptured phallus still shining redly in the candlelight. It glistened with her juices, standing as stiff as a totem that has done its magic.

'Are you all right, sweetheart?'

Bridgit dropped down beside her and slid an affectionate arm around her shoulders. Then Dan slumped down too, looking totally shagged. At that moment she fiercely loved them both. They were both so different from anyone she had ever met – so totally off-limits. For ten minutes they sat on the floor of the studio, a tangle of limbs, finishing the wine in the dark. Then slowly Jo became aware that above her Dan and Bridgit were kissing; she could feel the straining of their bodies towards each other and the soft, slapping sound of their mouths on skin. She didn't mind; in fact, she liked it. She was propped up between the rimy sweat of Dan's chest and the sweeter softness of Bridgit. Dreamily, she closed her eyes to concentrate on them subtly writhing against her.

'Do you want to help me?'

Bridgit was whispering to Dan. When they disengaged themselves from Jo's limbs, she didn't ask them why they were moving back up to the sculpture. She already knew.

For a while she listened to them – to those strange, instinctive sounds that no one ever needs to learn. Wordlessly, they communicated as Jo listened. Then, as Bridgit's breathless pants turned to little wails of excitement, she stood to watch them. Her eyes widened with arousal.

Bridgit had mounted the sculpture's cock, which still stood slick with her own juices. She was lovely in her abandonment; her crimson hair bouncing over white shoulders, brown-tipped nipples pointing hard into the air. Bridgit's eyes were closed as she thrust down on the object of her pleasure; her lips parted as she occasionally ran her pink tongue over berry-red painted lips.

She was thrusting quite slowly, her long white thighs arching and stretching so that the fierce red phallus showed only momentarily between the dark curls of her pubis.

Jo simply gaped, feeling a corresponding heat building up in her own body. Biting her lip, she began to rub her own cleft, quite unconsciously. It was impossible to watch someone so completely unrestrained without getting horny. Bridgit's pleasure was totally contagious.

Slowly, Bridgit opened her pale eyes and smiled lasciviously. But it was not Jo she wanted to watch her. It was Dan who responded, by placing the camera back on a podium and strolling over to her.

'Hmm, that looks good. You can't get enough, can you?' he said amiably.

'Never goes flat on me,' she laughed breathlessly, posing like a gymnast on a bizarre piece of apparatus. 'But something at both ends – now that would finish me off.'

'Oh, yes please. Come and get it.'

Sure enough, as Bridgit reached up to open Dan's jeans, again a rock-hard erection sprang out. She pulled him on to the sculpture so he knelt in front of her. Moaning and whispering, she nuzzled against the dark shadow of his hair and balls, rubbing her face into his crotch. Dan was looking down, watching her; his neck craning to see her make love to him with her mouth.

Jo was transfixed; never in her wildest fantasies had she imagined a live sex show that was anything like this. Her hand moved faster now, massaging herself, seeking out the sensitive bead.

Bridgit was bearing down on the sculptured phallus, pumping up and down as her strong thighs worked in a faster rhythm. In her mouth now was Dan's saliva-slick cock. At times, Jo could only see a tangle of scarlet hair but then when Bridgit shook it out of the way there was the fat, red girth of Dan's cock to be seen. Bridgit's mouth was wide, wide open as she moved her lips up and down it in the same rhythm as her dancing hips. Jo found herself opening her mouth too, totally mesmerised by the scene. My God, she found herself thinking, that must feel so incredible, to swallow two cocks at the same time.

Jo licked her lips and swallowed. Dan's cock looked so wet and tempting as Bridgit's mouth worked over it. Without thinking, she dug her fingers deep inside the puffy wetness of her lips. The sweet spasm of a small orgasm made her gasp. But a moment later she was hungry again. Her fingers slid easily back between the heat of her lips towards her empty entrance. That was the problem. She wanted more than thin, short fingers in there. She wanted something wide and hard. No, more than that – she wanted something she couldn't control. Something wild and fast and totally off-limits. Her eyes couldn't move away from Dan's cock. She wanted it so much that her guts twisted with desire.

Unsurprisingly, Bridgit could not take much more. Her hips jerked frantically. She was grinding her face into Dan's crotch, trying to pull more and more of him into her eager mouth. With a sudden wail, she reached her climax. Jo watched, fascinated. As Bridgit disentangled herself and sat up straight, her smiling face was flushed and happy.

'Wow. I think I need a rest.' A little shakily, she clambered over to where Jo was standing.

'You OK, sweetheart?' Close up, Bridgit smelled of sweet, pungent sex.

'Yeah. Definitely.' Jo shook her head. 'This is incredible.'

'Yeah?' Bridgit laughed and then leaned forward to kiss her. It felt so totally natural that Jo kissed her back. 'We love you being here too, don't we Dan?'

He was checking over the camera, but sauntered over when he heard his name. Jo noticed his cock was still jabbing up, out of his flies. There had been no time for its hardness to subside. She tried not to look at it. After all, it really wasn't hers. It belonged to Bridgit.

'What did you say?'

Jo stole a glance up to his face but blushed when her eyes met his. He was watching her in that slow, sardonic manner of his. Was he laughing at her?

'I said we love Jo being here, don't we?' There was no jokiness about Bridgit. Her arm was slung around Jo's shoulder. Dan looked down at the two naked women. Jo could have sworn she saw his cock twitch in appreciation.

'Sure.' He crouched down low on his haunches. Jo studiously tried to avoid looking at him below waist level. 'Have you two got it together yet?' he asked.

Bridgit smiled down at Jo, lifting her eyebrows conspiratorially.

'Baby, I'm shagged at the moment. I think Dan's trying to ask my permission. What do you think of his raging hard-on? Want to give it a go?'

It really was ridiculous, but Jo could feel her face glowing as bright red as Dan's scarlet erection.

'You mean – with me?'

This time Bridgit laughed out loud. 'Well, I think he's going to be disappointed if we just send him off to bed with a Kleenex. Be my guest. I'll see he behaves himself. I know, let's go and try out the she-wolf.'

Hand in hand they crossed the studio. Moving

through the aisles of strange, morphic figures, Jo was again reminded of Bridgit's words – that she would be exploring her unbridled instincts here. It was all coming incredibly true in a way she could never have believed possible.

Bridgit halted at a vast, furry shape that at first appeared to have no real animal form. She pulled Jo and Dan down beside her. It was like a soft and fluffy sofa. Only as she looked around herself, did Jo slowly recognise that above her loomed a vaguely wolf-like head and that the four arms of the sofa corresponded to the upright legs of an animal lying wantonly on its back. But it was a much more light-hearted piece of art than the wolf-man. It suggested comfort and soft-ness. In fact, Jo quickly realised, the she-wolf made a perfect place to have sex.

'Lie back on top of me,' Bridgit instructed, as she reclined on her back in the thick fur. Compliantly, Jo slithered over her, feeling the older woman cradle her in her arms. Her head rested comfortably on Bridgit's shoulder. She felt safe and warm in the knowledge that what was about to happen was completely in accord with Bridgit's wishes. Sighing, she kissed Bridgit's shoulder and looked up at Dan.

His face seemed oddly blank. He was now standing, watching them both, his eyes glazed and dreamy. Attempting to be seductive, Jo bent her right leg, revealing a tantalising glimpse of her slippery entrance.

Shaking his head in a kind of disbelief, Dan exhaled a mouthful of air. 'Jesus.' Then coming to himself, he smiled. 'Sorry. Just trying to catch the moment. Tremendous.'

After watching him pull off his jeans, Jo glanced apprehensively towards Bridgit. But she only smiled back sweetly and ran her fingers deftly along the length of Jo's body.

'I'll make sure he doesn't rush,' she whispered. 'Though he's absolutely dying to get inside you. I can tell.'

Dan had pulled a rubber on, and when he clambered on to the furry surface his cock looked strangely dark and taut. But Jo wanted it in her – as fast as he could ram it up inside her.

Lazily, he slumped down next to her and stared into her eyes. Again Jo felt herself colour up, looking away fast. He seemed to be searching her eyes, reaching into her soul before he got started. She felt a pang of envy that Bridgit had this gorgeous man to herself all of the time. Very tenderly, he reached up and stroked the side of her face.

'You want this?'

'Oh, yes.'

From behind her, Bridgit whispered, 'We want it to be good for you. We love you being here.'

'I love it too,' she said to both of them.

Like a revelation, she realised that for Bridgit and Dan this was more than some quick, pick-up opportunity to spice up a boring relationship. They were two real, richly experienced people who just didn't give a fuck about the rules and conventions of society. They obviously, totally loved each other. And weird as it seemed, this encounter tonight meant they loved Jo too, for a little while at least. The whole thing was sweet and fierce and completely mind-blowing.

Bridgit was idly fondling Jo's breasts and the responses running through her body were driving her silently crazy. As Bridgit pulled and rubbed her hardened nipples, Jo could see them standing up stiff and hot as they burned to be touched. When Dan reached out to grasp her hips, Jo heard herself gasp with anticipation. But he too seemed only interested in casually caressing her skin, sliding his open hand over the bony prominence of her pelvis and cupping the peachy roundness of her buttock. All of Jo's attention was fixed on the yearning – no, the agonised craving – that pulsed inside her cunt. In a kind of anguish, she began to arch her hips towards him, rocking gently as she moaned encouragement.

Still, as Bridgit tormented the hardened beads of her nipples, Dan explored her hips and then the sensitive pit of her stomach. His hand was barely inches from the line of her pubis, but he carefully avoided direct contact. When he finally let his fingers stray into the thin reddish hairline, Jo thought she might explode with rapture. Unable to stop herself, she reached down to find the elusive mystery of his cock.

As her fingers slipped around it, she heard his quick intake of breath. Glancing up into his face, she caught a momentary flutter of his eyelids as if he too found direct contact almost too much to bear.

Squeezing the long, rubber-cool length, she was amazed at its hardness. She could feel every bulge and vein, right down to the base where it flared out, hot and wide. Below hung two pendulous testicles that she cupped momentarily in her palms. Looking into Dan's face, she saw his eyes were closed and his lips were parted in a grimace of pleasure.

Suddenly he ran his hand down her pubis and ground into the parted lips of her sex. Rubbing greedily, he spread the wetness, making a long, slick channel for his entry. Groaning, he pulled her towards him, jabbing his cock between her parted thighs. Behind her, she could feel Bridgit too, pushing her towards him.

'Keep it slow,' Bridgit urged Dan, 'don't let go until I tell you.'

Reaching around Jo, she was pulling her thighs wide and lifting her hips high as Dan prepared to enter her. Jo felt oddly and deliciously helpless. The rubber-sealed tip of Dan's cock was jutting closer now, momentarily brushing against her swollen lips. Instinctively, she reached out to him, grasping his strong shoulders, pulling him closer.

Then she felt Bridgit's hands wind around her, reaching to part the glossy channel of her lips. Panting, Jo felt the hard cock-end nuzzle and then push against her. Gently, he pushed a little further as Jo dizzily hung on to his shoulders, trying to pull him deeper.

'Just leave it there.'

'No!' Jo cried out. The bulbous tip had done no more than pierce the tight circle of her entrance. It seemed to be hanging there, sending a million welcoming signals through her nervous system. The desire to bear down was irresistible.

Bridgit was trying to quiet her, smoothing down her hair. 'Just feel it, baby,' she crooned. 'Really feel it. It'll be worth it. OK, another inch.'

This time, as Dan pushed just an inch further, Jo bit her lip to stop a scream erupting from her throat. The sensation was unbelievable; the tension seemed to skewer her body. Every nerve ending was switched on full. Uncontrollably, she felt herself begin to tremble.

'OK, OK.' Bridgit smoothed back her hair. 'Just a little bit more.'

This time, as Dan pushed forward, a wave of crimson seemed to engulf Jo's brain. His wide-girthed cock was pushing the walls of her entrance apart, stimulating her in a way that Graham's rapid jabs or even her own frantic masturbatory antics had never done. She felt close to fainting.

Another inch. Jo was shaking now. Her frame juddered as Dan's cock eased inside her. It lay still and wide, stretching her softly gripping flesh. Then suddenly, as he eased it just a tiny way forward again, the violence of her orgasm began to rise. Gasping into Dan's shoulder, she felt her bared teeth graze his skin. It was too much – that unbearable stretching that drove her muscles into spasm.

'Come on, baby,' he whispered. 'Come on. Squeeze me dry.'

Gasping for air, she let her climax rip through her, grinding down on to him, biting her teeth deep into his shoulder, lifting her hips as wave after wave of pleasure ripped through her. She could hear him grunt too, as her pussy squeezed him relentlessly. Coming back down to earth, she gradually became aware of dribbles of wetness running down her thighs. She had, quite literally, come over him. Creamy juices were saturating his cock.

'Get out, now.'

Bridgit's voice. Woozily, Jo lifted her head from Dan's shoulder.

'No!' she wailed. Just as she realised what this latest instruction meant, Dan slid his big, fat, gorgeous cock out of her. She was agonisingly empty.

'It's OK,' crooned Bridgit, her breath hot inside Jo's ear. 'You just went up to the moon and back. But in a minute we'll have you dancing up to Saturn.' To back up her words, Bridgit's hands snaked down between her legs. 'Oh, you are gorgeous and wet. Jesus.'

Jo winced as fingers brushed her madly receptive clit.

'No,' she whispered. 'I can't take it yet.'

'You can,' Bridgit insisted, fluttering her fingers towards the deep, wet well of her entrance. 'That's how to get there. Overload your system.'

As three long, slender fingers slid inside her, Jo felt Dan wind back against her. The jabbing pressure of his cock against her stomach made her breath catch. Looking into her eyes, he sinuously slid his tongue into her gaping mouth. It felt primitive and so, so sexy. His tongue worked around her teeth and then rammed towards her throat in long, juicy jabs. At the same time, he reached down and pinched the tips of her nipples gently, pulling them into hard spikes.

It was true. She was overwhelmed with sensation again, already coasting towards another massive orgasm. When Bridgit's fingers slid out of her and began to make teasing, circular movements around her clit, Jo knew she was more than ready again.

Dan pulled his mouth off hers; it was because he was getting too close. She could feel it in the bucking spasms of his prick that rubbed like a hot pole against her stomach.

'God, I've got to go,' he said hoarsely. 'I'm going to have nothing left.'

'OK. Let me get her in position.'

Cradled as she was in Bridgit's arms, it was easy for Jo to be re-positioned with her buttocks between Bridgit's thighs and her knees bent upwards and outwards. Throughout, the older woman continued massaging her juice-heavy pussy, sending maddening sensations from the bud of her clit, circling down around her passage to tickle the further recesses of her newly aroused anus. By the time Dan's cock swung above her, Jo was crazed for it again, spreading her legs as wide as possible to get as much of Dan's cock inside her as she could.

This time, Dan drove into her. No subtlety, no teasing. Jo felt her lungs empty with the first thrust as it shot up her like a greased piston. Then it swung back and was immediately up again. Dan was over her, grinding into her, working his cock deeper and deeper inside.

'Oh, yes,' she moaned, lifting her thighs high above Bridgit's, trying to lock her ankles behind Dan's backside. This was what she wanted. A cock pounding into her so fast she could barely follow its rapid beat. And she could see that Dan was in ecstasy; jaw set and eyes closed in bliss.

Momentarily, he opened his eyes, staring far down into her soul.

'You ready for the big one?'

'Anything,' she panted, though it was hard to speak through the staccato jabs of his fucking.

In reply, she felt a wave of delight as Bridgit's fingers moved into the heat where their bodies joined. Glancing down, Jo could see the wildly primitive sight of Dan's cock thumping into her own purplish and open cunt. Exploring that slippery join was Bridgit's hand as it first of all circled the thick base of Dan's cock and then began to creep along the glistening surface of Jo's sex. Closing her eyes, Jo surrendered to the sensation.

Firstly her stiff clit was tickled, making Jo buck and shiver as if a thousand volts of electricity had just been fed into her. Then the fingers caressed the stretched inner skin of her thighs, making runnels of pleasure work from her toes up into the centre of her spine. Finally, the fingers worked around and underneath her, circling her anus in delicate, shiver-making strokes.

Above her, Dan was going crazy. He was giving her his full length now, sliding it back and forth so she got the full benefit of every inch. His chest was slapping against her breasts and each time he reached full penetration the hardness of his pubic bone ground against her. Jo started to lose it – nails digging in his shoulder, breathing running short and ragged.

At the same time there were those fingers – dainty,

insubstantial fingers – teasing and tormenting the puckered orifice of her backside. The combination of a pounding hard fuck and the delicate fluttering around her anus was driving her insane.

'I'm going to –' she managed. 'Oh, please –'

Bridgit knew what she wanted. She had obviously planned it all along. With a long, triumphant stab, she pushed inside Jo's rear, finger-fucking her virgin anus.

The sensation of Dan's cock rammed hard up her cunt and the fast, burning finger thrusting inside her backside sent her screaming over the edge. Jo's hips spasmed, her throat opened to a wordless cry; again and again she felt the hot penetration of both entrances. Her own juice was running over Dan's cock and over the fur of the sculpture. It was the most violent orgasm she had ever known, spinning on and on for long, slow-motion seconds.

When it subsided, Dan slowed inside her.

'I think you came.' He was smiling mockingly. 'Rest now.'

Gently, he pulled out and she felt his heat and power drain from her. Exhaustedly, Jo rolled over on to the thick fur and yawned. She was completely drained, though inside her passage she could still feel the burning pulse of her orgasm subsiding.

Next to her, she was aware of Dan and Bridgit getting together. Glancing across, she could see Bridgit kneeling in all her white-skinned beauty to mount Dan from above. The sound of their fucking was gently rhythmic and somehow comforting. As she curled in a ball beside them and closed her eyes, Jo could hear them whispering and sighing. It felt beautiful to be there, silently sharing in their ecstasy. Then, in a nest of warm fur and limbs, she finally fell asleep.

Chapter Six

Next morning, Jo woke late and ambled through the narrow corridors of the farmhouse to find the others. Bridgit was sitting in the low-beamed kitchen, opening her post.

'Hi. Sleep well?'

'Best in years.' Jo grinned. 'At home – I mean, at Northford – I often got up and roamed about at night. But here, I slept like the dead. If I stayed here, I'd be like Sleeping Beauty – out cold for years.'

'Have some coffee.' Bridgit lifted a jug off the wood-burning stove.

Jo suddenly realised that she might have sounded like a guest trying to overstay her welcome.

'Listen, don't worry, I'm going to get on my way today. No problem. Did you say there's a bus? I'll get going after breakfast.'

Bridgit patted the carved wooden bench. 'Sit down. There's no hurry. We can sort that out later. Well, you certainly look well. Like the cat that got the cream.'

Jo sat down and spooned some sugar in her mug. 'I guess that's what I am. The cat that got lucky. That's what I'm like,' she explained. 'My friend asked what animal I identify with and I told her straightaway that I'm a cat. I keep thinking about it. Pleasure loving but a bit solitary too.'

'Hmm, you look kind of feline with those green eyes. And you like danger too, you said.' Bridgit pushed some hunks of granary bread on the stovetop and watched them gradually crisp. 'You are going to have to watch that risk-loving tendency at Fenris Gate. I've been thinking this morning. Michael Ruthen is going to snaffle you up for breakfast.'

'I don't think so.'

'Oh, he's quite a character. And into all kinds of animal mysticism – nothing wrong with that, of course. That's my area, too. But a big difference between Michael and me is that I keep my desires under a kind of loose rein. You know, instinct is really important, but in the end, when you are really going for the ultimate experience, you need to keep hanging on to that thread of reason. You need to be able to find your way back. Do you follow me?'

'I don't know. Maybe. But I know you and Dan really go for it. Surely you let yourselves go completely?'

'No. I don't think we do. I want to tell you about some of the things that are important to me. But first, do you fancy some of these baked eggs?'

From out of the stove she produced a dish of soft-baked eggs with tomatoes and melted cheese. Piled high on a thick piece of toast, Jo laid into her breakfast, realising she was utterly famished. The food was incredibly good.

'Go on, tell me,' she continued, between mouthfuls of egg and toast.

Bridgit sat back, hugging her own mug of coffee. This morning she looked fresh and utterly comfortable with herself. Again, Jo admired her assurance and warm intelligence.

'Listen, I don't want to come over like a boring old lecturer, but I can see you are a bit of an adventurer, Jo. So am I. So is Dan. But I wish I'd known someone a bit more experienced than me when I started out on all of this. I don't want to sound like a puritan, but there are a couple of principles I follow. Like respect.'

Sitting forward, Bridgit connected directly with Jo, eye to eye.

'Jo, I really respect you and hope you respect us. You really are lovely and – oh, it's hard to find the words – inquisitive and inquiring and kind of vibrant. I genuinely love your company. I would never force you to do anything you don't quite clearly want to do. So that's important, Jo. To check people out for respect.'

'Sure.' More toast had come off the stove now. With big lumps of fresh butter and spoonfuls of honey it tasted unbelievably good.

'And then there's safety. Physical safety, for a start. I mean, our instincts can lead us along some pretty strange roads. And psychological safety too. It's just as important not to get beat up mentally as physically. And there are people out there who love to do both. Don't ask me why, they just do. So always make sure there's an escape route when you need it. When things get too heavy, you've got to know there's a road back. Promise me that, Jo?'

Jo swallowed down a huge bite of honeyed toast. 'I'm listening. Honest. So are you saying that if those two things are in place – you feel safe and there's respect between whoever's involved – everything is OK?'

Bridgit sipped some more coffee and thought about

it for a second. 'Yeah. That's what I'm saying. Basically, if it harms no one – do as thou will.'

'Wow. Sounds wonderful. I never really thought about it before. It sounds so easy.'

'Easy is not how I would describe it. I think there's a reckless side to you, Jo. That's the only reason I'm telling you this. And there's a crazy side to Michael Ruthen too. He is well into the idea of going as far as the mind and body can take it. To Michael there are no limits. I guess when you two get together, the impact could be pretty hot.'

Jo frowned in disbelief. 'I haven't even met this guy yet and you're pairing us off. Maybe I prefer women, anyway.'

She tried a sultry little smile, but Bridgit just shook her head in a kind of mockery.

'Do you know what my definition is of a bisexual? A very, very greedy person.' She laughed. 'It takes one to know one. Let's leave it at that.'

'OK,' Jo chuckled. 'And how do I get to find this superman? What do I need, the number seventeen bus or something?'

'Listen, I've got an idea. It's about six miles across country to Fenris Gate. And it's the most gorgeous spring day out there. What about taking the scenic route? I could walk with you the first half at least and you can easily get there by dinner time.'

'Sounds great. Like the right way to arrive. I'll just get my things together.'

It was true; it was the most beautiful, blue-skied, sun-basking day. But before setting off, Jo went in search of Dan, following the smell of paint and turps back to his studio.

'Hi,' she said shyly. 'I'll be getting off now.'

'Oh, right.' He wasn't flustered at all; he simply laid

down his brushes and started wiping his hands. 'So, you're off to Fenris Gate?'

'Yeah. Though from what Bridgit says, I think I had better watch out for this Michael guy.'

'Oh, I think he had better watch out for you.' There was that humorous little sparkle in his dark eyes again. 'Come here, then.'

He had his arms open wide and, although suddenly shy, Jo walked over and slid inside them. He hugged her warmly, like a best friend or brother.

'You take care, then.' He smiled down into her eyes and this time she succeeded in meeting his gaze for more than a second. 'I think you are going to have a wonderful summer down there. After that – see how you feel, Jo. There's your whole life left to live and your own way to do that. You are too young to get stuck.'

'Thank you,' she said, choking up a bit. 'I mean – for everything. Maybe if the time had been different, or if I met you somewhere else –'

It was a stupid confession, but she desperately wanted him to know she had got a little bit crazy about him.

'But you didn't, sweetheart. I met Bridgit and you are going to meet so many interesting people that it is enough to make an old guy like me sick with envy. OK. Get going. Only, if you ever need us, you know the road back.'

'Sure. Take care. And take care of Bridgit. She's a genius.'

'I know.'

'I'm glad you know.'

Outside, the spring sunshine danced along the lanes as Bridgit and Jo set off across the hills. It was an ancient and beautiful landscape of white-weathered

101

drystone walls and towering trees just coming into bud. Bridgit pointed out a long, purple ridge to the east, towards which they were heading.

'Fenris Gate is below Moersett Ridge. The whole place was a Viking settlement and there are lots of really interesting artefacts down there. That's partly why the place will have appealed to Michael. Stones have long memories, and magic works better where there is a history of magic.'

'Viking magic? That sounds weird. So you really believe in all this?'

'Hmm. I do. Since you passed through York you've been in old Viking territory. And up here, in the countryside, all those beliefs are even stronger. They get mixed in with farming traditions and observance of the seasons but the locals still live their lives pretty much as their heathen ancestors did. It's hard not to follow pagan beliefs when you just look around. You can almost feel the earth renewing herself – look at the hawthorn blossom, Jo, in the hedge. And see the wren there, still finishing her nest. It's no surprise that people often keep up the old ways here. Celebrating the Maytime, weaving corn at harvest, lighting bonfires at Samhain, summer's end.'

It was true enough. Looking around herself, Jo could see that the land really did look freshly green and lush and yet she knew it would change and decay back into winter as the seasons rolled along.

'Yes, there's some kind of force of spring here, definitely,' she agreed. 'A kind of life force. But magic? That's another thing entirely. Emmi said something about Michael and magic too. But in this day and age, I can't believe it.'

'Oh, you mean because we've got television and the Internet and a hired expert to explain everything away? But think about what most people haven't got.

No sense of connection with the earth and the ways of life their ancestors have pursued for thousands of years. The church means less and less to them, but there is still a yearning to celebrate the beauty of the world and the important times in our lives. Heathen myths and legends stay alive because they still speak to our souls of a time of wisdom, when our ancestors walked with both beasts and the gods. And when we enter that dreamlike state – whether through meditation, sexual ritual or sheer force of will – then it does seem to transport us into a world of magic.'

For a while, they walked along the buttercup-strewn path in silence. Then Bridgit took her arm.

'Tell me the truth, now. Last night. At your deepest, most dreamlike level, how did you feel?'

Jo had to think for a while before she answered.

'I felt like – like I was in some kind of timeless place. And that you and Dan were real but were also – I don't know – some kind of characters or role-players initiating me. God, this sounds like rubbish. But it was strange. I felt as if I recognised aspects of what was going on, even though I had never come across anything like it before. It was a kind of spooky déjà vu. I'm sorry. I just can't explain it in words.'

Bridgit took her hand. 'But you just have explained it perfectly. I'm so pleased for you. That illustrates precisely what I was saying. You see, our unconscious minds contain all human knowledge, past, present and future. In certain situations, such as rites, our mind can suddenly connect with that vast collective memory going back through ancient times to our very first ancestors. It's what I try to achieve with my art.'

'Yes, I felt that,' interrupted Jo. 'When I first walked through your studio, I felt strange echoes from the past – but it wasn't really my own past. None of those creatures had ever appeared to me before. They just felt familiar.'

'Exactly. And it's what Michael tries to do with his shamanic rites. Certain rituals secretly preserved by wise men and women can do this extremely powerfully. The effects can be quite extraordinary. Magical, in fact.'

It was with some foreboding that Jo parted from Bridgit at the head of the next valley. After a friendly kiss goodbye, Jo watched the dwindling figure retrace her steps towards her own farm. The worn old path ahead of Jo dropped steeply and the violet ridge of Moersett looked closer now. Once on her own, apprehensions fluttered around the edges of Jo's mind. She wondered how Colin and Graham had reacted to her disappearance. More seriously, she began to worry whether she had left any clue, however small, to her destination. But finally, she let her mind rest in the knowledge that Emmi had only spoken to her alone about Michael and his community. No one would ever be able to find her out here.

The path followed a long, rolling hillside down beside a stream where Jo stopped for a few moments to rest and drink from the clear spring. Whatever shadows her mind tried to cast, her new spirit of adventure rose up to scatter them. The sun was warm on her back and, as Bridgit had said, all of nature was waking up around her. It was hard not to believe that her own awakening was a part of the natural season too. Wandering from a dell of sapphire nodding bluebells back into the sunshine, she felt deep within her spirit that she was right to leave Northford and, at last, her true life was beginning. Her body felt strong and full of stamina; her mind cleared as exercise sharpened her senses. Whatever waits for me at Fenris Gate, she decided, I am more than ready to take it on.

Her first sighting of the community came as the sun was already dropping over the horizon of Moersett. Jo had climbed the last rough-hewn ridge and her view throughout the last half-hour had necessarily been fixed on the broken stones of the pathway. Now, as she raised her head and stopped on the final summit, she smiled as she gazed out across the fertile valley and grey stone buildings of Fenris. Like a pilgrim sighting a shrine, she was both glad and sorry that her journey was almost ended.

Fenris Gate was bigger than she had expected; a mass of red-tiled roofs surmounting squat and ancient buildings. The fields and paddocks were dotted with livestock and she could just see a few inhabitants gathered in the large yard near a vast, round building. For a few minutes, Jo sat on her haunches on the ground, carefully watching the scene. A flock of sheep cropped their way across a walled enclosure; smoke twisted from a chimney in the round building and also from the main farmhouse. The place looked so serene and pretty that Jo was almost disappointed. It was as if, after all Dan and Bridgit had implied, the place was simply too ordinary.

It was only later, when she entered the yard, that a few signs emerged that this was not some traditional farming community. The dozen or so people idling by the water pump were all young – none appeared older than twenty-five. And the friendly reception she got was utterly unlike the threats and warnings she might have got from local, traditional farmhands.

'Hi.' A couple of lads strolled over, still glowing from working in the sunshine. 'You want some help?'

The taller boy wore a ring in his ear and a black T-shirt over his broad frame. Like most of his friends, he wore a pair of worn shorts and sturdy workboots. His companion was a compact, oriental youth whose black eyes met hers inquisitively when he raised his shades up on to the top of his head.

'I'm just looking for a friend of mine.' Jo gladly dumped her bag on the cobbled ground. 'Emmi. Is she around?'

'Emmi? You mean little Emmi from that religious place? Oh yeah, she's round at the cookhouse. Hey, you're not Jo are you?' Jo nodded at the smaller lad's enquiry. 'Amazing. Emmi said you might come. Great to meet you, Jo. I'm Niall. And this is Rob.'

The next moment, Jo was pulled into an enormous hug – first from Niall, and then a moment later Rob embraced her. She could feel the heat radiating from taut, work-honed muscles.

'You here to stay?' Niall asked with a broad grin on his face.

'I hope so.' It was hard not to be swept up by the tide of their friendliness. By now a couple of the others had gathered round too. One of the girls offered to run round and fetch Emmi. Soon Jo had been introduced to them all by name. She noticed Michael was not one of them.

'Jo! Jo! My God. You've done it.'

It was Emmi, hurtling around the side of the building, running straight up the path towards her. In an instant they had grabbed hands and Jo was trying to tell her what had happened as fast as she was able.

'Listen, I'll take you up to my room,' Emmi interrupted. 'I want to show you everything. We can come back down later, for something to eat.'

'OK. Sounds good to me.'

Giving everyone a smile, Jo turned to leave with her friend.

'Everyone's so friendly,' she confided once they were out of earshot of the rest of the group.

'Exactly. Though friendly might be too tame a word

for it. They can just be a bit too up close and personal sometimes. That was Rob, was it, giving you the big bear hug?'

'I think so. But it's fine with me. I really like that attitude. I want to be with people like that. People who are open and free. I feel completely different already. I can tell straight off, Emmi. This is it. The place where I can really feel myself.'

'Yeah, sure,' Emmi nodded. 'Feel yourself. That's if the others will give you a night off,' she added sarcastically.

Jo still hadn't discovered the source of Emmi's strange mood when they met up with the others later that evening. The meeting room was in the old farmhouse; a long, candlelit room with bulging whitewashed walls and a long, polished oak table. The food was good but simple and the wine, which was passed around in large earthenware jugs, was rich and potent. Again, Jo found herself drawn to the people sitting around her; they offered her food and drink, made jokes and told funny stories. As the wine began to mellow her mood, Jo kept looking around for Michael but still there was no sign of him.

'So – where's our great leader?' she asked Emmi. She was picking at her food but drinking deeply.

'Oh, he'll be along soon enough. Don't worry, he'll soon spot you.'

The wine had done its part in melting Jo's inhibitions; also, she was getting more and more irritated by Emmi's low-key mood.

'OK, why not spill it – what's wrong?'

Emmi was playing with a little pile of crumbs on her plate with maddening self-absorption.

'Wrong?' The look on her face of being caught out said it all. 'There's nothing wrong. Honestly.'

Jo sank her face down close beside Emmi's with a sinking heart.

'Go on. You're not pleased to see me, is that it? If you've met someone else, just spit it out.'

A guilty squeeze under the table edge compressed Jo's hand.

'No way.' Emmi smiled. 'It's just – oh, you are not going to believe this. I was thinking of going back to Northford, Jo. I was starting to pack.' Suddenly Emmi's face darkened and she looked around quickly. 'You won't tell anyone, will you? I haven't said anything yet, to anyone. They don't like that sort of thing. Promise me? Don't say a thing.'

'Of course not,' Jo whispered. 'But why leave? And anyway, I'm here now. We can have a brilliant summer together. That's the whole idea.'

Leaning over, she kissed her softly on the lips. Maybe it was the wine, but the others suddenly seemed to fade away into darkness. When Emmi didn't pull away, she slid her tongue slowly inside the girl's soft mouth. It felt good – so good that Emmi gave a little gasp of pleasure. Jo could feel the muscles stiffen in Emmi's shoulders as she pushed back against Jo's tongue. The girl's fingers started to reach upwards beneath the table top towards Jo's thighs.

'Hey, Emmi, aren't you going to introduce your friend?'

The warm and confident male voice reluctantly broke into Jo's consciousness. Quickly, she broke away and looked up. At the other side of the table from them stood a man whom Jo immediately knew to be Michael. He was flanked by Niall and Rob.

'This is Jo,' Emmi announced with some attempt at warmth. 'Sorry, Michael, we were just making up for lost time.'

Michael was younger than Jo had expected; dark

cropped hair framed a face so intensely handsome that she could barely look at him. Yet, it was a very masculine face; his brows and eyelashes were dark and an evening shadow was growing on his chin and cheeks. But it was his eyes that dazzled. The palest, almond-shaped green, they had their own goldish light as they flickered slowly over Jo. For a long second, they lingered and she felt a kind of heat flame up and then die.

'I'm not surprised,' he drawled. 'She's beautiful.'

Then he was gone, disappearing up to the far end of the table where he sat with his little coterie. Jo sat still for a moment, trying to calm her feelings. After just that one long second's interaction, she knew she wanted him. The sensation was like desperate, stomach-clawing hunger. On the surface of her inner eye she projected his image again – the angular face that could have belonged to a model or an actor; the powerful, charismatic gaze. And then there was the directness of his compliment and the public way in which he had made it. In that one moment, she felt as if her life had lurched forward another ten years. She wanted him and was fairly sure he wanted her. And she decided then and there that she was going to get him.

'So – got over the impact yet?' It was Emmi talking in that mean, jealous way she seemed to have picked up. 'I mean, Michael's charm is rarely wasted.'

One thing the new Jo had decided since setting out was that she was no longer going to feel shame – or be coerced into feeling it.

'Listen, I thought you said everyone was attracted to him anyway?' she retorted. 'Yeah, I think he's attractive. Dead right. But for now,' she dropped her voice and slid her arm slowly round Emmi's waist, 'it's you I want to be with.'

'You sure of that?' Emmi's blue eyes were tinged with hurt. 'Only Michael is someone who gets deep under your skin, Jo. He'll get in your blood and change you. I know it. He won't be happy until he's got his claws in you.'

Jo laughed and shook her head, but what Emmi said was true. Even as the dishes were cleared and ambient music started up in the gloom, Jo was powerfully aware of the group laughing and talking at the far end of the table. Even as she and Emmi retreated to a dark corner seat to talk, she could feel them. Glancing up, she could see that others gravitated to Michael too, gathering like moths in the dusk. Jo just couldn't understand what Emmi's problem was; whenever she tried to find out directly what she disliked about Fenris Gate, she only replied with what sounded more like positives – people were too friendly, they lived outside normal rules, Michael's influence was too strong. Jo just thought it sounded too good to be true.

He sent Rob over. Jo could see Rob's tall frame approaching out of the corner of her eye. As he made his way directly towards her, she felt her heart jump up to her throat.

'Hi.' Even Rob shared something of Michael's charisma – a directness that stripped through all the petty conventions most people wasted so much time on. 'Michael would like to meet to you. Come over.'

That smile too. White-toothed and expectant. She didn't even look over to check out Emmi's disapproval.

'I'd love to.'

As they approached, Rob took her arm, as if to steer her through the casually mingling groups of friends. It was a subtle gesture, but Jo sensed more than good manners in it. These were people who would not ask your permission before they touched you. There was something voracious about them. They were madly tactile.

At the head of the table, Michael was leaning back in his chair, talking to a fair-haired girl who was making huge eyes at him. But Jo's momentary disappointment immediately disappeared when Michael's eyes fixed upon her. His whole body focussed on her. He cut the other girl dead.

'Jo, Jo. Come on, sit down.' He signalled for a chair to be pushed up beside him. 'A new member is always a big occasion.'

Sitting down beside him, she was aware of the nervous rictus of her smile. He was watching her closely. He seemed more alive than anyone she had ever met before.

'The day after tomorrow I'll welcome you properly. It's our feast. A new member deserves a part in the rite.'

Already she felt out of her depth. 'Oh, I hope I don't have to do anything,' she blurted. 'There's so much I need to learn. I don't know – maybe we should leave that until I know more.'

'There's nothing for you to know,' he said, so slowly that it contrasted sharply with her own gabbling. His voice, she realised, was deep and well educated. It certainly made people listen. 'All you have to do is feel.'

The others were pressing tightly around her. Rob's broad back was hot against her shoulder, pushing her closer to Michael. They were tightly packed together; she could almost smell the testosterone rising in the air.

She could see every detail of Michael's face. It fascinated her; as he uttered the word 'feel', he had shot her a glance so deep and piercing that she had looked away, feeling a blush rise on her face.

111

'It's an incredible coincidence,' he said softly, and this time she could feel his wine-warm breath on her cheek, 'that we share the same eyes.'

Shaking her head, she frowned. 'What do you mean?'

'That shade of green. We could be brother and sister.' Abruptly she looked into his eyes, staring deep into the emerald liquid that seemed to tear into her. When his hand reached out and clasped hers, she felt paralysed. 'It is a unique bond, Jo,' he said softly into her ear. 'As soon as I saw you, I knew you were different. That maybe in some other place we had met before or will meet again. Do you feel it?'

'Yes.' She spoke without thinking. 'I knew I had to meet you.' She could scarcely believe she was saying this. Yet some wild, urgent part of her desperately needed to speak honestly for once, without pretence. 'Since I first heard of you I had to meet you. And now I'm so glad I'm here.'

Glancing down, she could see that he was stroking her hand, very carefully, as if she were made of precious glass. Yet his hand, she could see, was large and very male, with dark hairs running almost to the knuckles. There was something peculiarly feral about him; although he displayed incredibly good manners, she sensed they were a veneer stretched over something far, far wilder. He was stroking her, physically and mentally, she decided. It was like being played with by a big cat. Underneath, there was brute power that he chose not to reveal until he wanted to.

'Your friend, Emmi,' he said, lowering his voice to a conspiratorial hoarseness that made her skin rise in goosebumps, 'believes in the rules of monogamy. She would like to keep you only for herself. My beliefs, and the ethos of this community, however, are based on true, spontaneous love and sharing.' He was watching her carefully. 'What do you say?'

There was no choice. Fondness for Emmi was as nothing compared to the new spirit of adventure she wanted to live by.

'I do care about respect. And I care for my own safety,' she confided. 'But after that, I want to be utterly free. Spirit – and body.'

'Oh, Jo. I knew it,' he said, cool eyes suddenly on fire. 'You are someone I have been waiting a long time to meet. We need to talk. But for now,' and with this his hand slipped from hers, 'you can return to your friend. But I will think of you tonight. Each night I spend time alone, trying to find my own way forward, on my own personal journey. In my meditations tonight,' he confided with a smile, 'I will conjure you.'

Jo returned to Emmi, but her mind remained firmly fixed on Michael. His persona seemed to cling to her all evening, directing all her thoughts. He left the hall shortly after their conversation and, soon after that, Jo suggested getting off to bed.

Outside the hall, in the brightly moonlit yard, Jo again felt a wave of gladness that she had come to Fenris Gate. A breeze ran through the silvered trees of the neighbouring forest; as they passed the stables she heard stamping and snuffling from behind the wooden doors.

'What's that?' she asked Emmi.

'That's Hengest. Michael's horse. Actually, he's incredible. Shall we say a quick hello?'

The truth was that even the mention of Michael's name sent a shiver through Jo's brain. Next moment Emmi had pulled back the bolts and they plunged into the darkness of Hengest's stall. It was warm and fusty in the stable, smelling of old hay and the animal's earthy scent.

'Hello, boy,' exclaimed Emmi, reaching out to stroke the creature whose thrusting nose shot forward in the darkness.

'Oh, he's beautiful.' Jo could just see the silken sheen of his coat in the moonlight. Hengest's eyes rolled at her as he shook his long face and then plunged it into her open palm. When his long, gritty tongue rolled out to taste her, she giggled drunkenly.

It was impossible not to associate the stallion with Michael. There was that same forceful energy and power in the animal. Reaching out to stroke his long neck, she could feel the pulse just below the smooth hide. It was almost erotic; she wanted to bury her face in his neck and feel his dark mane falling on her. Then she suddenly knew exactly what she wanted, seeing in her mind's eye a vivid imprint of how it should be.

It was here that she wanted Michael to have her – here in the darkness of the stable, up against Hengest's solid flank, surrendering to the crude animality of the moment. Because that was where her instincts would lead her – to this surrender. Whatever the animal inside Michael, it would meet the passion in her. Their human trappings were of no importance. With Michael she knew she could be her wildest, most excessive self.

Later that night, in Emmi's bed, Jo rested on one arm, staring down at Emmi's face. With her lips parted in the moonlight and her hair falling back on the pillow, she looked so lovely that Jo almost felt guilty for not enjoying her company as much as she had hoped. The atmosphere between them had, if anything, grown tenser. One problem was that Jo wanted sex – the kind of raw sex that Emmi herself had so recently shown her.

Straddling above Emmi's golden body, Jo started to kiss and suck her, feeling the girl's nipples harden and her pubis nudge eagerly against her. Urgently, she

114

reached down and ground her hand against the parted seam of her sex. She needed to reach inside her, to connect with whatever had been lost between them. But only very slowly did Emmi get juiced up so, impatiently, Jo slid down and started to add saliva to the salty skin of her inner lips. Pressing her mouth hard against the bud of her sex, she suddenly heard Emmi moan out loud that she should be more gentle. She was hurting her.

Gentle? Jo did not want to be gentle. She was hot for a completely physical session and disappointed that Emmi was so laid back. Politely, Jo started to give her some soft and docile strokes, taking her very slowly up to a sweet kind of pleasure. But it was not what she wanted. If she had been a guy, she would have wanted to give her a long, hard fuck. Or maybe that was what she herself wanted, she thought. The heat that had built up between her own legs all night was so fierce that maybe she needed some more intense action to give her some relief.

When Emmi's hand strayed down across her own stomach, Jo was already close to exploding. But tenderness was what Emmi wanted tonight and, as she caressed Jo, it was all she could do not to beg her to go faster and deeper, like a man. Lying with her eyes shut and her body spread across the mattress, Jo tried to be patient. Emmi's tongue had reached the tops of her thighs now and it was only with utter self-control that Jo could stop herself lifting her hips and grinding into her sweetly lapping face. The slowness was driving her crazy. Eagerly, she parted her legs wide, wishing Emmi would finger-fuck her, wanting hard penetration in her vagina, her anus, everywhere.

Now, feeling Emmi's maddeningly slow lapping take her higher and higher towards her climax, she shamefully thought of Michael. He had said he would conjure her – yet had he also, magically, conjured himself into her sexed-up brain? It felt like it. She was obsessed. Guiltily, she let the wave on wave from Emmi's sweet tongue drive her fantasies.

She wanted Michael. She wanted him to single her out and take her to that dark and earth-smelling place. Matching her own urgent need with his, he would push her into the dank hay and grasp her panties, pulling them off so she was raw and exposed to his greedy eyes. His cock would be thick and ready, waiting for her, desperate to get up against her. She wanted his cock hard inside her, slapping her backwards against Hengest's solid flank. She wanted him to pick up her legs and wrap them around his waist, driving so hard inside her that it hurt her spine and banged her swollen clit. She wanted to mate with him, like an animal, panting on heat with her mouth open and her entrance wet and ready. Then she wanted him to come inside her – marking her like an animal that was his and his alone.

With a breathless sigh, her orgasm ripped through her body, so intense that her empty passage squeezed hard on the emptiness she wanted Michael to fill. Curling up together, she soon heard Emmi drop off to sleep with long, sighing breaths. Then she lay thinking alone, still curiously unsatisfied. Michael still burned in her mind. It was only a matter of time. And when she wondered if he thought of her too, she knew the answer already. He had told her his mind was fixed hard upon her. She knew that somewhere in a darkened room in Fenris Gate, Michael was meditating silently. And the object of his thoughts, she smiled secretly, was undoubtedly herself.

Chapter Seven

*O*utside, the sun was rising above the low farm buildings clustered around the yard. A few members of the community were gathered at the pump, sunhats and plastic bottles of water at the ready.

'What's going on?' Jo asked, spotting Niall in his black shades.

'Oh, hi, Jo. Are you coming to help us in the fields? Spread some fertiliser and chop out some weeds. It's perfect weather.' That white-toothed smile again – so warm that it was almost intrusive. 'We don't use chemicals or machinery – it's all done by hand. It's hard work but a real laugh.'

'No way. I'm showing her round this morning,' cut in Emmi. 'She doesn't know where anything is.'

'OK.' Niall wasn't at all fazed by Emmi's rudeness. 'Maybe tomorrow. But later this afternoon we're riding up to Abel's Tarn. Have a swim, take a picnic – you know, chill after all the hard work. You fancy that, Jo?'

'Oh yeah. Count me in.' She got in before Emmi could object.

'Sound. We'll see you here, then. About three.'

Jo tried to lose the idea that she was missing out on something as the two girls took a tour round the farm. First, there was the cookhouse at the back of Michael's house, where Emmi often helped out. Jo noticed that although everyone did some work, the hours were easy and playtime was as important as worktime. People were expected to cook and clean up for themselves if they didn't eat in the big room with the others twice a day. Somehow it all seemed to work out – while a group of kids were doing food prep in the kitchen some others were sunbathing out in the meadow. Emmi told her that they worked in shifts and that way no one had to kill themselves.

'Everyone's slacking off now the weather's picking up. All the animals are out to grass fending for themselves, and the crops have taken well. Heaven for slackers, basically.'

They were watching one of the guys knocking down some bread, ready for the ovens. He was a big, bluff Liverpudlian with silver oven scars on his broad arms that showed he was used to the work.

'You nearly finished then, Kelly?'

'Dead right. Got enough on the go now to keep us going two days. I'm getting off to the tarn later. You seen that sun out there? What about you two?'

'Maybe.'

'Oh, I just don't get you, Emmi,' he retorted sharply. 'You've landed in fuckin' paradise and you still got a miserable face on you.' He turned to Jo. 'Honest, girl, you want to get out there and start having a good time.'

'Don't worry, I will.'

'Nice one. I'll see you up there.'

'OK.'

The rest of the morning really did feel as if Emmi

was deliberately keeping her away from wherever the action was. They took a look at the outside of Michael's house and then the paddocks and pastures where most of the livestock were happily grazing. Eventually, Jo made sure they wound their way back to the yard. Finding a long, low stone near the fence, she sat down on it to wait in the sunshine.

'You sitting down?' She patted the warm stone beside her.

'No thanks.' Jo turned away and pulled a sour face. Frankly, Emmi was really getting to her.

'So what is it now?' Jo complained. 'Scared you'll catch something? Oh come on, Emmi. You're being a complete pain.'

'I'm being a pain? Jo – you know nothing. Do you want to know a bit more about what goes on when the sun sets at lovely old Sunny Brook Farm? That thing you're sitting on, it's supposed to be some old anvil left by the Celts. Anyway, they use it now. There are iron rings – look. People get tied to it.'

'So?' Jo could see the iron rings. It was kind of interesting. 'Do people get hurt then, is that it?'

'Well, not exactly.'

'So, you mean it's a sex thing?'

'Yeah. Totally over the top.'

'Well, what do you want me to say? If it's not hurting anybody, why get worked up? I mean, I can't see anyone cowering around like they're unwilling prisoners here. Looks to me as if everyone's totally made up to be here – except you, that is.'

Emmi was sulking, kicking the toes of her trainers into the stones like a child. 'You'll find out,' she said in an aggrieved tone. 'You'll find out the hard way.'

'Look, they're here.' Jo pointed to a gaggle of people making their way down from the fields. Earlier they had seen them working in the distance. Only it didn't look like too hard work – most of them had been loafing on the grass. A few were carrying old-fashioned pitchforks and hoes; they all looked hot and weathered with bits of grass stuck to their clothes.

'You coming for a swim, then?'

'Forget it.' Emmi was still muttering to herself.

Jo got up and dusted herself down. Niall had given her a wave. The others were looking over.

'Listen, if you don't want to come along – then don't. I'm hot. I want a swim.'

Walking over to the others, Jo felt only a little guilty. After all, this prudishness of Emmi's was a quick change of face. Only a short while ago she had been banging on about animalistic sex and getting Jo to play with herself in public. Jesus, she could do with loosening up a bit. This whole attitude of hers was crazy. There was no way she was going to let Emmi stop her having a good time.

As a group, they refilled water bottles at the pump, went to collect some bread and cheese and fruit from the stores and then set off up the hillside. People were hot and happy, goofing about in the sunshine, telling stories and jokes. Jo walked with Niall and the fair-haired girl, Lyn. Soon enough, Lyn mentioned Michael, and Jo had to find out more.

'So how did all this start up?' she asked. 'Was it always Michael's place?'

'Oh yeah, for years now.' Lyn seemed as keen to talk about Michael, as Jo was to listen. 'He inherited it from someone. He was still at university. He was at Oxford, you know. He's incredibly clever. An expert on ancient folk history – for which, read magic. It took a few years to get everything going as well as this. I've been here two years.'

'And what about you, Niall?'

'About the same. I was one of Michael's students. I

persuaded my father to let me come over from Japan to study with him.'

'Wow. So you must know him really well.'

'Well, I know his mind pretty well. He's way ahead of his contemporaries. Where they speculate, he seeks to prove. His whole approach is so radical. There are even aspects of what we are doing here in farming that are part of his experiment. The way he has laid it out, right next to the old woodland, with the round-house facing east – all those things are based on old manuscripts which in turn were based on spoken accounts handed down through generations.'

'I had no idea.' Jo was impressed. 'But what strikes me is how well everyone gets on. I mean, you all seem pretty happy. Except Emmi, that is.'

But she was interrupted before she could finish her enquiry. Behind them clattered the sound of hoofs. Moving over to the side of the path, Jo made way for a rider on a tall grey stallion. Looking up, she saw the rider was Rob. He was wearing only shorts and a pair of sandals – no high boots or hat. Seated confidently in the saddle, he looked pretty impressive with his deep tan and glittering earring.

'Hi y'all.' He slid out of the saddle and started walking along with them. After a while he broke free of Niall and strolled over to Jo.

'Beautiful horse.'

'He sure is. Olaf's his name. I bought him last season to improve the bloodstock here. He's a beauty. Sired some first-rate foals.'

Jo let Rob walk between her and the tall, prancing stallion. He was as sleek as a sealion, with silver-grey flanks and a dark, wispy mane. Although Rob tried to keep him at close rein, he bucked his head up and down, snorting and whinnying each few minutes, eager to move on faster.

'So, were you one of Michael's students too?'

'Me? God, no. I'm Michael's cousin. I've lived on the farm or close by it all my life. I was one of the fittings, so to speak, when Michael took the place over.'

'So do you agree with all this – the way it's run and everything?'

'Agree?' Rob laughed. Jo had been attracted to him before, but somehow, now she knew he was part of Micheal's family, she wanted to know him even more. 'It's amazing. Listen, I'm going to have to let him run,' Rob apologised, as Olaf started to nudge closer to her, pushing his huge face in front of her. 'Do you want to ride down to the pool? It'll be more fun than walking.'

'But I haven't ridden for years,' Jo protested.

'Never mind,' Rob said, grinning. 'I'll steer. You just hold on tight.'

Clambering up in front of Rob, Jo found that any horsey skills she had once gained out in Africa seemed to have completely disappeared. Like an idiot, her foot slipped in the stirrup and then Rob had to give her an almighty heave to get her up in front of him. Once up there, it was very high. Olaf was a much bigger horse than any she had ever ridden before. And the track sloped steeply downhill, so Rob had to hold her tight to stop her slipping forward over the horse's neck. Still, Rob felt good so close up; nice and hard and strong behind her.

'Can't wait to reach the flat,' he said, pressing his mouth to her ear. 'Olaf's totally frisky today. He's just covered one of the mares and he's got a spring in more than his step.'

'Oh, right.' Jo didn't know what to say.

'Still, it always turns me on that. Getting the animals together. Watching them mate. Olaf's a horny bastard. Bit like his master.'

'And who's that? You or Michael?' Jo laughed. It was hard not to laugh at such heavyweight innuendo. It really was not subtle.

'Oh, me.' Rob was leaning towards her ear again, tickling it nicely. 'I'm the official horniest bastard here. And Michael – well he's the kind of resident sex-and-magic guru. You will have picked that up, I guess.'

'Not hard to work that one out.'

'He wants you to come over to the farmhouse tonight. That OK?'

'I suppose. But why?'

'There are a few of us who are kind of taking extra lessons with Michael. Not everyone wants to get completely involved, you know. Like Emmi. She's kind of dropped out.'

'Do you know why? She's kind of evasive.'

Jo listened, hoping to get a convincing answer. But it was no more forthcoming from Rob than from Emmi.

'Who knows? I wondered if it was because of you turning up. I mean, a relationship-type thing. It's obvious there's something going on between you two. People can get like that, you know, dropping their old friends and so on.'

'No, it's not that,' Jo said slowly. 'Something else has changed her.'

Rob was working his hand around her waist. 'I was watching you and Emmi the other night,' he started, breathing into her ear in a way that made her skin tingle. 'It was a real turn on. I know Michael thought so too.'

'You mean at dinner?'

'No, after. You were really starting to get it on.'

'What do you mean, Michael thought so too?'

'Oh, I can just tell these things. The way he looked when I brought you over. That weird, possessive way

123

he's got when he likes what he sees. But maybe I'm too fast off the markers. I mean, could be you only like girls.'

'You kill me.' Jo laughed. Anywhere else, she might have taken offence at all of this. But here – well, it was pointless pretending to be coy when everyone was so clearly up for it. 'Are you always so direct?'

'There's no point being any other way, is there? So, what about it. Are you ever into men?'

'Yeah. Sometimes.' Looking straight ahead she knew he couldn't see the grin breaking out across her face.

'So, we've got a sometimes,' he was saying. 'Well, what type?'

'Oh, I like a guy to be direct. And tall. With a tan. And maybe an earring too.' It took him a microsecond to take this in. Then he pushed his hand up her T-shirt like a snake after a free lunch and ran his broad fingers over her bare midriff, seeking out her breasts. Jo just closed her eyes, holding tight to the saddle, her body deliciously melting in the sun.

By the time they reached the pool and slid off Olaf's back, Jo could hardly stand. Rapidly, she took in the place. It was a lovely, deep, greenish tarn with a shingle shore. Dark foliage hung over the water; it looked cool and mysterious.

During the last part of their ride, Rob had dropped the reins to sink his other hand into Jo's crotch, rubbing frantically until she was frightened her wetness was going to break through the thin fabric of her shorts. Behind her backside, she had felt the growing hardness of Rob's cock digging hard between her cheeks. He had squirmed against her, trying to get some relief as he pressed up close.

But now something mischievous told Jo not to give in too easily.

'Let's have a swim first,' she announced, although her body was raging with pent-up need.

'What? Do we have to?' He reached out for her arm but she wriggled away. In a second she was on the shore, kicking her shorts and suntop off. The water felt freezing, like an icy shower after the intense heat of the afternoon. Screaming with laughter at the cold, she let the water lap up over her knees and then her thighs until it reached the hot junction between her legs. It was no use lingering; Rob was right behind her, splashing into the shallows like an exuberant kid at the seaside.

'Hey, wait for me!' His fingers just grazed her bare backside as she launched full frontally into the green water. The cold knocked the breath out of her, but still she pulled a few strong strokes with her arms to get away from him. It was complete sensual luxury to glide through the dark water, feeling it play across every nook and cranny of her nakedness. Glancing down, she could see the pale fluorescence of her limbs glowing greenish below the surface.

'Jo, stop.' Rob was catching up with her, launching forward with a powerful crawl stroke. Between a mixture of laughter and mad panic, she found herself slowing down so that in a few seconds he grabbed her leg.

'No!' she shrieked as he upended her. They were a thrashing mass in the water as she felt Rob grasp her waist. Next moment he lifted her up, pulling her tight towards him, his mouth sliding over hers. When his tongue forced its way between her lips, Jo felt her whole body weaken and droop forwards over him. He was slippery and hard all around her, driving up against the softness of her body. The coldness had forced her nipples to shoot out stiffly; the sensation of them bumping against his hard chest made her shiver

125

with desire. Immediately, he reached down and grasped his erect cock, trying to manoevre her on to it. She kicked her legs away, beneath the surface.

'No,' she gasped. 'Not here.'

Looking up into his face, his expression was blank with need. Close up, he was madly attractive; she could see the gold strands in his sun-bleached hair and the clear-blue intensity of his eyes.

'Where, then?' he asked quickly.

'Oh, in the sun.' It gave her a few seconds, as he cogitated over this, to wriggle free of his grasp. But as she swam rapidly away, all she could think about was the tantalising hardness of his big cock as it had brushed against her stomach.

Swimming beneath the overhanging foliage, she entered what appeared to be a second pool surrounded by masses of tall rushes. Rob was not far behind her and again his strong crawl stroke soon launched him towards her. When his fingers reached out and caught at the cheek of her buttocks she turned and said, 'Over there.'

Ahead lay a shingle bank in the midst of a forest of tall rushes. As the water grew shallower, Jo's knees bumped along the bottom of the pool. As she scrambled for the bank, she could hear Rob coming up fast behind her. Finally, his fingers locked around her ankle.

'Let go,' she said in a kind of mock alarm.

'That depends.' He was pulling himself up towards her. She was held down on all fours, her hands on the shingle shore, her knees still in the shallows. 'It depends on what you give me.'

Skilfully, his grip grew tighter as his other hand found her waist. Once there, it locked impassively around her. She could feel herself panting, not entirely from the cold. This was exciting, more exciting a pursuit than anything that had happened before. And Jesus, she hardly knew the guy. That gave it all an extra thrill that she had never anticipated.

As his body rose out of the water and locked up against hers, Jo's eyes closed involuntarily. The sensation of his cock swinging against her buttocks was incredible. It was almost enough to make her wet herself with anticipation.

Quickly, his hand plunged forwards and found the open lips around her entrance. With no preliminaries at all, he rammed a couple of thick, stubby fingers inside her. Jo started to moan; it was so good she backed up to them, driving down to be massaged on to them.

'You feel fucking gorgeous,' he breathed, working his fingers around. 'There's no running away now. You're gonna get it.'

She wasn't about to argue. All she could think was that if he didn't get inside her quickly, she was going to come on his fingers. And that would be a kind of waste.

No fear. Rob wasn't into the long-drawn-out etiquette of foreplay. Tilting his cock up in his hand, he knelt behind her, slid his fingers out of her and pressed the fat end of his cock up against her entrance. Jo could hear herself starting to pant. She was so close to a climax that just to feel the wideness of his glans sent a surge of pleasure to the ends of her fingers and toes.

'Ooh, lovely,' he was murmuring, as he pushed harder. 'Lovely and wet.'

Suddenly he rammed it inside her, right to the hilt. Jo groaned. Jesus, he was well built, stretching her with the solid width of it. And the length of it seemed to lift her rear end, impaling her right down towards her stomach. Dropping her head nearly down to the ground, she thought only of pleasure. He started to pull back – and then slapped forwards, sending it shooting the full length again. He was working up speed now, driving in and out with long, confident thrusts.

Little anguished pants were coming out of Jo's mouth. Rob had got hold of her waist now and was pulling her back on to his cock. There was no stopping it now. The rhythm of their fucking was fast and steady. She could hear him too; he was starting to moan under his breath. She snaked her hand down between her legs and found her pussy. It felt stretched and puffy while the thick meat of his cock pumped on and on. Gently, she reached out and brushed her clit with a slippery finger. She could feel her muscles tighten round his cock. Again she rubbed – and again.

Her head was dropping into the shingle. Rob's hands swung down and he started to claw at her tits, pinching the points of her nipples. Suddenly it was too much. Every stroke of his cock was driving her higher. Yelps of pleasure erupted out of her throat. He was driving his prick as far as it could go now, thrusting it like a piston up her slippery channel. On and on, his full length humped inside her, his groin slapping against the cheeks of her buttocks. Adjusting the angle, he seemed to skewer her so deeply that she gave a scream of delight. Now his fat balls were banging up against her with each full thrust, swinging back and forth. There was no stopping the build-up of pleasure inside her. With a spasm so violent that she nearly threw him off, she came. All through her orgasm he dug it away, grinding inside her.

'That's it, baby,' he was moaning, abrading the deepest part of her with the end of his cock. 'Take it all, take it all the way.'

'Slow down,' she moaned, trying to pull away. As

her orgasm died, she was desperate for a few seconds' rest. In the end, she had to slide forward away from him and pull herself free. He just would not stop hammering it on and on inside her.

Wriggling around to look at him, for the first time Jo realised she maybe really had given an invite to the official horniest bastard at Fenris Gate. He was kneeling up, staring at her with a kind of manic intensity. Without his clothes on, he looked fantastic, from the broad tanned shoulders to the packed muscles of his stomach. And below that, his cock was standing to ramrod attention, just waiting for her to give it some more action. Jo was amazed, but also relieved, to see he'd pulled on a condom. Jesus, she had been so completely off her head that it had slipped her mind.

'OK, let's try it this way.'

There was no comfort break for Jo. Reaching down, Rob pulled her thighs wide and pummelled his cock straight inside her. Just the sensation of entry was enough to arouse her again. Looking down, she could see the gorgeous action as it pistoned in and out of her wide-open lips. She started to cry out, grabbing his wide shoulders, meeting his long lunges with some steady action of her own. Looking up at his face, she could see he was completely sexed-out: eyes blank, mouth open, jaw tight. Then, suddenly, he reached down and started kissing her, driving his tongue to the back of her throat. It was something she loved; the hard pressure on her mouth while he fucked her relentlessly. Eagerly, she lifted her legs, sliding them up the sides of his body until her calves rested on his shoulders. Now it was deep – so deep that her whole pussy burned with pleasure.

'Oh, I'm nearly there,' he whispered, pulling off her mouth to nibble and lick her ear.

'Yeah, yeah, me too,' she moaned. 'Don't stop.'

He kept it going; same pace, same long, pounding strokes. Jamming her groin up tight beneath him, she felt his pubic bone grind back across her lips. It felt unbelievable. She could hear herself making little yelping noises as he stoked up the fire towards a raging explosion.

She heard his climax erupting in sudden deep groans from his chest. On and on he pounded his cock into her.

'Jo,' he moaned. 'Oh, baby. Take it.'

With a guttural cry he mashed into her, giving her short jabbing strokes as he spurted into the rubber. As soon as he slowed, she whispered to him.

'Shit, I was almost there.' She felt slightly cheated, though it was no one's fault.

'OK. No sweat.'

He was still in his post-fuck stupor but squelched out of her and pulled off the rubber. Next second his broad hand found her pussy and fat fingers worked up inside her. At the same time, he put pressure on her clit. Jo just opened her legs wide and let him finger-fuck her to heaven. She was already red-hot and it seemed to take only seconds rather than minutes before she was whimpering at heaven's door while the pad of his thumb massaged her clit through a heart-stopping orgasm. As he pulled his hand out of her and pulled her into the sweet-sweat-scented crook of his shoulder, she decided one thing. She liked Rob. He was more than OK. In fact, she fancied him nearly as much as Michael Ruthen.

Night fell increasingly later now that the better weather was well on its way. As Jo stepped through the twilight towards the farmhouse, the sky was a deep violet against which sillhouetted trees waved in

130

lacy blackness. The dying hum of a small aircraft disappearing over Moersett made her halt on the path and watch its wings glint in the last rays of the sun. It was the first sight or sound from beyond Fenris Gate she had heard since her arrival. They were living miles from any human contact; Dan and Bridgit were at least a half-day's walk away across the pitch-black moors. In the other direction, all she knew was that somewhere beyond the deep swathe of forest lay the open sea. The realisation of her isolation made her feel both a little fearful and excited. After all, whatever happened here, no one from outside was going to stop it.

Inside the farmhouse, paraffin lamps illuminated narrow, quarry-tiled passages. Then, finally, she heard voices behind the door. Inside, Michael was at the centre of a small group of now familiar faces: Rob, Niall, Lyn and two or three others who all hung out together.

'Hi, Jo. Help yourself to a drink.' Michael waved her over towards one of the familiar earthenware jugs. Jo enjoyed the strong wine that accompanied nearly every meal or meeting. It was made from hedge berries, she was told, and infused with special herbs. One thing she noticed was that it was more potent than ordinary wine. It freed inhibitions, certainly, but also made Jo feel powerfully aware of others around her and their emotions and reactions. And after drinking, she always fell into deep, blissful sleep punctuated only by vividly colourful dreams.

But tonight, just seeing Michael again was enough to excite her. Returning with her cup full of wine, he indicated a seat close by him and she moved into the warmth of his orbit. Just that smile was enough to make her skin rise in goosebumps; there was something deliciously predatory in that white-toothed greeting. Snatching a quick glance up into his pale eyes, she hoped he would manipulate the situation so that they could spend some time alone. She needed him, like she needed food or air. There was something about him that erased all the rational functions in her brain.

'We were just talking about tomorrow's spring festival, Jo,' Michael explained. 'Niall has been researching some old texts on Beltane. Go ahead, Niall.' The young student started to read from a sheet of closely typed paper. It sounded to Jo like an obscure history essay. He was talking about folklore customs and gods and goddesses, but much of the detail was lost on Jo. Fragments of the account were familiar – the May queen traditions, circle dances and maypoles. But as Niall moved on to strange tales of fertility and castration and a bizarre account of a strangled god's sinking into the seething bog, she concentrated more and more on just looking around herself.

Michael's house was warmly furnished, with old-fashioned lamps and ethnic rugs and fabrics on the walls. Pictures too, of mythic subjects covered the walls and a variety of carved and feathered objects were displayed in cabinets. There was nothing uncanny about the place at all, considering Michael was said to be a practitioner of magic. The only unusual aspect to the room was that a raging fire was built up in the stone hearth. Given the time of year, Jo was surprised that they wasted the wood.

Rob was still wearing only his shorts and sandals, and most of the others were similarly half-dressed. Only Michael still wore his black jeans, buckled belt and white T-shirt. The firelight cast red shadows across naked arms and limbs. A few of the group sat on the floor at Michael's feet, with arms and legs casually twisted around each other. Gender seemed to make no difference; even staunchly heterosexual Rob languidly rested his arm on Niall's shoulder. There was something reminiscent of an animal pack, she thought, about the way they all slumped down together in easy physical closeness.

Only once, when Niall described in erotic terms the mating of stallion and mare along with the similarly earthy mating of a god and mortal maiden, did Jo feel herself being watched. She looked up to find Rob staring at her, smirking with his eyebrows raised cheekily. Suppressing a smile, she looked down, fixing her eyes carefully on her hands. Just the memory of her encounter with Rob turned her on. Bizarrely, she felt attracted to both of them – Rob and Michael. Then she wondered why indeed she should question it? After all, as everyone constantly told her, at Fenris Gate there was no need to keep desire trapped in traditional one-on-one coupledom.

There were a few questions after Niall finished reading. Michael wanted to know if he had come across any other references to animals beyond the tales of stallions and mares. Niall said he hadn't. Then, after a few more questions, Michael thanked Niall and the group relaxed and started to disperse.

'Now, I need to show you something,' Michael said, leaning over towards Jo.

'Oh, right.' Her heart began to thump. She was desperate to be alone with him. Rob's hints that Michael was sexually aware of her had been on her mind all afternoon. Even wonderful sex with Rob couldn't stop her body tingling as he spoke to her. It was as if he could mainline straight into the ache of her need.

After getting up, he reached for her hand. The sensation of being touched by him felt wonderful, just as it had the previous evening.

'I need to show you the forest.'

Outside, the air was still warm although the sun had long since set. In the trees above them, the cries of bats pierced the air as they circled and swooped in search of insect prey. Expectantly, Jo let Michael lead her up the path in silence, longing for the moment when he would reach out and take her.

It was almost pitch-dark as they climbed the path which was no more than a pale blur streaking ahead of them. She was aware of his longer legs pulling her forward as he strode up the pathway, avoiding the low-hanging branches as the forest thickened around them.

He only stopped when they reached the summit of a hill and, momentarily, the moon slid out from behind a silvered cloud.

'It's warm and dry here.'

He pulled her down on to a patch of sun-warmed grass; he was sitting with his legs bent and Jo snuggled cosily between them. From their vantage point on the hill, they could look down on the waving mass of treetops below them. The feeling of his strong chest and cradling arms made her feel utterly protected.

'I need to tell you about tomorrow, Jo.' Wrapped so comfortably in his arms, Jo listened to the seductive resonance of his voice.

'I've been working for some time on different ways to achieve what's called shapeshifting,' he explained. 'That means we try, as part of our ritual work, to get in touch with our familiar spirits. What I need to tell you is that this is not just some kind of mass hypnosis or groupthink experience. There is no doubt at all that some identity change is taking place.'

'I really don't understand,' Jo butted in.

He laid his arms loosely around her shoulders and Jo sank her forehead against the taut muscles of his upper arm. He felt warm to the touch; tenderly she rubbed against it, enjoying the sinewy smoothness of his flesh. She almost wished he would just shut up – she needed him so badly. Ever since she had set eyes on him she had longed to be like this; completely alone, enfolded in his arms.

'Here. I want you to have this.' Michael reached into his pocket and dropped something into her open palm.

'My God, what is it?' It looked and felt like a bent hook or maybe a heavy half-moon earring.

'It's a tooth. The tooth of a wildcat. Your animal spirit is a cat, I know.'

Jo listened carefully, amazed that he knew this without being told.

'I want you to keep that by you all day tomorrow. Go down there to the woods and spend some time meditating on the nature of your animal spirit. This is a serious matter,' he insisted, suddenly grave. 'You may find that your animal spirit, what the Norse seers called your *fylgia* or fetch, overwhelms you when we start the ritual. It may overpower the human part of your nature and you may perceive the world as that creature.'

'You say I may. Does this actually happen? I mean, has anyone else experienced this?'

'All of those who were at the house tonight. They all transform into their animal spirits.'

Of course. She had known it all along at some unconscious level. Now it was so apparent. Since first watching the smaller group around Michael, she had guessed there was something different about them. They were so tactile, so oddly feral. The thought of joining them made adrenaline pump around her veins. This was amazing.

'I think I knew. This is so incredible. It's what I've always wanted.'

135

'Hold on, Jo. I sense in you a quality to walk in that strange world that is very unusual. From our first meeting – no, even when Emmi first spoke of you – I could sense the lure of the cat spirit that is your fetch. I think you will find it easy to change. Maybe too easy.'

She was staring down at the forest where the black crowns of the trees rolled like a sea in a sudden breeze. Tomorrow, she would go down there and meditate on her spirit, as Michael had instructed her. The thought strangely thrilled her. The oddest sense flashed into her mind that down there she would love to prowl free through the undergrowth. She could almost feel the tickle of twigs and leaves beneath her furry belly. Her whiskers too would twitch and tingle in the darkness, guiding her along to – to what?

'Tell me. What is it like?'

'I can't tell you that. If it is meant to be, you will experience it.'

'I mean, will I see the world as I do now? Or is it somehow different – I don't know, more primitive?'

'You have some kind of far-sightedness, Jo. You are right, the world is oddly different when we fare forth. It has always been night when I have travelled there; it is indeed a primitive place of strange landscapes and unpredictable weathers. The world we call the real world is only one view of a complex of different planes and times that co-exist within the living universe. The elemental worlds that we travel to in ritual can be dangerous, so we must keep to the path that is laid out for travellers. It is not wise to stray from the path.'

'I promise I won't,' she declared suddenly, not knowing how or why she was so sure of this. Then she rested her head back against his shoulder, watching the stars glimmer and shine above the forest roof.

'I want you,' he said suddenly, reaching down to kiss the sensitive back of her neck.

Smiling to herself, she settled back, sighing with a kind of relief that he had finally declared himself. As he nuzzled his lips against the little hollow at the top of her spine, her whole body was suddenly bathed in warm, syrupy delight. Gently, he extended his tongue and licked upwards, towards her hairline. The nerves in her spine trembled.

'So do I want you,' she declared, suddenly twisting round to receive the full power of his kisses. But instead, he only reached up with his fingertips and sealed her lips gently.

'Not yet. Tomorrow I will need all my strength. As will you. It is not yet time.'

Then, abruptly, he rose from the ground, pulling her upright too. Jo felt bereft and disappointed. She wished they could just sink down again on the grass and she could tear into his smooth skin and hard muscle.

'But I need you,' she complained.

Patiently, Michael turned to her, taking both her hands loosely in his. 'It is necessary. When the time comes, you will know why we have waited.'

Chastely, he kissed her with dry lips on her forehead. But as she leaned against him, Jo felt, like a bolt of lightening shooting straight to her overheated sex, the hardened bulk of his cock. So, he was a man too. All this reticence was only a sign of strength.

'If you want, go and see Rob,' Michael said, hearing her sudden intake of breath as she brushed against his hard-on. 'He thinks of you now. He wants you too.'

'I was going back to Emmi.'

'Emmi is going to leave.'

Momentarily shocked, Jo then realised this was true. It certainly didn't need anyone with second sight to work that mystery out. But Jo had been trying not to face up to the obvious fact ever since she had arrived here. For some reason, Emmi was no longer a part of Fenris Gate.

'I suppose she is.'

'So, take your pleasure among us now. That will be best,' he continued, as he turned and led her back down the slope to the golden lights of the farmhouse. 'It will be safest for you now to stay only with your own kind.'

Chapter Eight

Next evening, Jo found Emmi out at the paddock. She was leaning on the gate, kicking her trainers into the air, her round rear-end sticking up through her shorts. She pretended not to hear Jo, growing suddenly intent on twisting strands of grass around her fingers like plaited rings.

Jo smacked her taut backside affectionately. The startled giggle was reassuring; maybe they were still friends.

'So, what's happening?' She settled against the gate next to Emmi, trying to get a fix on her mood from the expression on her face. But her friend was keeping her blue eyes blank, gazing out across the pasture. The light softened her face like a golden-lit, soft-focus advert. Above, the sky was glowing with the pink luminosity of a dying sunny day. A couple of the ponies were cropping the grass serenely as the trees darkened to black silhouettes against the sky.

'Oh, the usual circus. They got Hengest to cover Freya this afternoon. Quite a performance. Everyone got off on that.' Emmi's voice was a singsong of heavy sarcasm. 'Bet you're sorry you missed *that*. So where were you all day?'

'In the forest.'

'Oh. Who with? Rob or Michael? Or the whole gang?'

'On my own, actually.'

It was true. All day she had wandered through the dappled shade and sunlight of the ancient woods, stopping only occasionally to sit against a tree trunk and concentrate on her task. Niall had given her a sheaf of papers containing notes and references about cats: from their worship in Ancient Egypt to torture and death at the hands of witch-hunters, she found that the cat had been equally feared and revered. With a curious sense of recognition, Jo had read of people's fascination with the lascivious animal, surrounded by the ring of caterwauling suitors attracted by her heated appetite that lasted for days on end.

Then, in a tranquil clearing among rustling leaves, she had held the cat's tooth tight and meditated on her familiar spirit. As the heavy branches above her head waved and creaked, Jo had used all the power of her mind to give shape to the animal part of her spirit. In her inner eye, she had conjured a fast and feline shape, dashing on all fours through the long grass. The sweet scent of mown grass and damp, turned earth had filled her nostrils and, all around her, she heard birds calling through the branches and smaller creatures scrabbling along the ground. Then, a sudden awareness had struck her: she was not alone. The forest was alive with activity. The trees were breathing and growing. The sunlight was casting benevolent rays across all living things.

But there had been something more. Abruptly, Jo had snapped her eyes open. The sensation of being watched had been so intense that she jumped quickly

140

to her feet, peering all around into the shadowy arches surrounding the glade. But nothing had stirred. Breathing fast, she had listened intently. Only the gentle rustling and stirring of the forest could be heard. And yet, as Jo had turned and hurriedly made her return to the bustle of the farm, she knew she had not imagined the presence. It was only now, in the warm evening next to sceptical Emmi that she began to wonder if her imagination was beginning to run ridiculously wild.

'Oh, I'm surprised you were on your own,' Emmi continued viciously. 'I thought you would all be out there in the woods, getting some practice in. You know, for the big animal fest tonight.'

'Look.' Jo turned and lifted a strand of the girl's fair hair. 'I'm looking forward to tonight; I'm not going to pretend I'm not. And if you don't want to get involved, I can respect that. But what Michael's talking about – it's amazing. A journey I feel I've been waiting for all my life. I'm not going to miss it. But it's not just that, is it? You've got to come out with it. What's eating you?'

'Well you're not for a start.'

It was impossible not to laugh at Emmi's aggrieved simper.

'And that's it? We can soon sort that out.' Laughing, Jo slid a hand into the hot crease at the juncture of Emmi's thighs. But, all petulance, Emmi backed away.

'You know what I mean.' She jutted her chin away as she spoke. 'It's just you, Jo. You're so – into all this Fenris stuff. There's nothing left for me.'

Sliding her arms around the girl, Jo felt heat glow from under her T-shirt. Emmi's body retained the day's heat like the sunwarmed Celtic stones over by the riverside. Suddenly Michael's advice not to mix with Emmi seemed so vague that she told herself she

141

hardly needed to follow it. After all, she had come to Fenris Gate to be with the girl.

'Come on. I really, really want to be with you.' Sliding her open palm upwards, she felt the swell of Emmi's small breast under the thin fabric. Through the soft sports bra she could just pinch the hardening lump of her nipple. It made a warm little electric shock trigger around Jo's clit. Since her rejection by Michael, she had been walking around in the swelter of her own heat. If her blood was simmering hot through her veins, then her sex was close to boiling over.

With a lizard-flick of her tongue, Jo skimmed across the girl's lips, tasting only strawberry-flavour lipstick before Emmi twisted away. Pushing closer, Jo continued massaging the stiff prominence of her nipple and tried again, sinking into the wet softness of Emmi's mouth. This time she succeeded in locking her mouth against Emmi's, brushing her slippery lips back and forth and sending her stiff tongue on a little foray into the heat and wetness beyond.

Like a skilled masseuse, she felt the girl's body slump with pleasure. Gently, Jo slid her hands over Emmi's shorts, feeling the hard muscle underneath the curves. Pulling the girl's hips towards her, she could think of nothing but the wetness that was oozing between her own legs. She wanted this to go on – the lovely deep kissing, the gentle grinding of Emmi's pubis into her own aching mound – but she wanted more – and faster too.

Freeing her mouth, she whispered, 'Let's get naked.'

Emmi grinned, in that naughty-little-girl conspiratorial way of hers. 'Not here!' she hissed. Then she giggled. 'Where?'

Glancing around, Jo spotted the open door to the stables. In a moment she had dragged Emmi over to it and bundled her through the door. Inside hung a deep gloom, save for magical golden sunrays piercing the gaps in the roof. Michael's stallion, Hengest, was a darker shadow, jostling in his stall.

Mesmerised, Jo watched the girl dance slowly along the aisle of the stable, sending motes dancing up into the air. Finally turning to face her, Emmi pulled her T-shirt up, watching Jo's reaction as her hair tumbled down over the straps of her white bra. In a second she had it unclipped and two soft and lovely breasts pouted from her chest. Sliding down shorts and panties in one fast movement she soon stood grinning and beautiful, trailing her fingertips up from her hips over her waist to her rapidly hardening nipples. Throwing her own clothes into a heap on the floor, Jo slid her backside on to the natural cushion of a few straw bales and pulled Emmi on to her so she straddled her thighs.

The girl's nipples tasted salty from the day's heat but soon Jo sucked through that to hard, candy-button flesh. Nuzzling the hot gap between her breasts, licking around the swells, Jo felt the ends of Emmi's hair tickle her face. She could hear Emmi make little panting noises whenever she caught a sweet nipple in her mouth, twisting it with her tongue and flicking the tip lazily from side to side. And behind her she could hear Hengest snuffling as he pawed around in his straw.

Suddenly, Emmi reached down and sought her mouth. Kissing deeply with jaw wide, Jo felt the girl rub her excited breasts over her own hardening nipples. Almost ashamed at the force of her craving, Jo stifled a groan as pleasure sparked between her abraded red nipples and the throbbing centre between her thighs. Looking down, she could see the pale curls of Emmi's pubic hair where it rubbed across her belly.

There were telltale smears of wetness too, where the girl was pressing slowly against her.

'Lie back,' Emmi whispered. 'I want to get right up inside you.'

Slipping down across the straw, Jo lay with knees hunched up to reveal the sticky parting at her middle. She felt utterly vulnerable; her eyes glazed, her body simply waiting.

As Emmi slid down to kiss her thigh, it hit Jo like a slap how wonderful this really was; how to be with another girl was truly the sweetest thing. She could hardly recollect why she was so hung up about Michael. Gently, Emmi began to kiss and lick the very softest, most sensitive skin hidden deep inside her thighs. Very quickly, Jo's hips began to arch and press, coaxing Emmi deeper and deeper towards the rich, crimson seam. When Emmi reached up and gently parted the slippery folds, Jo gave a little cry of pleasure that turned to a moan as the girl's tongue connected with sticky flesh. It was so easy to ride off on that river of pleasure. Licking deep into her channel, lapping up her honey, the girl forced Jo's muscle to tighten and quiver. Moving her tender tongue tip back and forth from the bony front of her opening to the deep chasm at her rear, Emmi teased Jo's flesh until all her control disappeared and she bore down desperately into the girl's face.

Jo felt nothing but the red river of sex; luxuriating in the blind loss of reason. She could feel her own thigh muscles involuntarily tighten around Emmi's head and little rhythmic sobs erupting from her mouth whenever her tongue brushed against her clit. Now Jo wanted to let go and reach her peak. Her own desire was so great; she could feel her body shuddering with suppressed need. Arching her back, she opened her

144

thighs to an aching wideness. All she needed to do was let go.

Emmi pulled the aching little bead between her lips, while a sympathetic spasm of pleasure rolled through Jo's pelvis. Now, very slowly, Emmi worked the tip of her tongue back and forth, while Jo's breath grew laboured and ragged. Slowly, Emmi worked her hand up her thigh until she could slide it neatly inside Jo. Then, very quickly, she penetrated. Pushing two stiff fingers into Jo's tight but slippery passage she began to work the girl in a way she knew she could not stand for long. A flutter of muscles began to work around her fingers. But Emmi flicked her tongue more slowly, not faster. And her stiff fingers worked deeper but slower too. Instead of fast, Jo's orgasm erupted as slowly as a giant cresting wave. With a cry and involuntary gasp for air, Jo's pelvis shot up from the straw as wave after wave of convulsions began to build, awaiting release any second.

'Oh please,' she began to beg. 'Don't stop, yes; just that.'

She was arched and panting, feeling every lazy tongue lap, ready and teetering on the brink – when Emmi came to a dead stop. For a lust-confused moment she thought the girl was tormenting her on purpose.

'Go on,' she begged. Barely another few strokes and she would be there. 'Oh, on my knees; just do it. Do it now.'

Blinking, she opened glazed eyes. Michael was standing above them as stiff and tall as an apparition. That was why Emmi had retreated, curling up on her knees, slipping her T-shirt over hot, spiky nipples.

Michael's eyes washed over the wet nakedness of her body, devouring the sight, unable to snap his eyes away. She was stretched open and vulnerable, pale on the straw bed with breasts swollen high on her rib-cage. Almost painfully, she slid her legs together tight, feeling moist runnels dribble down her thigh. She felt nauseous with frustration.

'Sorry, Jo,' he said haltingly.

Jo stared at him angrily through eyes blurred with tears. It was unbelievable – she was nearly crying with frustration. She felt like a bomb, all primed to explode when the fuse is suddenly snuffed out. Her body was an agony of swollen, pulsing heat.

'Yeah?' she snarled, dragging herself up from the straw, aware of her breasts bouncing as she sat up.

'I've got to take Hengest out. Look, I'm not trying to cramp you two. It's after six. Late already for his gallop.'

To make matters worse, she could see that Emmi, in an utterly pointless tantrum, had hustled on her clothes and was making a quick getaway. Great. Bad temperedly, Jo groped around for her own clothes. She had dropped them somewhere; it was hard to see. The door slammed as Emmi got away.

But Michael had not moved. Like a statue, he stood above her, lust-darkened eyes working over her, appreciating her nakedness. Suddenly she felt like the cat he had described as her spirit. A vivid image sprang up in her mind, of stretching and rolling on her back, pawing the air, allowing Michael tantalising glimpses of her hidden treasure. But in the real world she reined in her instincts, only a tiny gesture of arousal getting past her defences as her thigh invol-untarily slumped open a loose, provocative inch.

He saw it, licked his dry lips, and his mouth hung open for long seconds. He had just caught another tantalising glimpse of her glistening seam and his eyes locked on to it, hungry and wanting.

'We have to wait,' he said hoarsely. 'You know that.'

'I need my clothes then,' she said, but the words came out strangely lacking in force, as if it was his choice to allow or disallow this.

For one endless moment more, he just looked, eyes tracing the spit-stiffened crimson of her nipples, the soft freckled belly and pink and puffy lure of her sex. In that instant she glimpsed victory, sensing that even he could not now withdraw.

'Your clothes,' he repeated, blinking like a sleepwalker.

Then he broke the spell, leaving her hot and desperate while he picked them up from the stable floor. Inside her head she howled, abruptly aware that she wanted only him – and not this sickening ebbing of her lust into nothing.

Dismissively now, he dropped her clothes down on to her lap and went to fetch Hengest's harness. Standing shakily, Jo pulled on her shorts but found Michael wasn't even watching her dress as she reluctantly pressed her breasts into her halter-neck top. But still she couldn't drag herself away. As fast as lightening her lust had been redirected. She needed Michael like a junkie needs a fix.

Michael coolly strode back with Hengest's gear. 'Look what you've done.'

She should go. There was still something taut and unspoken between them from last night. She knew she should go and find Emmi.

'What?' She couldn't think why she was still hanging around, elbow perched on the animal stall so her body stretched long and lean for him to admire.

He only had to nod his head towards Hengest's hindquarters.

'My God,' she gasped in admiration. The animal sported a massive erection.

'He must have smelled you two.' Michael grinned wickedly. 'The scent's driven him mad. Come and have a look.'

'I don't know.' Jo backed away slowly. Not because she didn't want to see, but because even just the outline of the stallion's phallus sent a surge of excitement through her abdomen so sharp that it hurt.

'Did you know, the Norse people used to keep the phalluses of their most powerful stallions as a fetish? It's such an incredibly potent object. The source of so much power.'

He held out his strong arm and Jo felt herself slipping her hand into his and approaching the horse with slightly unsteady footsteps.

'Look,' he said. She could feel his calloused hand gripping hers tightly, pulling her nearer. Close by, she could feel the warmth of Hengest's shining flank rippling against her bare arm. Timorously, she glanced down and gazed in awe at the massive organ. Like a gigantic tube of leathery brown flesh, it danced between Hengest's hind legs. Feeling herself grow breathless, Jo pulled back, not a little scared of the horse's huge length and girth. She guessed it was nearly eighteen inches long and as thick as an elephant's trunk.

'Touch it,' Michael whispered suddenly.

'What?' She was genuinely shocked. 'You must be joking.'

'It's a sacred object, more especially when it's erect. Its power will help you tonight, when you enter the rite. Remember, the more primitive, the stronger the magic.'

He was speaking as if this were just an ordinary situation, as if he had just asked her to touch a bowl of incense or a ritual candle. She gazed again at the dark and mysterious phallus, wondering if it really was just another component of magical ritual. But to her it looked more than that; like something that made her blood pound fast in her head, that made her fingers tingle with excitement to think they might actually reach out and stroke that incredibly stiffened phallus.

Stooping a little, she gazed round-eyed at the strange organ, marvelling at its tapering length and thick, muscular base. Her hand, as it reached the rubbery surface, looked tiny and white, unable to stretch around the solid girth.

'Oh.' Jo almost felt her knees buckle. Inside her, her muscles grabbed on emptiness and her juices seethed. Timidly, she explored the vein-thickened base and then let her fingers crawl all the long way along its tautly stretched surface to the tip. She could not believe that this was really happening; it was something she realised she had wanted to do ever since she arrived at Fenris Gate.

'It's a good thing he's due to cover Freya again tomorrow. So it's not such a bad thing you've given him a raging hard-on,' Michael said huskily. 'If not, I'd be tempted to suggest you relieve the poor brute of his load.'

Did Michael really mean what she thought he meant? Just a momentary image of taking this further, of letting her hand work back and forth along the horse's magnificent shaft, made her dizzy. Sure enough, she could see his huge testicles swinging like swollen bags of leather between his legs. Trying to control her responses, she began to massage the tip of his cock, though its circumference was too large to grasp. As her open palm cradled the strangely wrinkled skin, Hengest suddenly whinnied appreciatively, shooting the huge cock forward into her hand. It burned her with its speed, rushing its full length through her fingers. Terror and excitement ran like lightening through her nervous system.

With a startled jump, Jo drew back.

'Are you OK?'

She knew that to Michael's eyes she must look pale and faint. 'I think I've got to go,' she mumbled, struggling to get away. 'I need some fresh air.'

'OK.' He slipped his arm around her in concern. 'If you want, we can both take him out for a gallop. I need to speak to you anyway, Jo. Here, let's go outside.'

Outside, she took big lungfuls of warm, spring-scented air. Out here, it was still bright in the fading sunlight and what had happened in the stable felt like a peculiar dream. Only when Michael went back to fetch Hengest for his exercise did she silently explore the damp circle on her palm. Sticky and warm, it made her legs weak with excitement as she remembered again the feral power of the animal, thrusting greedily into her inquisitive hand.

'Here you are, boy,' Michael soothed, guiding Hengest out of the stable door. It seemed that Hengest gave her an appreciative whinny too, as he clipped out on to the cobbles. 'If we take him for a quick canter I can drop you at the roundhouse in time for the feast.'

Warily, Jo took a look at the horse's belly and was relieved to see that all that was left of his hard-on was a mere hand's length of reddish tip protruding out of his animal sheath.

From the saddle, Michael gave her a hand up so she could ride in front of him. As the smooth leather stretched the parting at her crotch, Jo inwardly groaned. It had suddenly dawned on her that Michael was going to give her no opportunity to find Emmi before the rite. Neither was there any possibility of his touching her. The thought of passing the whole evening in this frustrated state appalled her.

'Look,' she blurted over her shoulder, 'I could do with going back for a shower.'

But, as Michael clicked his heels, he said, 'Take a shower under the pump in the yard, Jo. It's going to save time. Listen, there's something I need to say.'

Leading Hengest carefully down the path to the meadow, Michael slid his arms loosely around her waist and Jo had to do her best to concentrate.

'I want you to be especially careful tonight, Jo. You know we've talked about a road appearing when humans fare forth? And about the importance of not stepping off that road? Well, I think tonight we should not even go to the road. It's enough to stay in the precincts of the house, or at the very most move only to the boundaries of the yard, which I can guard inside a warding circle.'

'Yes, sure.' Jo already found it incredible that tonight she would run in the skin of her own shamanic cat spirit. 'But what's the matter? Are you worried about something?'

'I did some preparatory work last night. Took a look at the lay of the land, so to speak. And I can't be sure, but there was a presence I could sense. Off the road, for sure, but out there somewhere, in the elemental world.'

It felt comfortable with Michael cradling her in his arms, confiding his cares to her. And out here in the dappled green of a warm spring evening, it was easy to talk about these things as abstractions.

'But what kind of presence? Danger?'

'Oh, I don't think it's anything too bad. But we must be prudent; the empty body is vulnerable once the soul has fared forth. And there are tales enough of travellers to the other worlds who unwisely trusted strangers. The roads between the worlds are dangerous and any wound received in faring will appear in the earthly body. So I want you to stay by me, Jo, and I'll look out for you.'

'Thanks.'

'OK. Time to let Hengest go.'

With a dig of his heels, he let the stallion off the bit; in a few paces Jo's hair was flattened in the wind and the horse galloped eagerly over the gently undulating pasture.

She was violently aware of Michael's skin pressing through his shirt close against her spine and the hardness of his thighs pushing against her bare legs. For a while she allowed herself to enjoy it, pressing her head back against his chest. But as Hengest's motion quickened, the rhythmic slap of the hard leather saddle jutting into her excitedly spread lips began to drive her crazy. She wanted to writhe on the beating saddle, press her poor tormented self tightly against its unforgiving hardness. As the seam of her shorts began to dig into the sensitive inner lips she slumped backwards, terrified she might reach some kind of unwelcome, involuntary orgasm if this went on and on.

Only when they trotted up to the roundhouse could Jo finally relax a little, slipping on trembling knees from Hengest's high back. Hot, damp and uncomfortable, she staggered to the pump that leaked drips on to the cobbles. Not giving a thought to anyone's reaction, she slid off her shorts and top and crouched under a spray of freezing water. God, she was sticky with congealed, fermenting sex. Even as she rubbed against her soaking panties she could feel the heaviness of her own secretions. But at least she was cool. Then, slinking like a cat to the sunniest spot, she picked up her shorts and top and settled on the wall, where in a few minutes the warm rays of the sinking sun dried her down, leaving her fresh and ready for the events of the night.

Inside the roundhouse Jo sat in the circle, her stomach full from feasting and head already fuzzy from glasses of herb-infused wine. There was a fierce expectancy in the smoke-filled room; ten or so of the community waited for Michael, either excitedly chatting in whispers or silently meditating in readiness for their transformation. At the far side of the room a vast fire burned. Smoke from the fire and the ritual incense made Jo feel pleasantly sleepy. In her hand, she constantly stroked the cat's tooth Michael had given her, replaying again and again the tales she had learned of the gods and their feline helpmates.

Suddenly the room fell silent. At the sound of a soft but insistent drumbeat, Michael strode into the centre of the circle. A headdress in the style of a wild dog covered most of his face and as he moved to the centre, Jo experienced his strangeness; his presence as both man and beast.

Lyn began the chant. Jo joined the warm surge and fall of the incantation, losing herself in its ebb and flow. As they chanted, a wide wooden bowl of liquid was passed around the circle. Once it reached Jo, she grasped it carefully and raised it to her lips. The drink was cool and bitter; tasting of pungent leaves and berries. After drinking deeply, she wiped her lips on the back of her hand and passed it on to the next person.

Michael was silent for a long time, breathing steadily. When he spoke, it was slow and steady, a rhythmic accompaniment to their incantation.

'In the name of the Old Ones I cast a ring of

fire. Let no evil powers enter herein nor abide within its boundary.'

As he spoke, he raised his arm, pointing his index finger forwards. Slowly he moved around the circle, drawing the ring in the air until he joined the two ends. There was nothing to see but, as the loop was completed, Jo felt a satisfying sense of closure, as if they were all sealed inside a tall cylinder of heavy-duty glass. She could hear the spit and crackle of the fire but could no longer drag her eyes away from Michael towards the flames.

He seemed to rest awhile, standing in front of the fire with eyes closed. Then he lifted his arms, drawing a shape above them in the air; a faint afterglow burned Jo's retina as she glimpsed the sacred flame. Her mind felt alert, almost bursting with excitement but her body sat deadly still and lethargic. In the furthest recesses of her brain, she was aware of a change in her consciousness, yet her mind was utterly in the present, with no desire to analyse what was happening around or to her. Intently, she watched him slide off his robes. Then, standing before them naked, he motioned them to do the same.

'Take off your human skins.'

A tiny part of her mind was surprised that she slipped off her clothes so readily. Already, the archaic part of her acquiesced, following the ritual like a long-forgotten bedtime story. When he motioned them all to lie down, she did so, uncaring of the consequences.

Again she felt the tall walls of protection arching above her. Time passed; he was at the altar, blessing the instruments of ritual, calling forth spirits. Then he moved around them, whispering to each. Eagerly, she awaited his approach. Never for one moment did she doubt the strong magic coursing through the room.

Finally, he was over her, astride her thighs. The tall

silhouette of his torso transfixed her. The heavy warmth of lust suffusing her abdomen returned and she twisted her pelvis restlessly, feeling his hard muscle press into her. Above, the dog's head snarled, eyes glistening and teeth sharp. Reluctantly, she lay heavy and still, in some state between dozing and rapture.

'Feel your hide beneath the skin,' he growled. 'See yourself in your true form. Breathe it into yourself, feel your spirit awaken.'

With every inward breath, she transformed. The surface of her skin tingled in waves as fur sprouted like silky hair; as nails tapered to spiny claws; then her hearing grew madly acute as her ears twitched, picking up distant sounds far into the night.

Then his voice was distant, addressing them all. He was calling them; no longer speaking in the human tongue. Rather, it was an urgent command to waken up and run.

Rising, she felt her cat spirit move above the dormant frame of her human self. Her eyes opened on a world of vivid colour and shapes. As if a thousand arc lights shone down on them, she saw in minute detail her fellows in the pack, circling and padding around the confines of the circle. At the centre was a taller, shaggy figure. With long grey mane and flashing eyes, the pack leader stood straight, a long tongue lolling from his snout, surveying the snuffling and yapping mass of his brood as they explored their new-found powers.

Daintily, she sprang forward on all four paws, feeling the hardness of the earth beneath her. In a few bounds she was at his side, pressing her nose to his muzzle in a gesture of friendship and trying to lick the wetness of his snout.

With a velveted paw he cuffed the side of her head.

Startled, she jumped back, tail springing into the air. He had not hurt her but she felt the admonishment. Retreating, she watched him as he lifted his long neck and drew blackened gums back over his teeth. She had a sudden, disturbed vision that she knew this creature from some other, even stranger place. But, studying his eyes as cold as jade-stone and his lean, slow-rippling hide, she was maybe wrong. Perhaps she did not know him at all.

A waft of air reached her nose, carrying a rich scent of shorn grass, horses and ripening blossom. The big doors were open. In a long bound she reached the fragrant air, feeling the night chill ruffle her fur in exquisite waves. The rest of the pack also scampered out into the yard, some running in excited circles, others curiously pushing noses to the fence. The night was spectacular; starshine glittered over the mysterious patterns of the bordering forest; a myriad of night-sounds rustled and hooted, making her long ears twitch with excitement.

Hypnotically, she found herself pawing at the fence. There was something irresistible out there. Above, the dazzling face of the moon suddenly slid from behind a silvered cloud. With claws raking the wooden struts she felt an electrifying shiver pass through her sinews. On the breeze she caught a scent so delicious and inviting that her neck lifted long and taut, bearing her twitching nose high into the air.

Behind her, she felt others of the pack jostle and bump against her furry hindquarters. A black dog lolloped up to her, eyes sparkling and long tongue warmly licking her face. Despite a dim knowledge of his difference in kind, she nuzzled against his neck. Then another creature, heavy-set as a wildcat, nipped her ear affectionately, trying to drag her backwards to play in the moonlit area of the yard. After shaking herself free of his attentions she braced up against the fence, breathing in the feral scent from the forest, she longed to join whatever it was that hunted wild and free, out there in the starshine.

Suddenly, from close beside her, the pack leader growled. Dropping her head, she eyed him curiously. He was sending the other creatures away with an imperious snarl. Now just they two occupied the yard's perimeter. With a long, sinuous motion he rubbed the furry smoothness of his jaw along her browbone. She could smell his hot jowls and feel their heat. Involuntarily, she crouched low, feeling the nerve endings beneath her fur shiver with pleasure.

With the tip of his nose, he prodded her forward against the fence. It seemed to her that he wanted her there, as close as she could physically be to the tantalising presence hidden in the thousands of sappy, rustling leaves. Then, when she was tight against the wooden struts, she felt him whip round, nuzzling the cold tip of his nose against her rear passage. Eagerly, she quivered.

A long, hot tongue scorched the open passage beneath her tail. She felt her own tongue drip slackly from her jaws. Her tail began to bat gently to and fro, as he snuffled around her hindquarters. Her new body felt sturdily compact; her four legs securely grounded while her gaping rear sent out provocative scents. Mesmerised, she felt a savage pleasure course through her system. Again, there was the hot intrusion of his tongue into her fur-fringed passage, lapping deep inside her like a snaky probe. Her animal body loved it, pushing back blindly into his dripping snout. Still she sensed a presence beyond the fence; the hint of a movement and the crackle of branches. The rough tonguing between her back legs only made her more eager to find whatever it was that prowled out there,

157

sending his scent to her on the breeze with its promise of a wild and secret union.

Rapidly, the pack leader loped up beside her. Pressing her nose against his muzzle, she wanted only to communicate her affection for him. But he was gazing out into the night; pale eyes traversing the thickets for the creature they could both sense was watching them. Suddenly, a branch cracked and her companion's pointed ears pricked up, twitching to attention. But it was impossible to see the creature.

So that was it, she quickly realised. He had aroused her to attract the outsider's attention. He was using her. She was scented bait, dangling in the wind.

Much later, she wandered through the forest. At first the rain was a pleasant spattering on the leaves, releasing the fresh scent of sharp sap. Then it began to pour, driving needles of cold, sharp water into her fur. Rain began to drip from the end of her nose as she twitched her whiskers, trying to shake it from her blinking eyes.

She had strayed from the road. How this had happened, she was no longer sure. The pads of her paws now felt soft, slippery mud instead of hard stone. And the further she strayed along shadowy paths, the more and more lost she became.

It was with relief that she dragged her sodden body towards a glistening expanse in the distance. Hopeful of rediscovering the road, she entered a patch of moonlight where the trees shrank back from a clearing of flattened grass. But there was nothing else.

And yet – dark shapes flitted behind the branches, always just outside the range of her vision. There were two of them. Two male cats. A tall, rangy tawny who glared at her out of the darkness and a grey-jowled black, as dark as midnight.

They moved out towards her. Their fleeting shapes

surrounded her, whirling and circling, eyes reflecting green in the moonlight. Jo stiffened, her four legs locking, the claws at the ends of her four paws raking hard into the ground. The rain lashed down on her coat and she knew she must look even smaller and more pathetic now, without the thick fluffiness of fur. Somehow, her instincts told her, she had to show her attackers that she posed no threat. Skulking down in a posture of submission was the only safe response she could imagine.

But it was no use. The bigger cat, the tiger-striped tawny, was padding around her, knocking into her bony shoulders and dripping whiskers. His eyes were cold emeralds; his open jaws a glimmer of sparkling fangs. Jo dropped her head, feeling the curving length of her vertebrae stretch. Suddenly, she felt Tiger Stripe prowl around her again, only this time he stopped at her rear. With a long, hot flick, his tongue swiped her rear just where her sex throbbed expectantly. With a whip of her tail she tried to ward him off. But now the black tom was nuzzling the scent in her cheeks, sniffing and rubbing his wide, craggy face against hers.

Again, she felt the trace of a cold nose and then a hot tongue burning against her rear. Desperately, she tried to bat Tiger Stripe away, but this time found her tail was oddly disobedient. Whenever she tried to lower it, it quickly flung itself up again. In fact, with her tail standing stiff as a poker in the rain-lashed air, she could feel her back end uptilted; it was as if she were trying to attract these predatory toms to her hot little hole, rather than repel them. Disturbed and panicked, she tried to inch her way forward away from the intrusive tongue. But she couldn't move. Her legs had locked – all four of them. The only parts of her she could move were her twisting head and the hindquarters which seemed to have a life of their pulsing and quivering own.

Tiger Stripe bounded in front of her. Timorously, she swung her head low, trying to avoid his enthusiastic tongue. With a deep growl, he suddenly nipped her ear and she screamed back in a strange, unintelligible tongue. Another growl vibrated in her ears, deep and commanding. This time Tiger-Stripe reared up, pawing her head. Horrified, Jo smelt the feral scent of his underbelly and saw a dangling silhouette below his fur. The animal's phallus was long and hard, a taut erection jutting out of his furry sheath.

Shaking her head, she began to spit, hissing like a kettle at the creature. But when she tried again to run away, still her legs would not move. Worse, Black was intent on her rear end now, rubbing his rough, sandpaper tongue inside her, trying to lap up her tantalising secretions.

When it happened, it happened so quickly that she had no warning. Only half aware of his movements, she felt Black pull away. The next moment he threw himself like a dead weight on to her thin back. His massive body knocked the breath from her lungs, so that for a few moments she slumped, wheezing, to the ground. Then, crying incoherently, she tried to shake him off, but only momentarily did he lose his hold. Almost instantly, she felt two sets of claws like iron hooks penetrate her sodden shoulders. Above her, Black was sliding along her arched spine, trying to gain a satisfactory purchase on her slippery back.

Suddenly, she felt it; a hot stiffness humping against the back of her rear legs. With his claws fully open, Black was dragging himself up her full length, jutting his animal cock against her in a desperate search for her tantalising passage.

Screaming and spitting, she tried to wriggle away

from the relentless thrusting. Shock almost paralysed her as she felt the hard tip probe deftly against her entrance. Looking around for Tiger Stripe, she saw he had retired to the side of them, gingerly licking his fat erection, waiting his turn.

With a cry of pain she felt the hot tip slide into her moist rear. Growling deep in his throat, the animal began a rapid thrusting, humping deeper and deeper inside her. It burnt inside her flesh; painful and strangely sharp, yet so rapid and deep she would have collapsed to the ground had her four legs not locked in a permanent stasis. Above her neck she could feel the creature breathe hotly, drooling on to her twisting neck. Adjusting his hold to get a deeper penetration, her assailant slid his paws around her belly, where for the first time she felt the row of little pink nipples shiver and grow erect.

The hammer blows to her belly were awakening in her some distant memory. In some other place, she had longed for exactly this. Now it was happening. His cock adjusted to a deeper angle and she felt herself begin to tremble – not with fear but a wave of exquisite pleasure. The pain had subsided; she could now feel a hot liquid coating the animal's hard organ. It was lubricating their pleasure, helping him drive it to the deepest, most sensitive parts of her body. And the speed at which he was thrusting was almost mechanical, like a motor running at full throttle. She began to cry out in a high-pitched yowl, feeling the fur on her back rise like iron-filings beneath a magnet.

Her assailant seemed to respond to her cries, worrying the back of her neck with his teeth, pulling himself ever higher and deeper inside her. His cock was sliding at full stretch now, pleasuring her from her pulsing entrance to a deep, incandescent spot far inside her belly. She began to scream in weird, undulating cries. An awareness swept over her that here she could be herself utterly. She could cry to the moon; perform like a bitch on heat; ram her starving body as far as it could go on this incredible, animal-humping creature. She could behave like an animal. The miracle had happened. At last – she was an animal.

His shaft seemed to be swelling. It was a strange sensation, as if an orange was growing inside her passage. Wider and wider she felt her inner channel stretch. Delicious sensations swam around her furry belly. The black cat halted now, his member stuck fast inside her, pulsing with a giddy regularity. She had never been so full before; her rear legs were almost lifted as the animal forced the walls of her passage apart.

Suddenly, she was aware of Tiger Stripe slinking around her, rubbing his cheek to hers and jutting his sharp jaw against her furry brow. He was hot and ready too, he seemed to be saying. He could scent her sex and was waiting urgently to mount her next. Gingerly, he stopped in front of her and lifted his leg to worry his dangling erection with his long tongue.

With a sensation like a hot tap filling her, Black's cock erupted inside her. Jet after jet of heat sprayed her sensitive channel, making her cry and shake with pleasure. Gently, as the pressure lessened, Black began to hump inside her again, sliding back and forth inside her jissom-slippery hole.

At last, she thought, this is it. Screaming in words and sounds she no longer understood, she was entirely animal. The cock was still working her relentlessly, filling her to overflowing, sliding like a piston spraying hot oil. Above her, the animal's fur rasped against her coat and she could feel his hot tongue lolling on her back. She could tell he was almost completely, luxuriously spent.

When he finally pulled out of her, she screamed. With jaws wide and gums pulled back over bared teeth, she writhed in agony. The pain from the barbs on his retreating cock was excruciating. Her whole channel throbbed as if a jagged knife had just been twisted brutally inside her. Panting, she felt threads of sticky come dragging on her fur. But before she could even stretch round and clean herself, Tiger Stripe casually whipped around to her rear, grasped her fur and threw himself on to her back. Trying to shake him off, she heard him hiss as his molten cock battled to find some relief. Feverish with excitement, she could feel the stinging rain and puddles beneath her paws but all of this was as nothing compared to the wild heat in her loins.

This time Tiger Stripe's tongue-hardened cock found its housing rapidly. The savage pain in her passage only seemed to make her heat burn hotter. Getting himself comfortable above her, he settled down to ride her as hard and fast as his fellow tom had done, giving her a deep and relentless hammering. On and on he bounced back and forth, faster than anything she could ever imagine. When he too, began to shoot a rain of hot seed, she squealed and shivered in a series of climaxes so powerful that her brain reeled in a maelstrom of pleasure. On and on her climax raged as she felt her spunk-filled passage spasm in waves along the length of the animal's phallus. It was a flood of never-ending delight.

Abruptly, she became aware of the brightness of light fluttering behind her eyelids. She squeezed her eyes shut against the light, trying to get back to the rain-sodden clearing, trying to keep the thrills of pleasure alive in the meltdown of her body. But it was no use. Her eyes opened on the sun-drenched room she shared with Emmi. The last convulsions of her pelvis ebbed away as she slid her own slippery fingers from the grip of her hole. With a sigh, she threw back her arm behind her head, enjoying the pulsating afterglow of what she now guessed to have been an amazing series of climaxes that had erupted as she slept.

It must have been something in the drink, she mused, that set off wild and intense dreams. Last night had been so wonderful, her transformation so vivid that it was hard, now, to believe she was only human. And yet she could remember clearly the end of the rite, when Michael had undone the ring of protection and she had risen, shaky-limbed, to marvel at the strangeness of her human body as she once more walked on two unsteady feet.

Emmi had been asleep when she returned, twisted in a spiral of bedclothes with her head buried deep in her pillow. Restlessly, Jo had paced the room, feeling the moon beating insistently through the window. Flashbacks had played on and off from her experience as a cat spirit; memories of wonderfully acute senses and a lithe and supple body that longed for the freedom to roam untrammelled through the scent-soaked world. More than anything, she had wanted to open her throat and howl to the shining disc of the moon. But when she had looked down at her own tanned and slender arms and the elongated length of her body, she felt disappointed and confused. She felt only half-alive. To have even glimpsed life as an animal had given her an appetite she felt she could never, ever satisfy.

Chapter Nine

There was a knock at the door.

'Jo? You there?' It was Niall's voice.

Jo pulled the sheets up around her sticky body, wondering if she still bore the scent of sex as strongly as she had.

'Yeah?'

Niall slid his face round the door.

'Hi. Wasn't it amazing? What do you think?'

Patting the bed, Jo slid over so he could sit down. Grasping her knees, Jo looked at Niall's coarse black crop and even blacker almond eyes. He had a strange resemblance to – had he been that friendly black dog?

'Just incredible. Listen, do you still feel weird?'

'How do you mean?'

'Oh, you know, strange sensations – oh, to put it bluntly, massively horny.' She giggled.

A wide smile broke out over Niall's face.

'Now you mention it. I woke up with a raging hard-on. And despite – you know . . .'

'Having a wank?'

'Yeah, all right.' A blush was starting to rise over

the smooth copper of his oriental skin. Despite his obvious intelligence, he was not quite so earthy as Rob.

'And you can't get rid of it, right?'

'OK, nuff said, Jo. What you trying to do, crucify me?'

She couldn't help but laugh. He was twitchy with embarrassment.

'Listen to yourself. Remember last night? How we acted like inhibitions didn't even exist. Why, if I were my spirit again, all these barriers would be down and – well, we'd really show our feelings.'

With this, she leaned forward and jokingly nuzzled against Niall's face. Sweetly, he poked his tongue out and stroked it against her cheek in a long, slick lick. Then their two mouths suddenly slid together with an impact that made a thousand volts of pleasure jolt through Jo's system. Inside her mouth, Niall's tongue felt as wide and rough as a dog's, twisting down to her throat while his fingers reached for her, raking her neck excitedly. As he grabbed at her breasts she felt them grow in pleasure and harden. He was squashing them, trying to pull her up against his wiry body. Eagerly, she slid on to all fours, lapping her tongue into his open mouth.

'Oh God,' he was saying, his eyes round as he looked down at her smooth freckled body and pointed, dangling breasts disengaging from the bed-clothes. Frantically, he fumbled with his trousers. With her spine lengthened and rump jutting out backward Jo felt again something like the pulse of animal blood running through her system. When Niall freed the rubbery pink length of his cock she dipped her head and sniffed it before giving it a slow, exploratory lick.

Niall groaned uncontrollably. Pointing her tongue,

166

Jo slid it around the little slit at the tip and then began to work her lips over the domed end. She felt his frantic fingers reach under her chest, kneading at her soft breasts. In response, acute pleasure made her push down, sliding her mouth as far down his shaft as she could get it, feeling the end gag against the back of her throat.

'That is so – nice,' he crooned, reaching down and cradling her head in his hands. Gently, he moved her up and down, so her wet lips slid along the smooth length, creating a licentious sense of fullness in her mouth and throat. But soon, a warning twitch from the base made her pull back.

'Yeah, I think there's only so much you can stand.'

He was staring down at her, eyes heavy and unfocussed. Quickly, she slid on to the floor and began to drag his pants and boots off. It felt great to be naked, crawling around on the floor.

While Niall slid to the edge of the bed, Jo pulled his slim brown thighs apart and began to nuzzle against his cock and balls, feeling his wiry black hair tickle her face. All she wanted to do was lick and suck him, but at the same time, keep him under control, always on the edge, with that final moment savoured for her own delectation.

Now, looking at the stiffness of his cock, she began to delicately lick along its length, smelling the saltiness and enjoying the little grunts of pleasure she could hear from above. His prick had the unveined smoothness of a young boy. When she slid the tip into her mouth, a few drops of briny pre-come seemed to scorch her tongue, sending ripples of excitement down her throat to the fluttering pit of her stomach. Gently, she moved down to the wrinkled sacs of his testicles and cupped first one and then the other in her hot mouth. She could hear him raking the bedclothes with his nails and see his inner thigh muscles tighten with excitement.

Again, she felt the warning signs; a rhythmic jerk of his cock and the tight swelling of his balls. He just stared at her palely when she got up from the floor, climbed on to his lap and slid her thighs around his waist, lowering her crotch against the top of his thighs. She needed to use his cock; she needed it inside her. Looking down at it greedily, she wondered what it would feel like; it was baby-smooth and pink with a little curve and nice fat juicy head.

She swiftly twisted round, picked up her bag, pulled out a silver-foiled packet and handed it to Niall. He was equally quick in undoing the condom and pulling it on.

Shifting her hips upward, she felt the rubber-sealed tip of his prick scorch against her own ruby coloured slit. She was drenched now; just the sight and feel of his cock against her made her breath run fast. And close in front of her now, she could see Niall's face, slack and almost pained with anticipation.

With a subtle shift of her pelvis, she ground her clitoris against the spongy head, rubbing with delicate, mind-blowing strokes. Then his hands suddenly gripped her arms and the strangled cry from his throat told her he was boiling over. Deftly, she slid forwards and bore down, feeling the round head slide effortlessly into her juice-filled channel.

'Ooh,' she moaned, riding upwards again, feeling it slip out momentarily before she jammed it in again. 'You feel good and thick.'

Niall seemed beyond speech; he had grabbed her waist and was trying to pull her downwards so she could get the full length inside her. But Jo just tormented him, dancing the rim of her entrance around his throbbing cock-end, feeling her muscles tighten and pinch him while his face contorted in a kind of ecstatic agony.

'Please,' he begged. 'Please, Jo. Honest, I'm gonna spunk outside you in a minute.'

'Now that would be a waste.' She giggled, rotated her pelvis so a few gorgeous inches were sucked inside her and then pulled off him, leaving him twitching. He looked as if he was going to pass out.

Suddenly at the edge of his tolerance, he clawed at her waist and pulled her down hard. His cock shot up inside her like a tight bolt sliding home. For a long second she gasped, feeling the rod-like length ramming firmly up against her waist. When his hips shifted she found hers did too, setting up an urgent rhythm, pumping up and down along the slick meatiness of his length.

'Ooh, that's amazing,' she groaned.

All the frustration of the last few days had built up, had tightened her muscles until all she longed for was this – a really good, hard fuck. Gingerly, she pressed forward, wrapping her thighs around his slim waist, locking her ankles hard so she could feel the fat base of his cock jammed inside her entrance. They were tightly bound now, her pussy squeezing hard around him, abrading his cock with juicy pressure. They couldn't get any deeper, their faces damp and close, their tongues occasionally flicking out like little cocks, their bellies slapping hard and fast together.

Deep inside her, Jo could feel his bulbous head stoking up some hidden, magical spot; it was the place that nothing but a living cock could touch and it made her guts melt with pleasure.

'Don't stop,' she whispered. 'Go on, go on.'

She was so nearly there, her pussy lips were

169

stretched across his crotch and her clit was catching on his fuzzy pubic bone. And it was still there, scorching inside her, the thick tip of his cock banging away.

The moment came when she knew she was on the edge, when if Michael himself had stormed into the room, she would not have been able to hold herself back. Pleasure exploded from her centre, so violently that she arched her neck and screamed. Miraculously, Niall kept hammering his cock like a piston. As her muscles convulsed she felt herself rebound back again and again into a crazy paroxysm so intense that she wanted to weep with relief.

Hardly aware of her surroundings, she heard Niall cry out gutturally too, jerking his cock forward to empty his load inside the rubber. Just as her own climax died into scorching after-waves of pleasure, she experienced the gorgeous sensation of his coming far up inside her, with a series of long, juddering thrusts.

For a while they just clung to each other, still upright, panting and shaking.

'God, that was amazing,' he sighed. 'I never, ever knew. You know – that it could feel like that.'

'Yeah.' She laughed. 'I'm amazed I'm still in one piece.'

Her channel felt sore and used as she slid off him. Collapsing back down on to the bed, the two of them flopped back, sheenily naked, totally shagged.

'And to think, I bet you only came up to tell me to get to work.'

He smiled with his eyes closed and she glanced at his slender, hairless body with its coffee-coloured nipples. He really was cute.

'No, I really did come up to tell you something.

Christ, I'm glad I did now. That was something else. I mean, like nothing before.'

She tried not to keep staring at his lusciousness. His cock was deflating rapidly but still there was something as hot as hell building up inside her again. He looked good enough to eat up, all over again.

'That was it,' he continued sleepily, flipping his arm across his forehead. 'It's Michael. He wants to see you. I'm to give you the message to go over to his place tonight, about nine. Something about last night.'

Michael. Just the thought of seeing Michael excited her. She could tell him about her cat dream. And how she had felt when she was dreaming, even how she felt when she woke up. Yes, she looked forward to telling him all about it. Just thinking about it made her horny all over again.

Michael was excited too, but not in the way Jo would have wished for.

'Jo, tell me honestly, what did you see in the forest last night?'

He was watching her intently, leaning forward in his chair as they sat in the ethnic sprawl of the farmhouse sitting room. His pale eyes were intense, narrowing in concentration.

'Well, there was something there, definitely. I could hear it. It was watching me.'

'No,' he snapped. 'Listen to me. What did you actually see?'

It was hard to form her thoughts coherently when he was always controlling her. And she very much wanted to say whatever Michael wanted to hear. But it was no use.

'Nothing,' she admitted. 'I sensed a presence very,

171

very strongly. And I heard it moving through the leaves up to the fence. But, no, I didn't actually see it.'

Sighing, Michael pushed his knuckles against his teeth and stared into the empty hearth.

'Maybe it was just my suggestion to you that something would be out there. You were bound to imagine it and now we can't tell what's real and what isn't.'

Jo had been curled up in the opposite armchair, but now she sprang forward, reaching out to touch his arm.

'No, no, no. It was there Michael. I didn't even remember what you told me. The only question is – what is it?'

He lifted his brows, just perceptibly. 'I've got a hunch that this is a really big breakthrough. For years now, I've been working towards this point, trying different shapeshifting techniques, gathering power. This is something I've been waiting for, for years.

Sometimes spirits can be raised that are quite out of the ordinary. Something wild and untamed. A wolf maybe, possibly a varg, a kind of lone wolf living outside the bounds even of the elemental world's edicts. As far back as medieval times, the Venerable Bede wrote about the early Christians failing here because of the wild beasts lurking around the place. And there are local legends too, of a spectral beast or *barguest* reported over centuries. Some of the sightings were around the time of some witchcraft activity, so it could be that someone broke down the boundaries and this entity broke through into our world then. Maybe the same thing has happened again. On the other hand, I didn't see anything either. But the power I was sensing, it was enough to knock me over. I've never encountered anything like it before.'

'But surely, when we go back again, we can both look out for it? When's the next rite going to be?'

'That's just it, Jo.' He was shaking his head. 'When the group rites take place I need to look out for everyone. It's a sacred responsibility, you understand. I can't just work with the group on their transformation and then neglect them because I'm searching for this creature.'

'So what are you going to do?'

'That's why I've asked you here now, on your own. You see, I sense at the very deepest levels that together we can get in touch with this creature. If we go alone, then at least I'm only looking out for you. I promise, Jo, I'll do all in my powers to protect you. But of course, there are no guarantees. This is not risk free. And you need to do it of your own free will.' Suddenly, he drew back, shaking his head. 'Listen. Forget I ever said anything. It's unfair to involve you. Forget it.'

'No.' She dropped on to her knees in front of him and took his hand in hers. She would do anything in the world for him. 'I want to. I want to do it. Just tell me what to do.'

Together they went through the insect-speckled dusk to the empty roundhouse. Only as Michael began to build up the fire did she fully begin to wonder at her role in all of this. During the Beltane rite he had pushed her up against the fence as some kind of bait. Not for the first time, she wondered at her own impulsiveness. She had enthusiastically agreed to do something, but what exactly, she wasn't sure.

'Michael, why do you need me?'

He looked up at her from the fire, his eyes golden and lively. 'It's the closest he's ever come, moving towards you at Beltane. And you – you are sensitive

173

to him, Jo. I don't know what it is, but there's something drawing him to you.'

He had taken off his shirt in the heat and now Jo watched him greedily as he laid out his ritual instruments. As she sipped at the bowl of ritual drink, she noted again that, unlike Niall, Michael was a full-grown man, with all the power of a well-honed body. The muscles in his back twisted beneath his fire-lit skin as he moved. Above the seam of his trousers she could see the hair-matted sheen of his belly; she felt herself melt in anticipation.

Once again, Michael drew the magical ring of protection in the air and Jo found herself drifting into a state of pleasurable languor. When the signal came for her to undress, only the tiniest fragment of her mind acknowledged that she was now alone with Michael and that they were a naked man and woman.

The first change in the rite came when Michael led her outside, while still in her human form. Taking his hand, she was calm and happy, feeling the night breeze play and tease across her naked skin. When they stopped at the old stone anvil, Jo let Michael lead her on to it, feeling the heat of the day radiate from the ancient stone. She knew that the group sometimes used the stone as an altar, paying tribute to its heathen origins. But for now, Jo let herself be laid down flat on her back, staring mesmerically at the beauty of the stars.

She was aware of Michael continuing his rite, chanting and whispering above her. Then, as before, he climbed above her, straddling her thighs.

'I need to bind you,' he whispered from behind the dog mask. 'I need to keep you safe in one place.'

His silhouette against the starlit night pierced her mind. She would do anything that he asked, anything at all. As he reached for her wrists, a shiver of anticipation ran from her spine down to her toes. Her wrists felt soft and vulnerable beneath the thick cord. As he drew her arms up above her head, she felt her torso lengthen provocatively and she whimpered a little with fear and pleasure. Her whole body felt taut and responsive. She was aware of her breasts riding high on her ribs, her nipples stiff, just beneath her eyeline. Deftly, he tied the cord through iron rings bolted strategically into the stone. When Michael slid down and grasped her ankles, she gasped out loud, not with surprise but with seething enjoyment. He yanked her ankles up roughly and positioned her with knees bent double and thighs vulnerably wide. When the cords tightened around her ankles she was completely secure, with her bottom just perched on the edge of the sun-warmed stone.

For a long moment he stood before her; a magical shape in the darkness with the hide of the dog's head brushing his naked man's shoulders. The outline of his half-hardened phallus twitched in front of his belly.

'Feel your hide beneath the skin,' he instructed at last. 'Awaken in your true form.'

When the moment of transformation erupted, Jo welcomed it with every cell of her body. It was like returning from the stresses of an acting role to the habitual comforts of her own, true identity. The sinuous length of her limbs felt so right; as she slapped her tail against the stone, it was like welcoming back an essential part of her anatomy. She began to purr, rubbing her long spine sensuously against the stone.

The pack leader's transformation was also complete. On the ground in front of her, the huge dog circled back and forth, occasionally lifting his muzzle to sniff the night air. When his eyes caught a ray of moonlight they glowed a luminously pale, preternatural green. Then, with a swish of his erect tail, he padded out towards the fence and hoisted his shaggy forepaws on to the struts, surveying the blackness beyond. She could sense that he had caught a scent of the creature; that there was something out there in the rustling leaves of the forest.

Stretching her neck up from the stone, she began to call him back. A curious rush of emotions struggled for expression: fear of abandonment, shamelessness, crazed sexual heat. She could feel her legs pulled roughly apart, leaving her sex wide and exposed. Again, she called to him, thrashing her tail against the hard rock.

With nostrils wide, he returned, savouring her scent as it rose from her lubriciously parted legs. Despite the bonds, she wriggled her hindquarters wantonly, edging her pink seam to the very edge of the stone ledge. With a thrill as sharp as pain she felt his cold nose momentarily dip against her wet passage. A yowl of pleasure erupted from her throat. Next moment, a fiery tongue snaked up against her sensitive inner skin, forcing its way inside her. Like a roughened, flexible cock, the dog's tongue began to lick her passage, pushing rhythmically deeper, lapping up her hot secretions. It was like paradise; she arched her back, panting up at the sky. On and on the tongue extended, curling upward at the tip as it sucked droplets of her juice back down to his greedy jaws. Uncontrollably, she thrust herself against his muzzle. The next moment, he rammed his tongue full length inside her, pushing his rubbery snout against her fur-fringed opening. The pleasure was unbearable. With an unintelligible scream, she lost control, muscles spurting molten juice over his digging tongue. In a matter of seconds, his rough tonguing had brought her to an explosive orgasm.

In the burning afterglow of her climax, she closed her eyes while the pulsing of her inner muscles quieted. It was when she wanted to squeeze her legs indulgently together, gathering every last drop of sweetness from her orgasm, that she first noticed the tightness of the bonds. And that they were around her ankles, not her paws. Suddenly she knew that whatever her eyes and ears told her, she was still a human being. Trying to relax, she closed her eyes against the dazzle of the constellations and wished herself forcefully back into her feline shape. Again she experienced the sinuous lengthening of her limbs, the twitch of her ears and flick of her tail. But like morning sounds cutting into a dream, when she opened her eyes, this was quickly followed by the realisation that the cord was not digging into paws but ankles, and that her arms were not fur-soft but smooth and hairless.

But of the pack leader's transformation there was no doubt. She could just see him, paws up at the fence once more, ears erect as he surveyed the darkened forest. His tail was whisking slowly back and forth, almost touching the ground as his proud head swivelled from left to right, trying to track his prey. Then, abruptly, his tail stopped stiffly and began to tremble.

Swiftly padding back towards her, the huge dog seemed suddenly intent on lavishing her with affection. His great, rough tongue ran down her face in great spit-laden dollops of tenderness. Extending her own rough little feline tongue, she kissed him back, pressing her cold nose into his furry cheek, purring as he pressed against her whiskers. With a friendly whimper, he drew back, his jaws grinning widely around his lolling tongue. A short, sharp bark drew her attention. He wanted to tell her something, but what it was she could not understand. Later, she guessed he had been trying to prepare her by softening the blow. But when she saw what he did next, it was not difficult to guess what he had planned for her.

Spinning round to catch his tail, he frustratedly threw his haunches down on the ground, cocked his rear leg and began to nuzzle his under-regions. From her prone position she could see the outline of a long, stiff member flexing beneath his jerking tongue. Shifting round and round on the ground, he was masturbating himself, drawing his organ out of its furry sheath with eager, doggy tongue-licks. She now realised what he had been trying to communicate – that it was nearly time to penetrate her. Her head began to reel.

Instinctively, she began to pull at the cords. With blinding certainty she knew they held her bare ankles. She was not a cat; she was a naked woman tied to the stone out in the yard. But Michael was no longer Michael. Instead, there was a magically transformed canine licking his cock in readiness to mount her. She began to cry out. But the only sound she could hear was a raucous caterwauling, shrieking into the night.

The pack leader coolly rose from the ground and padded over to her. Then, with an agile leap, he sprang on to her prone body, straddling her with his four, slender legs. Again, he reached down and licked her face gently, his doggy tongue entering her parted lips in a wet French kiss as he licked inside her mouth. With a quiet whimper he edged forward, the sharpness of his claws clacking against the hard stone. Writhing apprehensively beneath him, she wondered what he was about to do. Then she felt it, dragging across her belly like a handless arm, jolting its tip across her naked body. As his cock pressed insistently against the pit of her stomach, her body prickled with animal heat. The strange organ felt burning hot and damp, leaving a trail of wetness on her skin. Paralysed, she felt him edge up her body, shifting his hindlegs to squeeze his cock across her scorching nipples, moving in rhythmic little jerks that betrayed the growing urgency of his need.

Inch by inch, he dragged his cock up to her neck until, with forepaws at the very edge of the stone, he squatted above her. It bumped against her jaw. Shaking her head, she tried to twist away from it, wailing in trepidation. Again it prodded her, this time brushing her whiskers, then hitting her face. A dreadful conflict wracked her as she realised what he wanted. She was unbearably excited, in a fever of weakness. From above her, he whimpered imploringly, jutting the hot, rubbery cock against her mouth. It smelled of clean dog, of fresh, juicy animal. Panting, she felt her cheek nudge against the damp tip. She stole a look at it. It was long and stiff and particularly thick in girth. A trail of liquid wet her face, sending an agonised explosion of lust down between her legs. Out of her mind, she opened her jaw. Shooting out her tongue, she sought the bulging length of his cock. The tip of her tongue found it and made maddened, rasping contact.

Slackly, her mouth opened around it and she let him edge it in. She was convinced that she had to prevent him seeing how overwhelmed she was. All her instincts were to roll her tongue around it, suck it and pull it inside her, but some deep-seated inhibition stopped her. Instead, she lay passively, while he slid it inside her parted lips. Then, very slowly, he began to work it back and forth.

Her whole body felt transformed; burning with animal craving. Her clit was heavy and swollen with desire; her parted opening squeezed hungrily on emptiness. Pleasure swam through her blood. The tip of the cock was pushing behind her teeth, forcing its way across her sensitive tongue, bulging against the roof of her mouth. She could barely breathe, but it was more from excitement than the way in which his bulk was constricting her airway. Involuntarily, she let her jaw open further. In reply he began to hump into her mouth, his hindquarters rocking rhythmically above her. The bulk of it almost gagged her, but she opened her throat further, taking it to the very back of her gullet.

What she was doing felt wrong, taboo, unlawful. But that only made it more arousing. Unable to stop herself, she began to wrap her tongue around the tapering meatiness of his cockhead. Eagerly, she explored its very tip, where a hot, clear liquid was dribbling into her mouth. It tasted clean and sweet and suddenly she rolled her tongue aside and began to suck. Down between her legs she felt a corresponding dribble of juice escape from her twitching passage. It was unbearable.

With a new urgency, he began to thrust his tip back and forth inside her mouth. Unimaginable sensations of pleasure rolled from her mouth down through her body to her ravenous centre. Moaning and twisting she gorged herself on him, lifting her long neck higher and higher to cram more and more tender meat into her open jaws. When she began to nip his shaft with her sharp little teeth he began to whine softly, worrying his prick in agitation. In reply she arched her neck and slid her jaw as far as it could go towards the thick, knotty base. With a yelp of pleasure, he suddenly jerked backwards, sliding himself free of her ravenous mouth.

In a moment he had leaped down to the ground and was padding around the stone on which she lay, whimpering plaintively. Again, an unearthly feline calling rose in her throat, crying out to him to come back to her. Hesitantly, he trotted to the fence and sniffed the scent from the forest. Then, with a snap of his head, he turned, yelping softly, telling her to be patient.

But that was no longer possible. Instinctively, she called again, howling up to the moon. She could just see him twitch impatiently, his long tail batting the night air. Then he turned, growling under his breath, eyes sparking. In a moment he had reached the stone.

With a sudden leap he was on her. The impact knocked the breath from her, stunning her for an almost insensible moment. His long claws struggled for purchase along her body, eventually grasping her middle. Above her was his long, heavy body; an enormous weight of rough-furred muscle straining to mount her. Suddenly she was distracted from the pain of his claws digging into her flesh; something was jabbing hotly against the inside of her leg. His phallus was humping against her, getting ever closer to her aching opening. In a frenzy, she writhed within the confines of the ropes, feeling the wet tip of his prick streak backwards and forwards against her leg. Then it rubbed frantically against the lips of her passage. Now she could feel what her eyes and mouth had already told her; his cock was so big that she knew it was going to hurt. Unable to escape, she closed her eyes and gritted her teeth.

She could feel his back legs dancing as he positioned his powerful body above her. He was yelping excitedly, trying to hit her tantalising slit. With a cry of abandonment, she pushed towards him, opening up for him as wide as she could.

With a frustrated growl, he found the slippery channel. Rapidly, he plunged the end of his cock inside her. The pain was tremendous; it felt gigantic, like a bludgeon striking her again and again. Growling again, he fucked even deeper, forcing the walls of her opening apart. This time his own lubricating juices cleared a way into the tight feline opening. But still, all she could feel was the mind-shattering burning of her passage being stretched as wide as it could be. Writhing beneath his onslaught, she longed for it to stop.

There was no way he could stop. She could feel long threads of doggy drool dripping on to her from his open jaws. His violent thrusting was getting faster now, his hindquarters jerking like a marionette. Almost unbearably, she felt his long, fast jabs push up and up her heated passage. It was getting so deep now, it was stretching her so wide – unbelievably, she heard a low cry of pleasure erupt from her own grinding jaw.

What had felt like pain glowed ever hotter within her as a strong, flowing pleasure. He was secure on his hindlegs now, penetrating her from the perfect, effortless angle. As if he could understand her pleasure, he began to yelp excitedly, driving into her so hard and fast that she rocked and bucked against the stone with only the bonds keeping her tied in place.

Now she could feel her own juices mixing with his, helping his cock glide effortlessly inside her as fast as his powerful muscles could drive it. Rolling her head from side to side, she drifted into a state of ecstasy; never had she known such overwhelming pleasure. Her pussy muscles tightened ecstatically around his long, burning shaft, squeezing wet juice along its length. In return he thrust even faster, humping his cock in a blur of speed.

She wanted all of it, every single red-hot inch. Pushing down, she felt a shower of blows pummelling inside her. With no idea whether she could take more, she wriggled and thrust, letting the massive organ pulverise her seething entrance. She cried and whimpered, driving him crazy with her teasing cavorting. The rough abrasion of his fur against her body made her weak with pleasure. Eagerly, she let him push his cock to its furthest depths each time he thrust, feeling a ball of fire build in her belly so powerful that she began to shake.

When his cock began to swell she whined plaintively. The pain returned, but this time twisted with searing pleasure. He stood motionless above her, panting with his long tongue lolling wetly. Like a filling balloon she could feel his cock grow, pushing the sides of her already stretched pussy further and further apart. It made her feel dizzy with lust, as well as fearful for her own body.

In the stillness she could suddenly hear a sound beyond his steady panting and the dry whispering of the leaves. Behind her canine lover, in the centre of the yard, something was stealthily moving. She hardly cared, so unbelievable were the sensations radiating from her overheated body. He was motionless inside her, pulsing gently, locked within her by the swollen knot. The sensation was exquisite, keeping her seconds from explosive orgasm.

The trigger came when he suddenly stretched his neck and flattened his ears; a strangled yelp erupted from his throat.

He could stand it no longer. His swollen balls hammered against her slippery rump. With a whine of release, a molten shot of juice sprayed inside her and she felt her muscles spasm frantically. Another and then another spurt scalded her spasming passage. Out of control now, she jerked against him, trying to climb his gorgeous, hot pole. She was grinding against his thick, hairy body, desperate to be filled. She could hear her own high-pitched cries as her climax ground on and on, as her tightened channel squeezed his sex mercilessly, milking it for every drop.

The sound again.

Momentarily opening her sharp cat's eyes, she could see the shape in the yard. It was watching her closely; a pair of piercing red eyes intent on the spectacle of the two animals fucking crazily in the open air.

Yet she was lost in her orgasm. He was still spurting crazily, filling her with hot jets of liquid. She could feel it flooding out of her, overflowing on to her twitching rump, bathing the stone beneath them in slippery wetness. It was melting her body into a state of bliss. Every time her convulsions seemed to slow down, she felt another delicious wave of spunk fill her and she buckled again. Her pelvis ground on and on as he finished, drilling into her with a final shower, skewering her flooded channel with his brutal bulk.

The sibilant sound dragged her momentarily from this ecstasy. It came from the red-eyed creature that watched, no more than a hulking black silhouette in the darkness. The narrowed eyes blinked. The hissing sound said so much – that he wanted her to know he watched, that he was on a knife-edge, that his frustration could not be held much longer.

But her senses were dragged back to the delights between her bound legs, where she rode a last, delicious flurry of fuck-strokes. The last few drops of his come oozed inside her. It made her stretch her long, leonine throat and scream one last time – knowing she was experiencing utterly abandoned, animalistic sex. And even better, knowing as she cried out that her secret watcher was being tormented, was being aroused and incited, to the very point of maddened pain.

Chapter Ten

Jo stretched her long body, uncurling in the warmth. Blinking her eyes, she stared for a moment at the unfamiliar view. A high, beamed ceiling with a polished pewter chandelier; gently swaying straw-coloured curtains; the deep comfort of crisp linen bedclothes. Frowning, she twisted over on her side.

Michael. He was lying beside her, still asleep. Hungrily, her eyes took in the masculine precision of his profile, the dark sweep of his eyelashes, the cool geometry of his cheekbones. In sleep, he appeared more vulnerable than awake; his lips pursed in a moist, pale pout. She longed to kiss him, but held back. It felt like a rare treat to be able to observe him quietly without having to deal with the power of his waking presence. It was like waking next to a sleeping panther or other seductive beast. She just wanted to hold the moment.

Vaguely, Jo tried to remember how she had arrived here. Her encounter on the stone anvil sprang back into her mind, prompting a pleasurable shiver through her body. Since then, she could only recollect a strange episode in the forest. Whether it had happened last night or was simply a vivid dream, she could not say.

She ran through the darkness, feeling the rapid power of her hindlegs speeding like a flying hare along the ground. To her cat senses, the woodland had a multitude of scents and shapes. It was alive with nocturnal creatures whose rich odours left exciting trails along the earth. Her eyes adjusted magically to the darkness and her whiskers guided her as fast as her four legs could carry her. The feeling of freedom was amazing. There was no limit to her energy; no constraint to her phenomenal speed.

As if with foreknowledge, she drove on towards the massive trunk of the tallest tree in the forest. Without halting, she sank her claws into the tender bark, scurrying up the vertical towards the first layer of branches. Her massively dilated eyes saw birds rise up from their nests in fright, hovering as they squawked. She felt all-powerful in that woodland world; a sharp-toothed, fleet-footed predator who could run faster and longer than any other creature of the night.

She climbed higher up the trunk, which gradually grew thinner beneath her piercing claws. Up there, the leaves rustled noisily in the breeze. No birds lived so high above the ground, only noisily scurrying insects. Clinging to the bark with all four sets of claws, she listened with swivelling ears as the tree swayed with a mournful groan. Enjoying every movement of her lithe body, she twisted gracefully round and edged along the tightrope of the thickest, steadiest bough. The pads of her toes felt secure on the knotty branch as her tail lifted to provide counterbalance. Only when the bough started to sink beneath her weight did she back up a little and settle down on her haunches to watch secretly from her leafy, hidden lair.

Parting her lips, she let the sweet breezes play along the roof of her mouth, tasting scents with her nerve endings, building up a fragrant map of the forest. She could smell water, grass, leaf mould and flowers. More potent was a family of badgers playing in a clearing. A hedgehog was also making her solitary way through the foliage. Mice and voles, moths and bats; all carried slighter but enticing scents.

Then she caught it. Very distant now; the potent scent of wild animal tingled across the roof of her mouth. Rolling her tongue, she tasted his scent. He was miles and miles away, at the far side of the forest. Still awake, he was prowling slowly, his pungent rear end towards her. His scent told her he was aroused but frustrated, burning off his excess energy in pointless stalking.

Suddenly, he turned. She caught the warmer scent of his open jaws and dripping teeth. His breath was rank. He was standing motionless. He had smelled her.

Across the darkness they watched each other without sight, sharing the subtle shifts in secretions that altered scents, making them irresistible. He was overpoweringly male, feral, animal. As her tongue flicked across the roof of her mouth, she salivated until her jaws were slack and sodden.

'Hi.'

Michael's eyelids had opened lazily. He was smiling up at her.

'Hi.' She grinned and snuggled back down under the covers. His chest was hard and furry to her touch. Reaching out, he stroked her naked shoulder.

'You were far away, just then. What could you see?'

For some reason, talking about the beast in the forest embarrassed her. She didn't even know if Michael had seen it last night.

'I was thinking about my cat senses,' was all she said. 'When I return to this human shape it all seems so empty. Scent and vision and hearing – almost everything has gone.'

'Has it?' He was stroking her neck appreciatively, pushing his thumb along the hollow at the base of her throat. 'And what about sex? Has all that heightened pleasure gone too?'

He was staring at her pale shoulders, dragging his hand around to the back of her neck.

'I don't know,' she breathed. 'Maybe I should find out.'

The emerald flash of his eyes connected with hers. Lifting himself on to one elbow, he arched above her. She was beneath the matted hair of his chest and armpits, his face intent upon hers as she felt herself melt down into the pillow. She was cradled beneath the power of his body. Lazily, he ran his fingertips down over her shoulder, avoiding her hard nipple, to the receptive flatness of her stomach.

'There's a whole lot more to find out,' he murmured, running his hand faster now, across the bone of her pelvis to the top of her thigh. 'So much more than you have ever dreamed of.'

She wanted to draw up her knees and make him touch her – but he seemed curiously slothful this morning. She guessed he wanted her, but it was not his style to take her quickly.

'What does it feel like when I take you in the rite?'

She looked up at him blankly. As if to prompt her, he slid his fingers across to the soft inner flesh of her thigh.

'Incredible. Like I'm on heat. I want it to go on

forever. The sensations are – almost too much too bear.'

It was starting again, already. Whatever satisfaction she received in the night, it was never enough. His thumb was stroking her inner thigh. A nerve started to jump in her leg. It was like a power station. The main switch had flicked on. The juice was flowing.

'You're lucky to transform to a cat. They are incredibly sexual. A queen can take dozens of toms, maybe fuck for a week. She can wear out twenty lovers. And could you take more?'

His eyes had turned to granite now. His thumb had started to stroke the outer edges of her parted lips. She wondered if he could feel the slickness already collecting there. Just the sight and scent of his body made her drip.

'Oh, I could take more,' she retorted. If this was a challenge, she was up for it.

'How much more?' His finger teased the seam of her sex. Twisting her hips provocatively, she sighed.

'Twice as much?' His finger ran across her swollen bud for a teasing microsecond.

'Oh yes,' she gasped.

Reaching down, he grasped his cock and sidled up above her so it lay across her stomach. It felt wonderfully heavy. Glancing down, she stared at it beneath the tented bedclothes. It was beautiful; crimson and damp, jutting up from the dark nest of hair at the pit of his belly. Suddenly she couldn't concentrate – just the promise of its inert weight made her blood beat fast. It was tickling her smooth skin. She could feel the coolness of his testicles brushing against her wet sex.

'Go inside me. Please.' Her voice was urgent. She couldn't believe herself. She was begging. Arching her back up high, his cock slid an inch or two downward towards her entrance.

'What about ten times as much?' His voice was still deadly calm. He was staring at her steadily. It was as if he had no feeling in his cock. Surely, she thought, any other man would let go, forget the inquisition and get down to it.

'What?' She had forgotten the question. Her brain was turning to hot nothingness.

'Would you carry on with the rites if I told you the sensations would be ten times more powerful?'

'Oh God, yes,' she urged, throwing her arms up above her head. She was stretched and exposed, twisting beneath him like her cat familiar when she called into the night for sex.

'Or twenty?'

'Try and stop me.'

'I'm glad, Jo,' he murmured, sliding down a couple of inches. His long, hard cock lay motionless on the open flower of her sex. 'Because I've chosen you for the Harvest Feast. You'll be at the centre of the rite for the entire group. It will be an incredible sexual experience for you. Unlike anything most women ever experience. You are very, very fortunate.'

'God, yes.' Lifting her knees up on either side of his hips she started to grind against him. The tip of his cock was bumping against her, tantalising the red-hot folds at her centre.

'Why me?' she asked suddenly, her brain working on a time delay far behind her body.

'I told you; you're unique,' he whispered. 'And just look at you. Bitch on heat, hot piece of tail – whatever you call it, it's you. You'll love it. And I knew from the start. I wanted it to be you.'

She was insanely churned up inside. When he said that he wanted it to be her, she felt so grateful that she almost cried. But she still wanted him so much to fuck her.

'Thank you,' she managed, eyes brimming.

Leaning down over her, he kissed her gravely. She sucked on his lips, her mouth a starving hole.

'Listen.' Abruptly pulling his lips from hers, he cupped her face, bringing her sharply back to the present. 'It's not a joke. Do you willingly agree?'

'Please, please get inside me,' she hissed. 'Of course I agree. I want it more than anything. Anything in the world.'

But when he thrust his cock inside her, she wondered how she could take ten times more sensation than this – or had he said twenty? – and not die of pleasure in the process.

Lost in a kind of blissful love affair with Michael and his coterie, the weeks of summer passed. In the midst of so much pleasure, it was easy to turn away from the uncomfortable thoughts of Emmi and her miserable isolation. Unthinkingly, Jo had taken Michael's advice to mix only with her 'own kind'. Then, one day in sweltering July, as she was strolling back to the farm from a swim at Abel's Tarn, she noticed Emmi striding off angrily towards the lane.

'Hey! Emmi!' Shouting, Jo started to jog after her. Her pace increased to a run when she noticed the girl was carrying a backpack along with a couple of canvass bags. In a few breathless minutes she had caught up with her.

'Hey! What's going on?' Blocking Emmi's route, Jo walked slowly backwards, glaring at her.

'Get out of my way. I'm surprised you're even bothered.'

Jo reached out towards the girl's arm. Emmi shook her away.

'Please,' Jo begged. 'Stop for one minute. Just tell me what's going on.'

'No! I'm going to miss the bus.'

Jo hated her when she was stubborn like this, but there was no way she was going to let her get away with just disappearing out of her life.

'OK,' Jo retorted. 'Then I'll walk with you.'

Side by side, the two girls strode along in silence until they reached the stone gateposts after which the farm was named. It was the first time Jo had left the community since her arrival. As they passed between the two monumental stone pillars, Emmi muttered sarcastically, 'Thank God for that.'

'Do you really hate it here?' Jo tried.

'You could say that.'

They were out on the lane, where the hedgerows were thick with hawthorn and wild flowers. The sun was beating down now that they were out in the open valley through which the main road ran.

'Let me give you a hand.' Jo reached out for Emmi's bags. She was obviously struggling in the heat. 'We'll get to Thorsby quicker, you know.'

Silently, Emmi handed over the canvass bags.

'Do you remember,' Jo said suddenly, 'when you said to me, all those weeks ago, that we shouldn't part bad friends?'

Emmi nodded silently.

'Well, I'm asking you the same now. Please, Emmi. I know I've been a bit of a selfish bitch. I came here to see you, and well – it's all gone to my head. But it can't be worth breaking up being friends over. I'm not going to stop you going or anything. Just tell me what's going on. I'll respect it. I promise.'

Emmi was still silent, striding forward with her lips tightly pressed together. What more did she want?

'And I'm sorry,' Jo blurted. 'Is that what you want me to say? I'm sorry for ignoring you and running around with the others all the time.'

'OK,' sighed Emmi. 'Apology accepted.' She turned and looked quickly over to Jo. 'Thanks for helping with the bags. Let's take the short cut across the meadow.'

Clambering over a wooden stile, the two girls set off across the broad sweep of a cowslip-scattered meadow.

'What time is your bus?' Jo eventually ventured.

'Half past. I've only got another ten minutes.'

'And then where are you heading?'

'Oh, I suppose I'll go back to Northford first. Get my head together on familiar ground. Then – oh, I don't know – maybe try college, maybe move south. Try and cadge some floor space at my cousin's in London.'

Jo wanted to rant and rave at this, but swallowed down her astonishment.

'I'm really surprised,' she said quietly. 'It's so beautiful here. I can't imagine going back to Northford.'

'Well, I'm really surprised you want to stay,' Emmi replied. 'You could always come with me.'

'No thanks,' she said much too quickly. 'You know,' she added more thoughtfully, 'I think you need to tell me all about this. You know, why you really want to go. It's something deeper than dislike, isn't it?'

'Oh, you don't want to know, Jo. Why should I spoil it all for you? Just go back and have a good time. Forget it.'

They were nearing the village now and Jo looked around uncomfortably. Fenris Gate was so delightfully self-enclosed that it was easy to forget that there was an outside world at all. It somehow seemed strange to see ordinary people going about their business – at Fenris Gate, she realised, there were no older people. And as well as being young, all of the community looked tanned and well, with the slow, good-tempered gait of people without a care or hurt in the world. The wine had something to do with it, she decided. But then there was the rest of the diet of mind-blowing magic and sex. It was as if Michael had invented the perfect recipe for an untroubled life.

Thorsby was no more than a cluster of houses along the road with a village green, a pub and a store. The single bus stop stood beside the ancient village cross next to the green. Dumping the bags, Emmi and Jo sat on the stone steps at its foot and waited. The road out of Thorsby was empty.

'You don't know what it means to me, to get away,' Emmi began. She was staring into the middle distance, shaking her head gently. 'Maybe I'm different from you. I'm certainly different from the rest of them.'

'What do you mean?'

'The transformation of course. Oh, you think that because I don't go off to the roundhouse with all of you, I haven't done it. Of course I have. My lovely spirit, the little doe. It's an unbelievable feeling, isn't it? I remember when I came back to Northford, it had just happened to me and I was dying to tell you. Michael had chosen me. And he needed me to be with him, alone. I was the chosen one for the next rite. I was dumb enough to be flattered, I suppose.'

This time, Jo didn't break the long silence. Her pulse had set off on a gallop. Part of her didn't want to know the rest of the story.

'And the sex was brilliant, though I think I was already getting a bit spooked. My theory is that it works easier for the guys. All that animalistic stuff is stronger in their genes or something. The thing is, Jo, there have been a whole string of girls who've been up for this. And they all opt out in the end. You are just the next one in the queue.'

Jo didn't want to know about the whole string of girls. She wanted to be special. Desperately, she tried to change the tack of the conversation.

'But what happened to you?'

'What happened to me is that when the festival came along and Michael did the rite, something went wrong. I didn't transform. It sounds straightforward. I just stayed as I am. So what? But it was just so awful.'

'Why?' Jo was surprised by the agitation in her own voice.

'Because they changed. All of them. The teeth and claws are real, Jo. It is not just some group hysteria. The fucking and the biting and the pain are all too real. So I tried to tell them. I tried to speak to Michael to tell him to stop it. And you know what I found out?'

Jo shook her head, feeling blood drain from her face.

'When the pack turn like that, when it gets in their blood, they can't even understand human language anymore. They just howl back in your face. You're not human to them. Just a bitch to use.'

'I don't believe it.' Jo stared at Emmi, her mind racing to find an answer. 'I've been thinking,' she retorted, 'about the drink we have at the rite. I mean, I'm not stupid enough to think it's just some harmless fruit cordial. It sounds to me like you had some kind of bad trip. So – it seemed scary that one time. Emmi, it's just an effect in your brain, like a bad dream or hallucination. No one at Fenris would ever harm you.'

'You really believe that?' The question hung in the air.

'Come with me,' Emmi suddenly urged, grabbing her hand. 'There's nothing back there that you need. There are loads of things we can do together. It'll be a scream. Look. Here's the bus.'

Sure enough, the green single-decker bus was meandering up the lane towards them.

'Come on, Jo. For your own sake. Just get on the

bus and get out of here. Michael doesn't care about you.'

'What do you mean?' She felt a jolt of anguish at Emmi's words. Glancing up, she could see the bus nearly upon them. 'Tell me! Why do you say that?'

'Are you coming?' Emmi stood up and stared down at her, blue eyes yearning.

'I don't know. Tell me first, why do you say that about Michael?'

'He's got his own agenda, Jo. The rest of us are just being used in some kind of experiment. It was something I heard Niall say once. About why Michael chose Fenris Gate. It's to do with sighting Fenris, he said. Now are you coming?'

The bus ground to a halt with a screech of brakes and the hiss of the folding doors springing open. Emmi backed up the steps, dragging her bags.

'Come on, Jo.' Emmi's face was pained. 'Please.'

Staring blankly, Jo found her feet had turned to stone. She wanted to stay. That was all there was to it – she wanted to stay with Michael.

'Move along, now,' the driver called. Emmi shook her head, eyes full of pain.

'Jo!'

'I can't.'

A moment later, Emmi had disappeared into the bus and the double doors sprang shut in Jo's face. Then with a dismissive puff of diesel, the vehicle rumbled back to life and sped away down the lane. The last glimpse Jo had of Emmi was a blurred vision of a blonde head through the smeared window. Then there was only the green shape of the bus receding down the lane. And then the lane was empty.

Looking about herself, Jo realised there was nothing to stay around in Thorsby for. Even if she had wanted

197

anything from the store, she had no money. At Fenris no one used money and she had happily handed over her few coins. And it was peculiar to be among strangers. The few villagers who ambled past seemed to eye her with an ugly hostility. Her instinct was to quickly get back to her own people.

On the way back, however, she paused at the Fenris Gate. Two totemic stone pillars stood at the entrance to the farm, like two monoliths from an ancient stone circle. Carved into the stone were ancient rune-like inscriptions and stick-like figures of men and animals. Crouching, Jo tried her best to decipher the story but it was too difficult, given the crudity of the carving and the spread of green lichen across the stone. Yet intuitively, she knew that it was significant. This was the Fenris Gate, after all. As she passed within the two pillars, she touched one of the stones with her finger-tips, then slowly pressed her body against it. She felt like a cat marking her return to her own, scent-marked territory.

During the next few days Jo found herself taking over Emmi's old room, but that appeared to be the only consequence of her friend's disappearance. There was no inquisition from Michael. When she told Rob and the others they only shrugged or quickly moved on to other subjects. No one wanted to talk about Emmi. For a few minutes, Jo recalled the authoritarian control freaks at the Northford Mission. Brother Colin had been frantic to find Emmi. But here, she decided, people were free and easy. Emmi had just not fitted in any more. But Jo didn't forget what Emmi had said.

A couple of weeks later, Jo was hanging out at the cottage Rob shared with Niall. She was up in one of the top rooms, lying on the bed, blissed out after an afternoon's swimming at the tarn. Rob was messing about with her hair, teasingly trying to come on to her, though they had fucked like rabbits early that afternoon in the sunshine. Dreamily, she shook her head and mouthed 'later'; she had already decided to stay with him that night. Then, suddenly, Jo realised Niall was in the room and she could ask him about Fenris, there and then, with a witness present to stop him trying to spin her a line.

'Niall?'

'Yeah.' He was making a fire up with pieces of paper rolled into balls and dried logs from the forest.

'What does Fenris mean? You know, as in Fenris Gate.'

He wasn't fazed or anything. He just explained it carefully in his usual clear, academic way.

'Fenris is the great wolf. The enemy of the gods. A kind of force of chaos.'

'So, he's not a real wolf?'

Niall laughed. 'Real enough to our ancestors. He's a kind of arch demon who lived in the underworld. Hel – the lowest of the Nine Worlds.'

'Hell? You mean like devils and roasting spits?'

'Not exactly. Spelt differently. Hel is the goddess of the underworld; she rules it – and it isn't full of hellfire. Instead, it's dark and misty, with a huge ice bridge in contrast to the fiery Rainbow Bridge to Valhalla. And Hel herself is strange; one half of her face is that of a beautiful goddess, and the other half of her face is just totally blank.'

'Weird.' Even Rob was listening now, settling back against the bedhead. 'Go on. And this wolf?'

'Loki, a kind of shadow brother of Odin, the King of the gods, fathered Fenris. He was supposed to be gigantically huge and an oracle foretold that he would bring about the end of the gods; but no chains they made could hold him.'

Niall was sitting cross-legged by the hearth now, as the flames caught and cast a flickering light across his face.

'So what happened?' Jo asked. Somehow she had known there would be a truth in the tale; that the creature, or whatever it was, was wild and untameable.

'According to the sibyl, the ancient prophetess, it started with a series of terrible portents. In a distant forest, an old giantess brought into the world a massive brood of young wolves, whose father was Fenris. The storytellers must have seen an eclipse because they tell of the wolves chasing the sun until eventually they possessed it, putting out its rays. Then came a long and terrible winter, probably an ice age, a time of war and blood and incest; what the prophetess calls a wolf age. When the Fenris wolf eventually breaks his chains the earth quakes and the last battle takes place, between the gods on the one side and giants and demons on the other. Odin goes after the Fenris wolf but when he tries to slaughter him, he's swallowed whole. Although Odin's son manages to kill the wolf, the end has come. The gods are slaughtered and even the stars fall out of the skies. When the giants set the world on fire, all is finished.'

They sat awhile, thinking about the story.

'But why is this place called Fenris?' Jo asked. 'And what's the gate?'

'I suppose the name Fenris became associated with wolves over time. There were wolves here, no doubt about it, in the forest. The famous sightings of spectral beasts in this locality may have been the remnants of an old pack. And the gate? Your guess is as good as mine. I've had a look at the inscriptions but they're fairly obscure. Probably Norse, and there are creatures like wolves on it too. Michael might know more. I know he's made a start at transcribing them. Ask him.'

'Yeah, yeah, sure.'

'I thought Michael said the wolf was a sign of luck?' Rob asked. 'You know, a sign of power.'

Niall nodded, watching them steadily.

'That's true as well. Maybe we always secretly admire what we fear. No doubt, to the old warriors the wolf was a symbol of brutal magic. A symbol to be engraved on your weapons. It was certainly considered lucky to see a wolf.'

'Oh.' Jo lay back and wondered. Only Rob settled down beside her and started messing about; dragging his splayed hand across her bare arm.

'What are you doing?' She smiled.

'I'm a wolf.' He grinned. 'Feel the power.'

'A sausage dog, more like.'

'I am not. I'm fucking ferocious. Watch out or I'll attack you.'

'Oh yeah?' Raising her eyebrows, she smirked. 'You and whose army?'

In a flash, Rob pounced, grabbing her shoulders and twisting her arm in a lock. Laughing hysterically, Jo twisted round, trying to wriggle away. It was no good. He was almost twice her size and powerfully strong.

'Let me go! You bastard!' she managed, trying unsuccessfully to knee his balls. But beneath the laughter, she had to admit it was dead, dead sexy. Rob's knee was pushing between her legs, parting her thighs. It was sending nice little charges of sexual electricity up to her pussy. Still she struggled, twisting and flailing. Then she noticed Niall had come over to sit on the bed.

'We're both going to attack you,' Rob whispered. It was his turn to smirk. Her arms were tightly held; as she squirmed, she began to feel an almost uncomfortably strong surge of arousal. 'Aren't we, Niall?'

'Yes.' Niall's voice was husky. When Jo managed to glance in his direction she could see he was flushed and excited.

'Get her knickers off.'

'Get lost,' Jo cried out, but there was a note of laughter in her voice that told them she was not completely serious. When she felt Niall's warm hands slide up her skirt, she had to bite her lip to stop herself whimpering with pleasure. He found the waistband and started to slide them down. She was sure they must already be damp; she was getting so turned on.

'How is she? I bet, despite all this "later" stuff, she's dying for it.'

A rough hand snaked up her thigh and slid between her lips. It made her buck with pleasure as fingers dug hard inches inside her.

'Gorgeous. All hot and ready.'

'You guys,' she managed, though Rob was trying to cover her mouth, 'are completely crazy.'

'You said it, babe. Do you want to go first, mate?'

She tried another kick to Rob's big, hairy balls but he saw it coming and dodged out of the way. Then she could hear the leather of his belt sliding out of its buckle.

'No, you go.' She could hear Niall's voice quavering a little. 'I'll keep her quiet.'

'Hmm.' Rob grabbed her waist and pulled her backwards so she was against his kneeling frame. His cock was standing up hard from his pants and in a second he had manhandled her against it, so she was still crouched forward in front of him on her hands and knees. His cock slid into her like a sharp knife into pulpy fruit. Uncontrollably, Jo cried out as it pummelled the full length inside her.

'Shut her up, hey?'

It felt so good to be used like this that Jo was close to sliding out of consciousness in seconds. When she felt Niall climb up in front of her she only stared at him with bleary, pre-orgasmic eyes. He was kneeling in front of her, pulling his own shorts down. Vaguely, she recognised the pert pinkness of his cock as it sprang out. Next moment, he grabbed her hair and pulled her face down to it. She started to suckle on it like a starving lamb.

The sensations building in her were almost too much to bear. Rob's fat cock always stretched her but tonight he just wanted to be selfish, driving into her while he rocked her waist, pulling her backside towards and away from him. The way they talked about her drove her crazy too. 'She won't last long,' Rob laughed to Niall. 'Fucked both ways, I reckon she'll come in less than a minute.'

Jesus. It was true. She couldn't get enough of Niall's juicy cock in her mouth; it was almost choking her. He had grabbed the base and was pumping his dick into her feverish mouth. Lapping her tongue around the head she felt her inner muscles start to clutch around Rob's cock.

'Come on,' Niall crooned, staring down at her with unblinking eyes. 'That's right, suck it, that's beautiful.'

Feverishly, he reached down and grabbed her nipples, pinching them deliciously. From nowhere, Jo felt her lungs gasp and then she was in it – a long, soaring orgasm, kept rolling by Rob's ceaseless hammering, hard and fast, deep up inside her where it felt so good. When she felt herself returning fully to the room, she wasn't sure what had happened – whether she had screamed or lashed out – only that her body was tingling from her clit to the tips of her toes and fingers. It had been incredible.

Rob pulled out and lifted her by the shoulders. 'Come on to me.'

He was lying back on the bed, his cock standing up like a big red lever. In case she hadn't heard too well, Niall helped her on to it, lifting her by the cheeks of her backside until her entrance was stretched above it. She couldn't pretend she didn't want it. It was like those nights with Michael. She wanted it again and again. When she let herself down on his cock, it pierced her with an explosion of pleasure. Eagerly, she began to work up and down on it, clenching her thighs around his narrow hips. Her clit was grinding against his groin; leaning forward, she began to work it against the hardness.

'I can't wait for the harvest rite,' Rob said, eyeing her steadily through a fringe of sun-bleached hair that had fallen over his forehead. 'You're going to love it. You're fucking insatiable.'

She felt insatiable. It was wonderful, because there was a never-ending supply of pleasure all around her to keep her going. Tonight she felt that whatever Michael had planned for the rite, she could take it. Her body burned at the thought of it. She wanted it to be as wild as he could make it, as off-limits as he could devise. Nothing could shock her. She wanted to be taken to the farthest extremes anyone could imagine.

But, still, she was surprised when she felt Niall nuzzle up against her back. He was slipping his hand where she and Rob were joined, massaging her swollen pussy lips and squeezing Rob's pumping cock. Not that she was shocked that Niall was fondling Rob's cock and his best friend was grunting and smiling; somehow it seemed normal, a part of the whole sharing and giving of pleasure. No – it was that Niall was getting his hand nice and wet from both of their juices and then, slowing her down a little, he began to probe his finger inside her tight anus.

'No,' she gasped, glancing over her shoulder.

'You'll love it. Honest. It's OK, I've got a rubber on.'

It was no good; she felt too full of Rob. His cock was bulging massively in her cunt. Whatever she had told herself a few minutes earlier, about being ready for anything, the hot little finger working up her backside was making her panic.

'I'm not sure I want to do this,' she pleaded to Niall.

But Rob's strong arms were still gripping her waist, making her dance on his cock like a marionette. And Niall, though slender, was wiry and strong too. When she felt the rubber-tipped end of his cock pressing between the cheeks of her buttocks, she tried to struggle, clawing to get off.

Rob just laughed. 'I told you. We're in an attacking mood. We get what we want.'

'I need to get wet.' Niall was panting. 'Let me in her a sec.'

She couldn't believe they were doing this to her. Gingerly, Rob pulled her forwards over him, so his cock slid out of her to stand hot and steaming between his legs. Next second, Niall bent forwards and slid in.

'Ooh,' he groaned. 'That is lovely.'

Below her, while Niall gave her a few good hard thrusts, she could see Rob watching her face. His mouth was open and dry. His hand slipped down to massage his own cock and balls while he watched her being fucked by his friend.

'OK, OK,' Rob said, suddenly impatient. 'I can't wait much longer. Give it her.'

The next few seconds were a maelstrom of ecstatic pain. Like a hammer blow, Rob drove his cock back up her, humping fast and furious, as if to make up for lost time. And behind her, Niall was driving the end of his cock between her cheeks, questing for her anus, lubricating its rim with her own juices and then piercing her second entrance like a skewer. Unbelievably, she felt it pass inside her. The head, no more, was lifting her backside, sending waves of pleasure all through her cramping muscles.

'I don't think –' she moaned. 'I can't –'

'Yeah, you can.' Rob laughed. 'Get in there, friend, or I'll do it myself.'

Oh God. No – she mustn't let Rob fuck her arse. In comparison to Rob's meat hammer, Niall's cock was boyish and slender, though long enough to delight anyone. Just the thought of Rob trying to get inside that rosy hole made her tighten fearfully.

'How do you like it, Jo?' At last Rob was no longer play-acting; he was talking to her straight, and those gorgeous eyes were connecting with her.

She shook her head wildly. The two of them were working in unison at last, setting a slowish but deep and erogenous stroke. Glancing down, she could see her tits were red and flushed, her nipples like scarlet buttons. The two cocks were sensational. There was nothing in her brain but the perception of double penetration, stoking up heat like an explosive furnace.

She just nodded down at Rob and gasped a smile. Niall was clinging to her back, driving more and more of his cock into her, scorching the virgin flesh with hard, rubber-cased power. Below her, Rob started to twitch, lifting his pelvis, driving faster, getting ready to come.

Keeping her eyes open until the very last second, she leaned forward to grind her clit across him, feeling the bulk of his cock probe for deepness, searching for the perfect angle from which to come inside her. She wanted to come with him. Eagerly, she bent forward and pushed a hard nipple against his mouth. Hungrily, he sucked, rolling his tongue round and round, bucking beneath her.

With rapid pants, Rob lost control; his cock seemed to climb inside her and then explode, as his mouth grimaced with pleasure. It was the trigger for her too. Letting herself go, she felt her sodden pussy work on him, felt her sorely pleasured anus relax to let Niall in another molten inch. The intensity dazzled her mind. Climaxing in a burning spasm, she felt them both, simultaneously, penetrate her body to the hilt.

But there was no deliverance from them when she came. Still Niall plunged on inside her, ploughing away, driving her on to Rob's inert body. She could hear him behind her, grunting with pleasure, feeding his tormented cock as far into her tight little hole as it could fit. All she could do was lie there, kissing Rob, who was lazily drifting off into a doze. As she too closed her eyes, her mind seemed to melt away to nothing but heat and pumping blood. Rob's tongue languidly flicked inside her mouth, thrusting like another little cock. Still Niall slapped against her back, pulling her thighs apart now, desperately trying to get better access. Then he reached forward and began to rub his finger fast against her clitoris.

'No,' she moaned, looking to Rob for vindication.

'Yes.' Rob grinned. 'Go on, Niall. Give it her.'

It was useless. She was trapped between them with no way out. As Niall eventually ground his way towards a noisy, jerking orgasm, he skilfully brought Jo with him too. Her clit just couldn't ignore the driving force in her back passage and Niall's fingers worked her until she wetly came all over them.

'God, am I tired.' She sighed, resting her head on Rob's broad shoulder. Niall was still flat out on top of her, going slowly flaccid inside her pulverised anus.

'Forget that.' Rob grinned mischievously. 'I'm only just waking up.'

And, to prove it, he pushed his cock up against the inside of her leg. It was newly erect and hard – very hard.

'No way,' Jo breathed.

'But this is nothing,' he joked wryly. 'You're going to have to get in training. We're only trying to get you ready for the rite.'

Chapter Eleven

She was with Michael. He had told her to keep herself apart for three long days and she had done so, sleeping in Emmi's old room and spending her days in the forest or wandering alone around the farm. The cornfields had turned from green to gold, sprinkled with the delicate frills of scarlet poppies. And each day she had watched the corn as it grew higher, knowing that the yellow fields held the key to her fate. For Michael had told her that when the harvest was ripe, it must be shorn. And she knew that when the corn fell, so must she take her part in the rite.

'Come and sit with me.'

He held out his arms and she slid into them gratefully, curling up on his knee in the big armchair in the farmhouse sitting room. For a while she just sat still, her head on his shoulder, feeling his warmth and closeness, feeling the pain of an anguished desire well up beneath her ribs. His fingers caressed her neck, drawing through the soft hairs at the nape like a fond man tickling his pet. If she had been in her cat form, she would have purred.

'Are you ready?' he asked softly. Raising pleading eyes, she looked into his beautiful face. The pale green eyes were steady.

'I think so.' She bit her lip. 'But, of course, I don't know what is going to happen.'

'But are you ready for that? For whatever I make happen?'

She was certainly ready for sexual release; after three days of abstinence her body was sick with need. Michael had made it clear that no one, not even Rob, should touch her. And the others had seemed to know too, and stayed apart from her. The promise of a sublime physical indulgence played through her mind constantly. When she imagined what that might be, she could barely still her fevered imagination. But there was more too, she guessed. Strange mysteries and maybe frightening aspects to the rite.

She looked to him for strength.

'How will it be?' she asked quietly.

'It will be incredible.' He kissed the top of her head and caressed her cheek. 'I will be with you, Jo.' His emerald eyes connected with hers at a deep, subterranean level. 'All the time I will be with you. When you feel others inside you, remember it is me. It is my will. My mind will support you.'

It was beautiful, this surrender. She never questioned it.

'Then I'm ready.'

He curled his arm around her and she wished they might stay like this forever, in front of the fire, with the impenetrable black night outside stretching over the forest.

'I looked at the corn today,' he murmured. 'And that is ready too. We will harvest tomorrow. Tonight is your last night apart.'

Sighing, she reached up to find his lips with hers

and when he let her, she pushed her tongue inside the warm gap of his lips.

'Just a kiss,' he murmured. Liquid heat enveloped her as his mouth fused with hers. Tortured by need, she pressed against him, feeling the hard muscle at the top of his arm abrade her constantly stiffened nipples. As his tongue mingled with hers she whimpered. Her legs were parting; her juices were seeping between her legs.

He pulled back and looked into her flushed face. 'Tomorrow you will have all you need. How do you feel?'

'I am in pain,' she said honestly. 'On fire. All I can think of is my body.'

'And are you completely abstinent?'

That had been the really cruel twist: she couldn't even have the small satisfaction of relieving herself. A few times, alone in the forest, she had been tempted. She had noticed everything – even smoothly phallic branches or stones. Crude as it seemed, she had longed to ram them up inside her. But Michael's instructions had overridden her urges.

'Yes.'

'And the creature we have spoken of – have you seen it again?'

For some reason, this was the only uncomfortable topic between them.

'Oh, no.'

No – she had not seen the creature. She wondered why Michael was obsessed with the single sense of sight. For, wandering through the sun-dappled glades, leaving a scent of keen arousal so strong that any feral creature could follow, she had heard him, smelled him, almost tasted him on the lush summer air. Sometimes she felt she was going crazy; that by the standards of society she was losing her mind. But that society seemed so far away and so remote from her new life at Fenris. It was harder now to tell dreams from waking. In dreams too, she had seen the creature, but all her fantasies of union with him never came to pass. She either drifted to another, inconclusive dream or awoke in dark confusion. When she woke, she sometimes imagined a faint but desperate howling. But, rising to watch at the window, she found no sign of him in the dark night.

'It is time to get ready.'

Gently, he lifted her aside and went to the table where a jug and beaker sat. As soon as she smelled it, Jo recognised the pungent ritual drink. She reached for it greedily. At last, she thought, as the bitter draught poured down her throat, my release can begin.

'This first drink tonight will make you sleep, Jo.' Michael reached out and took her hand. 'Then tomorrow you will drink again. They will come for you at the appointed hour.'

She could barely wait for the transformation to begin. Anticipation tingled through her nerves as he led her up the stairs. But it was with disappointment that they passed the door to Michael's room.

'Just one more night.' He smiled and showed her to a chastely single bed in a small whitewashed room she had not seen before. 'Now you must sleep.'

'Just one more kiss.' She slumped down on the bed and pulled his arms so he loomed above her. With every nerve in her body she wanted him inside her. He grasped her hair and stared into her face.

'Oh, you are greedy for experience, Jo.' He seemed to be studying her, scrutinising the desire so evident in her face. 'I want you too.'

His hand fell on the flatness of her stomach and trailed from there to her groin. 'Tell me, then. Which

212

do you prefer? My lovemaking here or the wildness of the pack?'

'They are so different,' she answered honestly.

She loved the tender intimacy of Michael's body when they spent long hours of ecstatic pleasure here in the farmhouse. But when the pack leader fucked her – then it was a frenzy – like nothing she had ever known existed.

'When I transform,' she added, 'then it is pure. No shame, no guilt, no self-awareness. There is nothing in the world to me but satisfaction.'

Just thinking about it, she rubbed her tingling pubis against his palm. She could tell from the way he licked his dry lips that he could feel her wetness. She wanted to open her legs and pull him into the wet ravine of her sex.

'You are a temptation,' he sighed. 'I could drink with you tonight and we could run across the hills. Completely free, completely abandoned.'

Arching her spine, she pushed her aching sex hard into his hand.

'Do it,' she urged. She could see the outline of his cock in his jeans; a huge erection that must be paining him too. Her small hand lifted to trace the shape of the hard bulge. It felt so solid beneath her fingertips that a jab of delight speared her. Wincing at the pressure, he closed his eyes.

'Or just let me suck you,' she whispered suddenly. 'We don't have to fuck.' She wanted to get down on the floor in front of him, on her knees. Her mind was filled with lewd images crowding her sex-soaked brain.

For a long second his transparent eyes considered. He was flushed too, his breathing faster now. He looked down the length of her body. 'You tempt me. Just looking at you. But in just a few blind strokes so much would be lost. I must not be weak. What is at stake is more important. We must save our power and release it at the appointed time. Rest, Jo. Try to sleep.'

But after he had left, she twisted awhile in a torment, feeling the drink work on her senses, making the images that danced in her brain grow ever more vivid. Finally, she rose and walked unsteadily to the window. The moon was almost as bright as day, hanging like a giant silver face up in the nightsky. It seemed to nod at her benignly, and then she knew that what Emmi had said was true. She was only another in a great line of girls to enter the rite, over centuries back to the earliest days. But it was a good feeling; it made her feel part of the round of seasons on the eternally spinning earth. The silver disc of the moon had seen it all before, so many times. Stumbling a little, she returned to the twisted coils of her bedclothes. In a few moments she had fallen into a deep and dreamless sleep.

Her next memory was of waking at dusk. Three girls were dressing her in a long, white dress. She felt drunk and unsteady but still they insisted she drank again from the jug. Her dulled mind was only mildly surprised to see the sun setting outside the window. Inside the room, three candles burned with golden tongues of light. In a recess at the back of Jo's mind she felt a tremor of fear. Of what, she was not sure. But somewhere out there, she sensed, something fearful waited.

A strange girl appeared before her, glowing in the golden light. Her hair was crowned with red poppies and corn marigolds and her skin was waxy pale. But when she moved to approach her, Jo realised the image was her own reflection in the dressing table mirror. She had been dressed as the harvest queen.

Yet she was no longer sure which aspect was herself and which was someone else – the mirror held a reflection of a character who had played this part in the rite time after time. Jo's identity seemed lost somehow, as if her former self had faded away into an insubstantial ghost.

Later, she was aware of travelling in a wooden cart, all through the sweet-smelling dusk behind a gently trotting mare. Waves of emotion filled her – joy and palpitating fear, sexual heat and a sickening apprehension. Above the fields, the sun was setting in a red ball, throwing long dusky shadows from the trees. Low on the horizon, she could just see the pale crescent of the moon gleaming phosphorescently.

She smelt the corn before they reached it; a sweet dust that danced on the air. With each step of the mare's hooves the scent grew stronger, filling the air with dry particles that parched her mouth. Then, as the sun finally dropped behind Moersett, the creaking wagon trundled along the rutted track and she passed through the gate.

Blinking, she looked around. Dark figures holding flaming torches aloft cried out in greeting. A few she recognised, but she could not see Michael. Yet, in a chamber of her mind, she remembered his words and repeated like a mantra that he would be with her through all the time of the rite. Somewhere, she knew, he was thinking of her. It made her feel more able to face the crowd as they clamoured around her, their faces as bright as masks in the light of flaming torches.

The girls helped her to stand and she rose with a galloping heart to dismount from the wagon. An instrument was thrust in her hand. She took it reluctantly, then saw it was the long, time-smoothed handle of a scythe. Near her feet, the rounded blade gleamed with a cruel smile. When she looked for guidance to those around her, they urged her to the centre of the field. Fearing that she would be asked to carry out some bloodthirsty sacrifice, it was with relief that she saw a single, uncut clump of wheat standing high in the centre of the field. Supported by her attendants, she walked as if across rippling water, over the circular lines of stubble to the last, corn-heavy sheaf.

All around her, the watchers began to chant in unison:

> The men are ready.
> The scythes are bent,
> The corn is great,
> Let the maiden be mowed . . .

Again and again they chanted, growing loud in the heavy evening air. Then they watched and waited as she struggled to cut the wheat. After a few awkward attempts, the knife-sharp blade of the scythe slid through the dry stalks and the rich grasses fell to the ground to a general cheer. The fallen wheat was quickly gathered and Jo stood, unsteadily, watching it being bound and woven into intricate shapes.

All turned as Michael arrived within the field. He was sitting tall on Hengest, the headdress of the dog above his bare chest and a flaming torch burning in his right hand. Then she knew that her mowing of the final sheaf was a sign – a kind of ending of the harvest and a beginning of the rite. As he approached she longed to reach out to him and bury her face against his skin. But she stood still between the girls who attended her, feeling the ground beneath her feet waver and swarm like the sea.

Michael dismounted and walked towards her in the silence. It was pitchy dark now, but she could see the

216

gleam of his eyes in the torchlight and the sheen of sweat on his shoulders and chest.

'Corn maiden,' he intoned steadily, 'do you feed us for another year?'

With this, he handed her a small cake of new-baked bread, scattered with the crisped ears of wheat straight from the field. Clutching it, she looked to him for guidance. When he led Hengest to her, Michael raised her hand to the stallion's mouth and, as he ate, she felt the horse's long, hot tongue lap into the creases of her crinkled palm. The rasping heat reminded her that she was also hungry now – not for food, which might sicken her empty stomach, but for the heat of contact. As Hengest nuzzled her, snuffling into her hand and nosing against her dress, she began to awaken. All the long hours of her stupor began to lift. Her mind remembered that she was here for a purpose.

'Corn maiden,' Michael said from behind the fierce countenance of the dog, 'do you make us vigorous for another year?'

Taking her arm, he led her forwards along the length of Hengest's flank to his rear quarters. Guiding her hand, he laid it on the animal's warm stomach. Frowning, she looked at him for guidance. She could see his lips part as he urged her. He was telling her to touch the beast. Shyly, she felt her face colour as the watchers crowded around her. Hengest was standing still, his head nodding as he tossed his mane. Looking down, she could see the creature was not entirely flaccid. Maybe it was the charged atmosphere out here in the field, or the mare's scent or her own aroma of suppressed desire, but Hengest was in a state of partial arousal. The scarlet tip of his phallus gleamed in the torchlight; his furry sheath was retracting rapidly. Jo looked at Michael timorously. If she were to touch the animal's phallus, she would be doing so in front of this crowd of eager spectators.

He nodded quickly, spurring her on. When she remained paralysed, he lifted her limp arm and moved it towards the animal's swinging genitals. Unable to escape, she took in a sharp breath of air and reached out. With eyes closed, she let her hand explore the pulsing length of the organ, feeling its velvety smooth skin covering the bulging mass. Just the thought of it – that she was caressing the gigantic phallus in front of all these people – made her feel faint with excitement. Even as she unsuccessfully tried to delicately pass her fingers around its fat girth, she could feel it growing. The creature obviously loved to be touched; with every second more and more of his huge appendage was extending out of his sheath, stretching long and scarlet from the receding covering of soft skin.

Michael motioned her to use her other hand as well. Fascinated by her effect on the animal, she reached out with both her hands and ran them up and down the veined shaft, feeling an excitement build between her legs as she did so. Around her, people were jostling for a view, marvelling at the size of the animal, admiring the way she ran her small hands along its shiny length from the thick base to the dripping tip.

The large opening at the end of his cock intrigued her. Cradling the thickened end in her hand, she felt drops of pre-come dribble on to her skin. Still Michael stood beside her, urging her to stroke the phallus. She could sense Hengest's agitation as she ran her hands up and down his shaft; the thick tube of flesh began to twitch and jerk, jabbing against her hands with an increasingly violent power.

Anxiously, she looked over to Michael. Surely he could not mean her to carry on tormenting the creature? The stallion was stamping his hooves now, scraping the dry earth. A whinny of pleasure escaped from his throat as she lasciviously squeezed the thick end, drawing a syrupy palmful of warm, potent seed.

Michael's touch drew her back. Breathless, she turned to him, ashamed now of her own wild thoughts. The gigantic phallus made her own entrance tighten ravenously, her eyes secretly measuring its fabulous girth and wondering, just wondering, if such a monster could ever inch its way into her own incredibly juiced-up entrance. Around her, too, she sensed that the air was thick with carnal interest as the spectators watched in silence as she caressed the animal. Although she could not see for sure, she guessed that the spectacle had aroused all who watched. She could almost smell the briny scent of sex growing thick in the night air.

'Corn maiden,' he addressed her for a third time, 'do you receive our seed for another year?'

Placing Hengest's bridle in her hand, Michael led her back towards the wagon. Now it seemed that the stallion was even more restless, pulling on his bridle and knocking his big, inquisitive face against her shoulder. Snorting and snuffling, he started to pull at his bit, leaning his long neck forward.

Back at the cart, she found that the mare had been unharnessed and was standing uncertainly, her tail whisking the air as the huge stallion approached. The crowd pushed against her flank, turning her so that her rear end faced Hengest's questing nose. As Jo realised what was about to take place, she felt the crowd's excitement infect her. Below her long white dress, she could feel her nipples press stiffly and her breasts swell roundly. She longed to see the gorgeous stallion take his pleasure. But the promise of it almost made her legs buckle with sexual heat.

A mass of hands helped the rutting animal raise his

huge body over the stationary mare. Jo could see that she was trembling, though her four legs had locked tight as soon as Hengest's rolling tongue had lapped greedily at her entrance. She could see hands pushing the stallion's fleshy rod towards his mate's lubricious entrance. Then a strong hand grabbed her wrist. It was Michael, guiding her towards Hengest's thick phallus. Eagerly, she pushed into the crowd, stretching to find the slippery pole that sprang proud and throbbing with life from the coarse pelt of his belly. Guiding it to the mare's entrance, she felt the warm natural lubricant that covered it from its arm-thick root to the dripping, questing end.

With a collective sigh of satisfaction from the spectators, Hengest's shaft sank out of sight. As he began to hump with short, sharp jabs he faltered on his hindlegs, shifting to find the ideal position. Now he was covering the mare, the crowd was wild, caressing both animals' smooth flanks, their hands dangerously questing to caress the primal beauty of frantically thrusting genitals.

Faint with desire, Jo looked around for Michael. Thick inside the press, she could feel bodies pushing against her as they heaved against the animals. More than once, she felt the jab of eager erections brushing against her and stray hands pressing against her dress, burrowing between her limbs and against her rounded buttocks. A wild frenzy was taking hold of the group, cries of encouragement filled the air and a strange, wordless sighing rose and fell as the beast ploughed faster and faster into his mate.

With a tug to her arm, one of her attendants pulled her free. She took her back to the cart where Jo was once again offered a cup of the bitter drink. It was no use pretending she wished to stay sober now – she too was getting wild with a rabid excitement. Gulping down the drink, she urged her body to transform and be done with this endless frustration. Knowing her dress was now in disarray and her face flushed and desperate, she looked about for Michael. But he was in the thick of those urging Hengest on – cheering in unison to the animal's pounding stroke, beating their scythes in time to the primeval spectacle of uninhibited mating. Then, as she watched, Hengest began to whinny and snort, his eyes rolling as he plunged ever deeper and slicker into the patient mare. With a sudden cry, Hengest bared his huge teeth, clamouring over the back of his mate, driving the massive leathery pole excruciatingly deep into the mare's entrance as he released his seed. Cries of congratulation rose from the onlookers as they helped to lift the quivering, snorting beasts apart.

As one, it seemed, the crowd of watchers turned to Jo. She was resting blearily on the edge of the wagon, her crown of flowers falling low on her forehead. The neckline of her dress had slipped to reveal a naked shoulder. When she saw them move resolutely over towards her, she heard herself moan wordlessly into the night. She knew that the next step in the ritual was to be centred on herself.

In the flickering light of raised torches, Michael moved intently before her. The dog's face confused her. She no longer knew or understood whether he was man or beast or both. Lazily, he unbuckled his silver belt and it seemed that all who saw the movement paused in their breath. He pulled out his shaft, which glowed scarlet and hard in the red light. She could not take her eyes off it. Her lips parted and she heard herself catch her breath excitedly.

At her sides, the girls pulled at her neckline, trying to open the fastenings and undress her. But Michael stepped forward impatiently and tore it from her

221

shoulders so it lay like shreds of cloth on the wooden edge of the cart. She stared up at him, trying to puzzle out the long, hairy muzzle and long, pointed ears. Whatever he was, she had to have him. She could smell the salty scent of his sex rising from his wetly gleaming cock-head. Above them, the moon rose bright, casting day-bright silver rays across her nakedness. Arching her back as she sat on the wagon's edge, she was aware of dozens of eyes devouring the darkly pert points of her nipples and her smoothly rounded thighs. As the moon beat down on her, she whimpered towards her animal lover. Lifting her feet to the edge of the wagon she displayed her wetly parted thighs. A collective sigh of drooling lust seemed to rise from the spectators as if they would all also love to penetrate that delicious, fur-fringed furrow.

Michael towered above her, but all she could think of was the craving in her sex. Twisting and moaning, she felt her cat spirit trying to break free, felt the insistent madness of animal heat burn through her smouldering body. Like the touch of a thousand volts, she felt him reach down and kiss the nakedness of her inner calf. Crying out, she opened her thighs wider. The snaking of his tongue worked up to her knee and then her soft inner thigh. Like a lizard taking a meandering route, his mouth idly worked its way to the parted entrance to her sex. With a flick of his stiff tongue he found the flower bud of her clitoris. Stifling a scream, she felt her spine jolt and her legs spasm; so long had she waited to be touched. But only slowly did he work his way to the slippery depths of her cunt, which lay slick-wet and ready for the most elaborate treats he could devise. Only with exquisite, drawn-out care did he lap his tongue across the tiny crevices and nerves of her inner lips.

It was too much to bear. As her clitoris was sparked

to the brink of a fierce, cock-hungry orgasm she cried out to him. 'Please. Inside me.'

But instead he only moved up and began to suck one by one on her nipples, all the time rubbing the pair with tender, teasing finger and thumb. All her brain was focussed on the wide ache of her entrance. She felt like nothing more than a bottomless seam to be filled; a tormented abyss that writhed in a pain that only a hard, fast fucking could cure. Nothing else mattered, not the wantonness of her movements, the loudness of her cries or the eager eyes of those who were slowly gaining confidence to crowd around the wagon and watch this spectacle as hungrily as they had watched Hengest mount his mare.

His mouth moved up over her throat, licking her cheeks and eyelids while she twisted her face beneath his dog mask, feeling a wild pleasure when his fat tongue rammed hard into her open mouth. Pulling his tongue into her mouth, she moaned from deep within, shuffling her pelvis higher and higher towards his swinging cock. When she felt it brush against her gaping entrance it felt huge and thick, as hard as an iron rod that would hurt and batter her. Now she could see faces around her as the watchers peered to see him enter her, their eyes shining and their expressions fixed with fascination.

Glancing down, she reached to caress his gorgeously inflexible penis. She stroked it down to the thick pelt at the base where her fingers could not encircle the root. Her hand explored all the vein-studded length until she cradled the low-swinging testicles that promised to release their seed inside her. She had never seen his organ so swollen with blood and lust. It stood as stiff as a hammer, giving off a feverish heat. It seemed to her to be a source of magical wonders, a potent fetish that would explode inside her with miraculous force.

Almost casually, he laid it on her entrance, pressing like a heavy weight on her stretched and exposed sex. She started to moan, writhing her naked hips, pushing down on it, wanting it in her. Around them, faces were peering inquisitively, eager to see the long fat rod disappear inside the small, puckered opening. The channel was as wet as a river now, and the heaviness of his member pressed into that fleshy course, pushing deliciously against her maddened clit.

Very gradually, his cock slipped between her straining lips. Pushing forward his hips, he forced the widened tip inside the entrance, stretching her flesh, making her back arch as she screamed.

'Oh God,' she cried. 'Go on. Oh, more.'

He sank inside her another inch and again she screamed as it scorched her sex-hungry body. As she twisted beneath him, she felt hands reach down and restrain her ankles and legs. They drifted over her body; across her trembling belly and taut, straining thighs. Fingers reached and cupped her sensitive breasts, tweaking the hard nipples cruelly.

Above her, Michael skewered another length inside her, making her muscles squeeze gratefully around it. She could feel her own wetness spilling outwards on to her thighs, dripping in hot runnels down between the cheeks of her backside. She was oozing with need. All she wanted was for him to let go and really drive inside her.

Still she was aware of hands digging into her body and the crowd about the wagon leering and reaching. Their eyes were glassy and round at the sight of their harvest maiden crying out as their leader tormented her with his wonderfully long and potent prick.

Above her, the face of the dog stared impassively as

he swung his cock deeper. More and more hands seemed to swarm across her body, clawing and kneading it, making every nerve ending burn with excitement. Panting, she closed her eyes. He was thrusting deeper and deeper into her lust-tightened passage. Jerking convulsively, she felt the smouldering shaft run up towards her abdomen like a battering ram, repeatedly hammering her with shattering, mind-searing blows. It was filling her every inch as she lifted her wide-stretched thighs, eager to feel it all the way from the swollen glans to that thickly upright base.

When it stopped, she cried out to the sky. With a massive jolt, his pelvis ground against her crotch, his swinging, spunk-heavy balls smacking into her. It was embedded up to the hilt, standing as hard as a pole inside her stretched entrance as her muscles deliciously quivered around it.

All around her, eyes were fixed on her magnificently receptive body. Closing her eyes, she felt her mind float away in a sensually maddened delirium. The roving fingers moving across her soft flesh felt like thousands of tiny animals rubbing and sucking her towards a state of massive release. Inside her, the cock felt like a gigantic python slumbering and quivering all the way from her cramped entrance to the sensitive pit of her stomach.

'Oh yes,' she moaned, as something slithered round her thrashing calf to the roundness of her thigh. It was long and smooth, far cooler than the feverish hands that grasped her wrists and ankles. As it moved like an unwinding coil up the firmness of her leg, she began to panic. In her mind's eye she could see it now – a smooth-scaled, flexible viper that quested for her sex with its constantly flickering tongue.

It reached the sodden heat of her groin, where the heavy mass of cock opened and stretched her entrance, leaving her wide and vulnerable. With a gasp she felt a little tongue flick out and probe her inner lips. Again it teased, brushing the slippery fur of her cunt, questing for the molten bud of her clitoris. Shrieking with pleasure, she felt the creature reach it. It was tickling it with its gentle tongue, making her buck and rise despite the impalement of the phallus that kept her staked to the edge of the wagon.

'What is it?' she moaned. But no one replied. Another cool slither was trailing up her left leg now, winding in circular coils towards her heated centre. In her confused mind she remembered the pack leader's long and flexible tail that sometimes slunk around the column of her leg like a winding briar. But this was a different sensation. When something else tickled her neck she flung her head from side to side, trying to free herself from a third, undulating intruder.

Then the snake reared its head above her face.

Screaming and writhing she tried to beat it off but her wrists were held secure. She could feel three of the vipers now: one had coiled around the top of her thigh to rest against her clitoris; another had travelled between the cheeks of her spread buttocks; the third was travelling across her throat, its sinuous body moving in pulses down her front.

She became aware that their touch was infinitely sensual. As one tapering snakehead wormed inside her juice-soaked anus, she groaned and sighed. A second still attached itself to her clit, sucking and tickling her most sensitive organ. And the motionless weight of the cock standing stiff and still inside her was maddening too. It was as if, since it stopped fucking her starving pussy, it was swelling; it was forcing the walls of her channel wider and wider apart.

Desperately, she looked to Michael for help. But

Michael was not there, only the fiercely impassive headdress of the pack leader. Wildly, she looked at the others who pawed around her, caressing her naked flesh and restraining her flailing limbs. But all she could see were long, dripping tongues and even longer, ramrod phalluses.

Blinking her eyes, she tried to clear her panic. Even when she told herself these were only hallucinations, it made no difference at all; they felt, looked, tasted and smelled real. She no longer knew what was human or animal, mortal or spectre. The three vipers seemed to pinion her as tightly as any chains. She was powerless beneath an ocean of animal lust; almost every inch of her body was being violated. And yet, she thought suddenly, wasn't this what she had wanted? What she had begged for and waited for? Going all the way; going way off-limits?

Beneath her spread buttock cheeks she felt the viper's head pulse inside her. It was climbing inside her passage now, making her gasp. Another was sliding across her breast, its tiny tongue flicking the hot beads of her nipples. It was too much to bear. Suddenly her hand was grabbed and a velvety smooth cock was thrust inside it. As she frantically squeezed it, her hand grew quickly wet as a gush of come spilled over it. Yet the next moment another replaced it, just as hard and urgent, just as ready to come at the touch of her magical hand. All around her were throngs of rampant cocks, jostling to press against her.

She could feel all three vipers now, slithering voluptuously around her. As one wriggled inside the tingling passage at her rear, she started to pant. Although the cock inside her remained stationery, she was growing frantic. Her clit could not bear much more torment, as the little head brushed against it and then

227

withdrew, creating waves of excitement that were damming up deep inside her nerves and bones.

'Please,' she started to beg, 'push inside me.' She was panting hard now. Her body was burning with sexual fire. When the third viper slithered from her breast up her throat to her face, she no longer thrashed against it. It was cool and sensual. It was seeking her deepest pleasure. When its forked little tongue met her own parched lips she opened them wide to welcome it.

Like a mouth-hungry cock, the viper thrust inside her lips. Moving in waves, it pressed over her tongue, pushing back towards her throat. Any disgust was overridden by lust now. Her mouth was being fucked just as coolly and expertly as her burning back passage. Letting her mouth fall slackly open she welcomed the creature, enjoying the sense of fullness in her mouth, anus and cunt.

Her only frustration was that he was not fucking her. The huge cock still stood stiff as a poleaxe inside her. She could not bear it any longer. Her body seemed to rise and heave with fiery pleasure. The little viper nesting in her pussy lips opened its jaws and gripped on her tiny bead of pleasure.

'Now, now,' she tried to whimper to the pack leader's impassive mask, though her mouth was pleasurably full and choked. And she heard the surrounding watchers murmur and sigh as she begged him. Yet he continued to stand as impassive as a statue.

At last she struggled to bear down on him, working her greedy pelvis. Like a piston, she pulled back and then bore down again, gasping as she felt the friction of her own delicious thrusting. At last, it seemed, the spectators understood too. Instead of holding her tight, they aided her, dragging her upwards to the apex of her withdrawal and then pulling her down roughly to smack down on his long shaft. She no longer knew what were fingers, cocks or even stranger creatures writhing across her abandoned body. Squirming up and down on the impassive cock she enjoyed its rod-like length, gyrating her hips in complete abandonment.

In her anus and mouth the strange dream-snakes danced too, throbbing in unison as she fucked. At her clit too, the nibbling of the viper's jaws made her burn in awesome waves of fire. All around her now were sighs and moans as the watchers pushed and pulled cocks around her, stroking them over her and pressing them into her slapping buttocks and breasts and panting face. She was a prisoner of them, trapped in a cage of phalluses, a captive of a frenzy to touch and suck and fuck her.

She was groaning into the night air now, her mouth stretched and pleasured by the mysterious kiss of the viper. Sliding up and down the stiff pole of the pack leader's cock, she suddenly felt it quiver and twitch. Joyfully, she thrust down on to it to receive every drop of that precious come. The impassive pack leader finally let out a groan of release. She could feel spurt after hot spurt of spunk gushing into her. At the same time, the serpent probing her rear entrance quivered exquisitely, as did the delicate little tongue of its mate that nipped at her clitoris.

Her climax seemed to lift her whole body up to the stars. Shooting spasms of delight burst from her cunt to the very ends of her toes. Her neck flung back and her spine arched convulsively. On and on, as the pack leader emptied every drop of his come into her, she climaxed ecstatically. She could also feel jets of warm spunk raining on to her belly, her legs, her face. After all her days of frustration, the sense of release was awesome. She could hear a high-pitched sound that rang through the night like a wailing siren. Then she realised it was coming from her own convulsing throat.

Gradually, her pulses slowed. But still every hair on her body stood on end. She could feel the sticky trail of his come dripping between her legs. She felt joyful and wild. Eagerly, she cried out again, howling up into the night. Then, with a flick of her tail, she clambered up on to the edge of the wagon and surveyed her beautiful, baying pack.

At last it had happened. The cat spirit had been woken inside her. Crying up to the moon she bared her sharp teeth and smelled the promise of the night. Her cat senses were alive to every sight around her and every scent carried on the warm air. Her human body had finally transformed. Whisking her tail high into the air, she began to purr.

Chapter Twelve

*L*ifting herself up on to her hindlegs, she raised her front paws and howled ecstatically. All of the pack was around her; jowls open, eyes gleaming excitedly. Jostling and yelping, they scrabbled with jagged claws at the edge of the wagon, begging her in a strange, instinctive language to come down and join them. With an airy leap, she joined their mass of hot, furry bodies, revelling in their fleshy scents and welcoming licks. It felt wonderful to lose herself in their swirling mass. They were nothing but a frenzy of hot, furry instincts, nuzzling and nipping and sniffing as they played in the corn-dusty darkness.

The pack leader stood a little aloof, surveying the mass of cavorting creatures. When he growled, they slowed and turned to him, something in the guttural command from his throat dragging back their attention. He had leaped up on to the wagon now; his dark silhouette was fierce against the moon. When his eyes flashed over towards her, they shone a vivid, unearthly green.

He was calling them with a cry that made her shiver

to the core of her graceful bones. His noble tones rose in the breeze, promising a reward both strange and delicious down in the forest. As one, they began to cry back to him, raising their ears and lifting their muzzles. Then, with a baying cry that split the night, he leaped down into their midst and they followed him. He was tearing off across the field with his pack pelting on behind.

It was a joy to run free. Her hindlegs powered her onwards, shooting her forwards as fast as a coursing hare. The warm breeze seemed slower than her hurtling body; she could barely feel the dry ground speeding beneath the pads of her feet. All around, the rest of the pack yelped and circled, jumped and howled.

When they reached the gate, the pack leader drew them on, not up the lane but over the sun-warm walls, across the meadows and under the fence. Human ways were not their ways now. Like a dark army they sped down towards the waving fronds of the forest, startling any night creatures that stood in their whirlwind path.

Jo felt as if she were flying, over walls and streams, under bushes and branches. Never did her human body give her such a sense of freedom. Her agile feet always found their balance and her magical senses relayed information to her limbs as fast as the twitch of a whisker. When they all flooded under the creaking boughs of the forest fringe, her small heart pounded with anticipation. The trees smelled of fluttering moths and lumbering, snuffling woodland creatures. But there was another underlying scent mingled with the warm aromas of rotted bark and overripe berries: the hot trail of the stalking creature whose musky odour made her pink nostrils dilate and tingle.

They were led to a clearing where the moon shone down on the mossy grass. Turning quickly, the pack leader halted, his long tongue dripping from his jowls. Panting, they clung around him, brushing against his long, shaggy pelt, questing with hot noses against each other's snouts and genitals. Then suddenly, it seemed to her, they all drew back.

She was in the centre of their circle, surrounded by dozens of green and amber eyes. Their warm breath reached her twitching nose, smelling of body heat and rising pulses. The pack leader was grinning with drooling lips, his black gums displayed in a seeming smile of lechery. Quivering on all her four legs, she began to back away slowly until, whipping round, she found that an unbroken ring of ravenous creatures surrounded her.

It was the pack leader who moved to her first. On long, elegant legs he walked daintily towards her and licked the tip of her nose gently. From somewhere in the dim recesses of her brain she remembered him from another time. He had communicated with her then, had told her that he would not desert her. Whimpering gently, she let him nuzzle her pointed chin and the sensitive scent glands within her cheeks. He felt good and strong, with a pungent, doggy smell. When he wound round to her middle, she started. His rough tongue was oddly abrasive as he explored her underside. He was nuzzling her softly quivering belly, his cold nose stroking her fur. Involuntarily, she felt a row of little pink nipples rise erectly. But she was reluctant to be taken like this, in the centre of a ring of onlookers. Nervously, she shook him away.

With a low growl he approached her again, winding round to her rear and questing into the moist little entrance beneath her tail. With an angry yowl, she shook her rump and tried to pull away. But his growl rose again. He nipped her tail with his teeth – not hurting anything but her pride.

She was horribly aware of the ring of glowing, unblinking eyes now. A raw scent rose from open jowls and a faint, steady panting could be heard. When the pack leader made another approach to her rear and pushed his face hard against her, thrusting his tongue deep against her soft, moist genitals, she meowed sharply. Yet, despite her protests, she could feel her tail rising and waving in a circular motion in the air, subliminally drawing attention to her deliciously scented entrance. But when she felt his heavy paws rise on her back, she struggled out of his clutch. She twisted round and batted him with sharp, unsheathed claws.

With an impatient bark deep from his chest, the pack leader froze behind her. Catching her breath, she tried to circle round so they could stand face to face. But with a commanding blow to her shoulder, he hooked one sharp set of claws hard into her fur. Yelling with pain, she began to struggle. But her efforts only resulted in a second stabbing blow to her other shoulder. His weight was above her now and although she struggled further, this only hurt her more. Then, very gently, he leaned over her and pulled the loose skin at the nape of her neck into his jaws. It was a quieting movement – the action of a fond parent dealing with a mischievous kitten. It stilled her; her muscles involuntarily relaxed. She was not able to override the instinctive mechanism; it was impossible to fight back.

He was hauling himself over her, and she could not resist it. Her body began to tremble as she felt his rough, furry underside drag heavily over her back. Although she could not move away, she was nevertheless beginning to respond to him. When the hot tip of

234

his cock brushed between her hindlegs she cried out, feeling it seesawing rapidly into the air. The grip on her neck tightened. His claws reached around her, imprisoning her round underbelly.

Again his erect member jabbed into her rear – too high this time, at the base of her tail. With an impatient snarl, he steadied his hindlegs and yanked her impatiently towards him. This time the red-hot tip found her tight little hole. With a yelp of pleasure he shot it home, squeezing it unmercifully into the constricted little gap.

Unable to stay silent, she opened her jaws with a long, ululating cry. Glancing around, she could see that the spectacle excited the ring of creatures. Her unearthly cries made them lift their tails and whimper. A few of the larger dogs were creeping forward now, trying not to catch her eye. Clearly the sight and scent of her being taken like this was too much to resist.

The pack leader's cock was heavily swollen as he tried to enter her. The jabbing motion was not enough to get more than the stumpy end inside her. Again he shifted his position, rising above her so she felt completely smothered by the arc of his belly and strong legs. Now he was angled deeply and with the next thrust of his rear she felt it slide further inside her, scorching her insides as it beat into her tight channel.

He started to hump hard and fast, pistoning in deeper and deeper until only the automatic locking of her legs kept her upright. His furry body was grinding into her, sending piercing sensations of pleasure deeper and deeper through her slender frame. Faster and faster it plunged, edging its animal bulk through the narrow entrance. As he danced on his hindlegs to get the best purchase, his thrusting reached a phenomenal speed. It felt like bliss; she was unable to follow what he was doing to her, she could only feel a massive wave of searing pressure driving up and up her sensitive channel.

Glancing blearily up from the ground, she saw that a few of the larger, more dominant animals had crept up close. Like a hunting game, they stalked her only when her eyes looked elsewhere. Now they stood as still as statues, their eyes glowing steadily.

Shivering with passion, she revelled in the situation. The nearest of her spectators, a smooth-coated black dog, was transfixed by her. As he sat rigidly on the ground, she could see the rubbery length of his member twitching against the grass. The sight flooded her channel with lubricating juices. In response, she felt the pack leader pound even harder into her, pushing her forwards across the grass. The claws of his forelegs rasped against her stomach as he locked his full, pounding length into her. When she felt his cock swell inside her, she dropped her head forwards nearly to the ground, so faint did the excitement make her. Yet still it rasped up and down, bringing her to a first, screaming and fur-raising orgasm.

Weakened, she tried to rise from her crushed position below his massive, pounding body. Looking up, she saw the black dog's wide-jawed leer just a hair's breadth away from her. She could smell his open jowls and see the cruel gleam of his teeth. Closer too was a pair of wild-looking creatures who watched her with unblinking, amber-lit eyes. As the pack leader worked his massive, knot-swollen cock inside her, they approached her, questing with hot noses, trying unsuccessfully to hump against her face and sides. The scents and silhouettes of their erect cocks drove her frantic. Again and again she let out a high-pitched, caterwauling shriek as she came. When she felt a hot jet of juice explode inside her, she writhed in ecstasy,

236

shaking her rear end and forcing it back on to his delicious shaft.

The pack leader panted above her for only a few moments before sliding down, leaving a trail of viscous fluid. But before she could twist round to clean herself, the black dog had mounted her, his forelegs sliding around her to lock beneath her belly. Despite her wails, he poked against her rear, quickly finding the wet opening and sliding inside.

It was impossible to withstand this second, animal pounding. After barely a few strokes she arched her rump with pleasure, feeling a new wave of burning fire flowing from his frenzied rod. The black dog's frustration seemed even more tightly pent; he panted above her, saliva dripping on her neck. Soon his bulge also burst, showering her in heated, slippery come.

Reeling, she staggered up to walk away. Her mind was in a fever; a series of orgasms had burnt all coherent thought from her brain. But a moment later, the next creature tugged at her neck. And then the next. Each time she took another mate, her body moved from sensations of feeble exhaustion to excruciating wantonness. Each pummelling cock awoke within her a new awareness of the truth of the situation – that she was being used like the animal she truly was. Deep within her flesh, she loved it. Her mind was nothing but heat and sensation, her flooded channel nothing but a quivering, squeezing receptacle. No matter how much she tried to retain some dignity, it took only a few eager thrusts from yet another mate for her to buck and shiver beneath the next onslaught, wailing with delight as she was ruthlessly serviced again and again.

She was crouching limply on the ground. Her heart still pounded and every cell in her body tingled warmly. From the ill-used hole at the junction of her legs, spine-tingling spasms continued to work their way through her body, driving all coherent thought from her brain.

When he approached her again, she raised her rump slavishly. If there was a chance of just one more cock, she wanted it. Her appetite was insatiable. She had no idea how many matings she had endured, but still her body pumped with languorous desire. Her brain had reached a steamy plateau; she was in a dreamlike state – drowsy and stupid with sex.

The pack leader dropped his head and gave her streaming orifice a cursory lick clean. Her whole body was wet and pulpy. When he tried to nudge her to her feet, she collapsed down on to her knees. It was no use – the channels of her nerves had been massively, brutally overloaded.

Grazing the top of her head with his sharp teeth, he grabbed the scruff of her neck again and lifted her. Curling below his wide jaws she hung foetally, like a newborn kitten as he carried her through the forest. For a long time she dozed, swinging lazily from his teeth. Only slowly, as the fresh air worked over her, did she begin to rouse. She became aware that he was carrying her into a dark and tangled part of the forest. Blinking her eyes, she began to wonder why she had never seen this area before.

He finally stopped by a small, round lake that gleamed phosphorescently in the moonlight. Sniffing and listening, she let herself be set down on the grass. She had no idea where she was. The trees were tall and matted with creepers, rising far up into the twinkling sky. Tottering forward on shaky legs, she began to explore her new surroundings. The night had grown bitterly cold. Even as she crept towards the water's edge, she felt her sense of smell vanishing.

Such a pall of cold surrounded the water that a thin veil of white mist rose over the tall grasses. All she could smell was chill vapour. Looking to the pack leader for reassurance, he nodded her onwards.

Yet all her senses told her something was wrong.

Instead of the reassuring rustle of woodland creatures, she could hear only the papery slither of vipers crawling in the undergrowth. No birds rustled in the treetops. No lazy fish hunted through the shallows; only night-hunting toads broke the surface of the lake. And, looking above her, the cheery nodding moon had disappeared.

With a start, she realised that the glowing patterns of stars that she used to guide her path across country were not in their rightful places. Crinkling her nose anxiously, she began to back slowly away from the chill edges of the water. If even the nightlights in the sky were crooked then she definitely needed to get back home to safety. She felt as if the very earth beneath her feet moved unsteadily. When she whirled round, a thick cloud of mist lay all about her. It was thick and choking, freezing and blinding.

She was entirely alone.

Calling out to him, she shrieked high and loud into the night. Sniffing the frozen air, she waited alertly for him to rescue her. Long moments passed. There was no sound, save the rustle of the tall grasses where unseen vipers kept their nests. Puzzled, she circled around and around, crying out quietly but clearly. There was neither sight nor sound of him. Then she stopped crying out. The sound of her thin little voice reverberated through the strange landscape in an eerie way that she hated. It seemed to announce to anyone out there, anyone or anything, that she was alone and unprotected.

Suddenly the awfulness of her situation hit her: she

was lost; she did not even know from which direction she had travelled. Fear cleared her brain and a few connections reawakened.

She had strayed off the road. This was the one thing she had promised herself she would never do. Through sheer stupidity and sexual heat she had broken her promise to herself.

Yet, at the same time, she felt betrayed. He had brought her here. This was a secret place that he knew, but she did not. Behind the indulgences of the night was some other, secret plan that he was silently hatching. It made her blood rise hot to her chilly fur. This was no casual accident. She had been carried here and abandoned.

She cried out to him one last time. It was a feeble, plaintive cry. If any creature with a heart had heard it then, surely, it would have been answered.

Only cold, unbroken silence replied.

Stifling the desire to cry with terror, she stood very still, her breath rising in steamy clouds from her open jaw. She had no idea what to do, or where to go. Throughout most of their journey here she had kept her eyes sleepily closed. All her animal resources were confounded in this place; she could not find a scent or follow her route by the lights in the sky.

Warily, she moved forward towards the only source of light. It was the faintly gleaming lake; the lake that glowed like no other water she had ever seen. With her whiskers twitching and her ears flat back against her skull, she pressed low to the ground, crouching her belly down against the long grasses, feeling the soil grow marshy and soft beneath her paws. For a few moments the white mist obscured her way ahead. Then suddenly it shifted and she found herself standing right at the water's edge. Ahead of her, shimmering in the pool was her own, wide-eyed reflection. The

240

shock of her appearance – rag-furred and shivering – made her cry out again, involuntarily.

A stone rattled behind her.

Wheeling round rapidly, she turned to face him. But a wall of solid mist blocked her view. Panting, she waited. There was no further movement. When the silence had lengthened to more than a score of rapid heartbeats, she convinced herself that nothing was there. Or that maybe a woodland creature – a mouse or a vole – had rattled against a rock.

Looking back into the water, she found herself drawn to the deep and mysterious reflections and images it held. The tall, thickly clad trees crowded the edges of the lake. Glimmering stars danced like strangers. And there – deep at the heart of the limpid waters – stood two long, shining shapes deep beneath the surface. Edging forward on her toes, she peered out to the centre. It was almost as if, she puzzled, two headstones or monoliths had been sunk far below the lake's surface.

Abruptly, she recognised the twin pillars. It was too dark and murky to read the inscriptions, but she knew them. She had rubbed herself against them; they were covered in runic script and images of man and beast.

Yet, it was not possible. That she should find herself in this upside-down, fantastical landscape was one thing, but to see the Fenris Gate? It was so crazy she wanted to bury her sore head in her paws and slump in misery down into the marshy ground. Yet that was what she could see. Illuminated by the lake's weird phosphorescence, the ancient stone pillars were those she had seen so often at the entrance to the farm. Somehow, she knew she was seeing them in their pure, magical form. They were indeed a gate to another, stranger land of mist and freezing cold. The magic of the night had awoken them. And somehow, she knew, she was trapped on the wrong side of that gate. He had brought her here and abandoned her. She had no idea how to find the path back to her real life.

The grasses behind her rustled, as if being parted. She watched her reflection start with surprise, her jaw falling open slackly. No longer did she dare to look round; she was frozen with terror.

Yet still a hopeful part of her believed it was him. That he had been searching for her. That he loved her and, though he had lost her, he had searched for her and found her. It had all been an unfortunate accident. She had betrayed him with these cold, disloyal thoughts.

Closer now, she heard the grasses bend and crack. Her heart galloped fit to burst. But still she could not turn the fibres of her neck. Her reflection was a statue, paralysed by the reflexes that strike the hunted listening to the hunter.

When she heard the pant of his breath, she knew. Her animal instincts were right; her human optimism was wrong. He had not returned for her. The creature behind her was something different, something wilder and way beyond the normal limits.

In a paroxysm of fright, she waited for him to find her. Not daring to move, she wondered if he might, by some fateful chance, not find her. After all, the mist was thick and the night dark. Cowering down by the water's edge, she made herself as small as she was able. Trying not to breathe, she waited. Her eyes were open and blindly staring into the lake.

As she stared into the water, his reflection appeared behind her. Huge, furry jowls swung above her, questing for his prey. Eyes that burned fiery, laser-red, bored into the darkness. His pointed tongue dripped from his mouth as he panted rhythmically like an engine.

The shock transfixed her. Every strand of fur on her body stood erect; her spine arched and lifted; her tail shot up like a bristling brush. Unable to stop herself, a shriek of terror tore out of her throat. It seemed to split the sky; it was an unearthly cry for help and mercy.

It was the creature of the forest – and yet, he too was changed. Larger and more fearsome, he towered over her, looking more like a demon than a warm-blooded creature.

Suddenly, her limbs unlocked. Fear goaded her limbs and she made a sudden lightening dash to the left, her four limbs galloping at full pelt.

But barely had she travelled for a few lung-bursting seconds before she was yanked back. Her tail was nearly pulled out from its root. He held it tight and was pulling her back towards him. Breathless with fear, she felt herself being hauled in like a fish on a line. Digging her claws into the ground, she shrieked and tried to pull away, but in seconds she was dragged back to the water's edge. She felt like a tiny mouse being tortured by a cruelly playful cat.

Still not daring to look at the creature with her naked eyes, she glimpsed him in the lurid surface of the water. Again, it made her stomach lurch with fear. She realised that she had never truly seen him before; he had only been a hint and a fantasy of something lurking in the undergrowth, watching her. Her imagination had filled in the void with erotic fancies. The reality of his terrible presence was quite different. He was not a half-tame noble savage.

He was a monster.

When she struggled, he swiped her with his claw. Talons like metal meathooks ravaged her shoulder.

Cowering beneath him, she huddled and waited. All she could hope for was that if he ripped open her throat it would be fast and efficient. Waiting for a quick and savage end, she sunk her head down between her paws. Above her, she could hear the deep bass rumble of his growl rolling in his barrel chest. The sound terrified her, with its threat of brutality and anger.

To her even greater horror, the creature began to wail. It was a weird, supernatural cry that started as a whimper and rose to an ear-shattering howl. Her ears flattened back against her skull as she closed her eyes, trying to blot out the horrible sound. He began to flail around, pushing her downwards, trapping her beneath the arch of his matted, scratchy pelt. Feeling horribly imprisoned, she began to edge forward on her crouching legs. But with another swipe of his claws, he held her firm beneath his belly.

A sensation of intense cold shot through her nether regions. Wriggling, she hissed loudly. But with an angry snarl, he shifted further over her. Again the strange feeling pierced her rear end. It was so cold that it almost burned her, drawing all sensations of warmth out of her flesh. He was rocking over her now and although half-crazy with terror, she began to wonder what it was he was trying to do.

Then she identified the icy coldness washing over her as something unbelievable. His genitals were inefficiently humping against her sodden rump. Rather than hot and blood bursting, his cock was preternaturally cold.

Hissing with fright, she struggled to break free. But his curled claws dug deep into her bony back and his sheer weight pinioned her to the ground. Wriggling and growling, she pushed downwards, bracing her feet, trying to create a space beneath him from which she could slither out and escape.

His response was to trap her tightly beneath his outstretched jaw. She could smell the icy rankness of his hairy muzzle. He seemed to be entirely covering her, imprisoning her beneath the claustrophobic pinion of his body. This time, when she felt the icy plunge of his genitals against her rump, she only snuffled weakly. He was just too powerful to battle with. Yet the size of him terrified her. If he was going to try to mate with her, she was sure he would simply rip her apart.

As he humped ineffectually against her, she began to feel the proportions of his phallus. It was hardening, though it was still cold against her fur. The blunt end chiselled between her back legs like a frozen log, trying to get a purchase within her body. Faintly, she hoped he might mistake the warm gap between her hindlegs for her entrance. After all, there was no possibility of his gaining proper entry. His cock was just as hugely in proportion to his body as her entrance was small inside her puny frame.

With a sideways tussle of his jaw, he began to howl again. His frustration was mounting as he thundered against her. Now his rump was going crazy, trying to find an entry for the massive, cold-blooded organ. She had completely crumpled now, beneath him, with her front buried close to the ground. As he thrust against her, the power was such that if his claws had not grabbed her, she would have been catapulted forward. As he continued to be thwarted, he began to yelp like an oversized puppy, high-pitched barks deafening her as he lifted his long neck to the sky.

In a moment of slow horror, she was aware of an icy pressure breaking between her hindlegs; it was knocking as hard as a hammer against her fur-fringed entrance. The effect was to make her try to arch her back, spitting and hissing as desperation flooded through her veins. Tightening his grip on her shoulders, his response was only to drive harder and faster, questing for her little orifice like a sledgehammer trying to bang its way inside a narrow pipe.

When it hit her, she almost shot out of his grip, so intense was her reaction. Yet still he held her, holding on grimly to her narrow shoulders. Like a slab of ice, the phallus plunged hard and fast against the pulpy wetness of her flesh. It was searing into her body, pushing past muscles and tissue as if she were made of soft dough.

Her body went into shock. A black veil seemed to fall over her eyes as her heart struggled to keep beating. The pain was so intense that momentarily all the nerves in her body seemed to collapse and numb. Her head nodded like a broken toy.

His cock ravaged the narrow hole. He appeared blind and deaf to any damage he was doing to her soft little body. With cold instinct, he worked the blunt bulk of his cock-end tight inside the vice of her little cunt, whining with pleasure as inch after solid inch rammed into hot, spongy flesh.

Her fright-widened eyes looked around wildly. Then she saw him, at the far side of the lake, standing as still as a sentinel. It was the pack leader, watching her as she was brutally taken.

Feeling faint with pain, she opened her slack jaws to cry out. But she could find no breath to even call to him. Her vision grew weak. She was no longer sure whether her eyes deceived her. Blinking, she tried to muster her strength. Yes – he was there, watching her coolly, standing impervious as she suffered.

'Michael!' She did not recognise the sound she made, but it came out of her jaws of its own volition.

246

Across the water, she saw him turn his head indecisively and then remain motionless. He had heard her, but refused her call. Her betrayal was truly complete.

Inside her, the massive cock-tip was grinding into her heat, working into the already stretched and spunk-slippery channel. Yet the size was unbearably too great. Above her, she could hear his yelps of protest as less than a third of his burgeoning rod managed to grind inside her. She was being smothered beneath the pounding onslaught of the creature. Any moment now, she imagined she would simply be torn asunder. It was impossible to imagine how he had even got the tip of his cock inside her. Writhing and crying, she began to call out to the pack leader across the water. Again she called out in a strange tongue.

'Michael! Help me.'

He was her only lifeline. Her cries were an unintelligible caterwauling of fear and desperation. But despite her pitiful cries, he only stared at her, transfixed by the monstrous hellhound pounding across her back.

The creature was clinging to her like a drowning man. She could feel icy saliva dripping from his open, panting jaws on to her head. He was howling with intermittent pleasure and frustration. As if to punish her further, he shifted his weight, bearing down from his massive hindlegs. He was lashing unmercifully at her slippery channel. The violence of his movements made her wonder if she was dying. Slowly – very slowly – he worked a further length inside her. The previous matings with the pack had softened and lubricated the deeper recesses of her passage. Now his frenzied jabs almost split her as he ground further and further up her fear-tightened pussy.

Her body slumped with shock and exhaustion. Yet

247

within her a small spark of passion began to burn. Incredibly, as her head bounced back and forth and her spine was subjected to blow after blow of shuddering weight, a wince of pleasure erupted in her stretched sex. Now almost half of the cold mass of his phallus was travelling like an oversized piston into the splayed softness of her channel. As pleasure built in her nervous system, she began to pant. It was impossible but true. A fiery delight was building up as the grim pain receded. The thunderous bulk of his cock pounded inside her magnificently; stretching and searing her hot recesses with massive, swelling might. Even his chilly coldness excited her. It was like being fucked by ice. It made her shiver and burn, all at once.

It was as if he sensed the change in her response. Her body was releasing hot, viscous juices all over the barrel of his cock. His whines of pleasure reached her flattened ears. He was growing rabid with excitement. Although only half of his member had squeezed inside her, the heat and pleasure to his tip was driving him frantic. Faster and faster his cock sped into her as his hindlegs danced and jerked.

Suddenly, an unbidden cry of abandonment issued out of her throat. This was pure bliss. Closing her eyes, she could just feel the draught as his massive balls swung back and forth behind her. Now she wanted him. Like a sex junkie, her body had wakened and craved the bliss of complete, hard satisfaction. His icy cock was paradise; a searing, jerking ride to rapture.

Although he was tightly wedged into her, her muscles now began to grip and tease him. The lubricious flow of her juices allowed him to jab even faster, pumping her rear like a machine. Soon both were howling wordlessly, gripped together by the swelling of his phallus. Beneath his furry chest, she tossed her head from one side to the other, utterly filled to bursting by the balloon-like swelling. Wave after wave of pleasure lifted her to ecstasy and back. She was lifted off the ground now, by the bulky barrel of his phallus. Her four paws scrabbled the earth, but all she could feel was her squirming channel. All she could think about was how ecstatic it would be to have him massively flood her when his moment of release finally came.

He was responding now to the writhing pressure of her vice-like walls. All her fears dissolved as she ground back against the gigantic length of cock, wanting more and more and more. Screaming, she felt him wedge a further massive plug of flesh inside her. Rocking back with her arched rump, she let him travel as far as he could inside her. His power was monumental. His coldness made her drool open-mouthed with excitement. The rough pelt of his fur and metallic claws only goaded her on, made her want to possess every inch of his icy flesh. Although she was dizzy and exhausted by his rabid pounding, still she knew she was experiencing a transcendent level of pleasure that she had never before known existed.

The creature raised his head and screamed with excitement. His cock was ready to burst inside her, pressing and pulsing with unexploded lust. He could stand no more. The tip had been abraded to the point of eruption. His massive, spunk-crammed balls were so tight that they were churning with arousal.

With an icy blast, a jet of come shot into her scalding hole.

Screaming with anguished delight, she felt her own blissful climax erupt. Ramming her furry little body back on to him, she let herself be bathed in spray after spray of cold, slippery liquid. It froze her genitals, making them jerk with delight. Strange animalistic grunts and gurgles were coming out of her throat. She was on another planet of delight; her body wanted every lewd and luscious drop of him. In febrile rapture, she fucked back on him, ramming his twitching cock to get every last pulse of his load. As she slammed backwards, trying to drive her opening to the root of his softening organ, yet another shot of come sprayed her, making her gasp and reel. She was awash with his viscous seed; as they both tried to fuck on and on, she felt it pour down out of her, dripping coldly between her shuddering hindlegs. Juice and come soaked her fur right down to the flushed pink skin.

Still he tried to bear down on her, fucking mercilessly as she tried to keep up with his mechanical speed and lightening jabs. Drool soaked her head and she could hear him panting raucously above her. He was still in a fucking-frenzy. His excitement only drove her to another, shuddering peak. She felt full of him, dripping with his precious seed, her whole body arching and shaking. Working her rear back on to him, she tried to grasp his deflating prick, greedily milking him for just one last eruption of thrilling spunk.

On and on her orgasm sailed, until the fire in her jerking passage exploded in pain. He was splitting her as he drove on into her. She seemed to be carrying all his massive weight. Though she collapsed forward with her face bouncing in the dirt, still he fucked on. Thankfully, at last his power was ebbing. His cock was slapping loosely inside her. With a final rush of racing jabs, he spewed a last trickle of juice inside her.

It was enough to send her into one last, piercing climax. She was being fucked into the ground. Her entrance was sopping and as soft as butter. The thought of it made her writhe on the earth in spasm after spasm of painful delight.

At last he pulled free. He raised himself on unsteady legs, whimpering like a puppy. Tottering beside her, he quickly gave her flooded opening a courteous, rough-tongued lick.

Then he was gone.

She was hot and blasted; her brain was swimming on tides of come-gushing lust. Spit dripped from her mouth, and her paws and underbelly were thick with dirt. A pool of liquid slowly dripped from her tortured rear.

Battered and satisfied, she drifted out of consciousness into a deep and dreamless sleep.

Chapter Thirteen

She rose like a diver from the murky depths of sleep. Pale daylight glowed behind the yellow curtains. Twisting round, Jo winced as a series of aches and bruises registered painfully on her consciousness. Hazily, she tried to piece together events since she had last lain here in the farmhouse on the eve of the harvest rite. Only fragments of memories swam in her brain and they quickly sank away. That she had transformed into her cat spirit, she was sure. And also that her body had given her pleasure that had built and built until it was almost a torture. There was evidence enough of that, in her stinging sex and tender thighs.

Frowning, she suddenly recollected a moment – when or where, she could not definitely say – when she had cried out for help. She had called out to Michael, that she could remember. He had seen her. The image of his impassive figure burned in her memory. Yet he had not come to her. He had remained motionless, ignoring her cries.

Little trickles of memory seeped back to form a

more coherent stream. Another, earlier moment of fear – when he had abandoned her. He had taken her off the narrow road into the dark tangle of a strange landscape. She had been lost and alone. Thankfully, she looked about herself at the familiar shapes of the room and the twinkle of earthly sunlight.

Twisting round further in the bed, she gazed at Michael as he slept. For the very first time, she discovered within herself a coldness towards him. His handsome face looked unfeeling in repose; without the animating light of his eyes, she sensed a frigid vanity about him. Suddenly everything he had ever said to her seemed intended only to make her carry out his will. He was utterly self-absorbed, utterly consumed by the Fenris obsession. In Bridgit's terms, he clearly did not respect her.

On a sudden impulse, she wanted never to speak to him again.

Sliding carefully out from beneath the sheets, she flinched as the pangs in her limbs became a sharp, unremitting throb. Yet that only fired her onwards. She dreaded waking him now. Once he woke, he would carry on in that same controlling manner of his. She did not want to have to hear him. And she had nothing left to say to him.

Moving to the door, she noticed his wallet lying open on the dresser. She halted and rapidly considered her position. She didn't want to steal from him, but then again, if she was ever to leave Fenris Gate, the only alternative was to wake him up and ask for money. Her conscience was salved by the notion that as soon as she could repay him, she would send the money back. But when she opened his wallet and found roll after roll of big fat notes, she felt less guilty about sliding out a couple of twenties. After all, it was obvious from the massive amount in his wallet that he would never even notice.

Tiptoeing out into the corridor, she crept silently along, looking for the narrow bedroom where she had left her final set of clothes. She even rejected the temptation of a long hot shower for fear of rousing him. Her whole being was intent on getting away. Feeling her way into the dimly lit bedroom, she scrabbled for her clothes and a towel and hurriedly dressed in the shadows.

Once outside, she strode across to the yard. The whole place was deserted, although it was well past dawn. Clearly the harvest celebrations had taken their toll on all of the community. Even the weather had shifted. Low cloud hung overhead, draining the air of summer's warmth. A grey tinge made the low outbuildings and drystone walls look oddly forbidding. No, she decided – she did not want to spend the long winter here. Just the first hint of autumn made her long for bustling, brightly lit streets, cosy pubs and central heating.

At the pump in the yard, she felt far enough away from the inhabited buildings to risk a quick wash.

'My God.'

Her voice sounded shaky. Peeling off her clothes, she gasped when she saw the sources of her pain. Her legs and stomach were savagely scratched and caked in mud. A sheen of flaky, dried fluid smeared most of her body. Purple bruises were beginning to erupt across her skin.

So much for hallucinations.

However much she mistrusted her addled memories, her body truly had been used in the most savage manner. Yet she could not deny that along with the wild brutality of last night's couplings had come a wonderful, blissful sense of satisfaction. Her body was bruised but at peace. Physical wellbeing soaked through every pore.

Jo rubbed away at the black streaks on her stomach and rear. She would go and find Emmi, she decided. Move south and start again. As the cold water spilled over her, the fresh pink skin beneath started to show through, clean and wholesome.

The sense of being watched hit her like a sharp blow.

Slowly raising water-dripping eyes, she reluctantly gazed out into the forest. The pit of her stomach lurched – the terrible thought occurred to her that she might never be free of the creature. Maybe it would come back, again and again. Whatever it was that Michael had freed might be impossible to send back once it had stalked her. Starting to shiver, she hurriedly gathered her clothes, horribly aware that she stood vulnerable and naked, here, at the edge of the forest curtain.

Among the branches, a slight movement caught her eye. Then, staring more carefully, she identified upright ears, a black nose and round, liquid eyes. They belonged to a young female deer. The doe was watching her inquisitively, her nose rising and twitching.

Jo grinned with relief. Standing motionless, her eyes met those of the shy woodland creature.

'Hello,' she whispered. 'Are you lost?'

With a last bat of her long-lashed eyes, the gentle creature rapidly sprang up on her slender legs and crashed back into the undergrowth. As she turned, Jo saw the white rump and tail of a tiny fawn, bouncing like a sprung coil after her.

The branches of dense foliage grew still once more. So, Jo mused, there were not only terrors in the forest. She was glad that her final memory of the place was an innocent one. Nature was not only potent and cruel – it nurtured the frail and gentle too.

This time it was a pleasure to reach Thorsby. Calling into the village shop, Jo broke into the first of her notes to buy a ham roll and a carton of orange juice. The chatter of villagers with the shopkeeper – about the threat of rain and a new baby in the village – seemed quaintly reassuring. But as she waited at the bus stop, Jo found herself still casting anxious glances back in the direction of Fenris. As she had passed through the twin gateposts she had paused briefly, trying one last time to detect a pattern in the carvings and scrawlings in the ancient stone.

The creature was there, she was sure of it – a large, four-footed monster with a curling tail and shaggy mane. The coils of a serpent wound near his feet and Jo wondered if the round shape surrounded by stick-like trees was the strange lake in which she had watched her own startled reflection.

But as her fingertips had trailed across the stone, scratching at the dried whorls of lichen, she had felt again the pressure of watching on her back. This time, when she whirled round towards the billowing trees, there was nothing to see but the quivering dance of heavy branches in the breeze. But she did not want to watch and wait too long. Eagerly, she passed one last time through the ancient boundary of the Fenris Gate.

At last the bus trundled up the lane, halting with whining brakes at the kerb. Clambering on, she threw a few coins in the driver's money tray.

'You can't pay with that,' he said cheerily, picking up a small brown lump. 'That's horrible. I'll get rid of it for you.' He reached across and opened the window of his driver's cab, ready to throw the tiny object out on to the road.

'No, no! Give it back. Please.' Jo held out her cupped palm, pleading. She had just recognised what it was, from the corner of her eye.

'All right, all right. But that's one pound eighty all the way.' He scrabbled together her change. 'So there's your twenty pence.'

Finding a seat, she felt the welcome rattle and grind of worn-out gears as the bus laboured up the lane out of Thorsby. She gripped the little object tightly in her palm.

The cat's tooth was all she had left in this world of her cat spirit – it was her only link with all the strange, mind-blowing experiences of the summer. Stroking it, she pondered why and how she had picked it up; she had intended to leave everything behind at Fenris. It must have been in her pocket all along.

Yet, as the bus accelerated into open country, edging ever closer to cities and crowds and traffic and busy, chaotic modern life – she was glad she clutched that one last token of her animal spirit. For the beautiful, ginger feline that Michael had transformed her into could remain a part of her still. Or maybe there was no cat spirit – only a magnificently wild aspect to her own personality that he discovered and allowed to run free.

It didn't matter, either way. She was no longer the gauche and awkward Jo of the Northford Mission House. Settling back into her seat, she pictured the amazing sights and experiences she was going to find at the end of her journey, where she could live her own life, wild and free. Back in civilisation, she thought, there were ample hunting grounds for a hot-blooded girl like herself. There would be interesting encounters, new sensations, attractive men. Just thinking about it made her feel hot and frisky. If she had been in her other form, she would have lifted her tail high into the air and purred with feline pleasure.

BLACK LACE NEW BOOKS

Published in May

INTENSE BLUE
Lyn Wood
£5.99

When Nan and Megan attend a residential art course as a 40th birthday present to themselves, they are plunged into a claustrophobic world of bizarre events and eccentric characters. There is a strong sexual undercurrent to the place, and it seems that many of the tutors are having affairs with their students – and each other. Nan gets caught up in a mystery she has to solve, but playing amateur detective only leads her into increasingly strange and sexual situations in this sometimes hilarious story of two women on a mission to discover what they really want in their lives.

ISBN 0 352 33496 7

THE NAKED TRUTH
Natasha Rostova
£5.99

Callie feels trapped living among the 'old money' socialites of the Savannah district. Her husband Logan is remote, cold and repressed – even if he is fabulously rich. One day she leaves him. Determined to change her life, she hides out at her sister's place. Meanwhile, Logan has hired a detective and is determined to get his wife back. But she is now treading a path of self-expression and exploring Voodoo. Will he want her back when he finds her? And what will she do when she learns the naked truth about Logan's shady past?

ISBN 0 352 33497 5

Published in June

ANIMAL PASSIONS
Martine Marquand
£5.99

Nineteen-year-old Jo runs away from the strict household where she's been brought up, and is initiated into a New Age pagan cult located in a rural farming community in England. Michael, the charismatic shaman leader, invites Jo to join him in a celebration of unbridled passion. As the summer heat intensifies, preparations are made for the midsummer festival, and Jo is keen to play a central role in the cult's bizarre rites. Will she ever want to return to normal society?

ISBN 0 352 33499 1

IN THE FLESH
Emma Holly
£5.99

Topless dancer Chloe is better at being bad than anyone David Imakita knows. To keep her, this Japanese-American businessman risks everything he owns: his career, his friends, his integrity. But will this unrepentant temptress overturn her wild ways and accept an opportunity to change her life, or will the secrets of her past resurface and destroy them both?

ISBN 0 352 33498 3

NO LADY
Saskia Hope
£5.99

Thirty-year-old Kate walks out of her job, dumps her boyfriend and goes in search of adventure. And she finds it. Held captive in the Pyrenees by a bunch of outlaws involved in smuggling art treasures, she finds the lovemaking is as rough as the landscape. Only a sense of danger can satisfy her ravenous passions, but she also has some plans of her own. A Black Lace special reprint.

ISBN 0 352 32857 6

To be published in July

PRIMAL SKIN
Leona Benkt Rhys
£5.99

Set in the mysterious northern and central Europe of the last Ice Age, *Primal Skin* is the story of a female Neanderthal shaman who is on a quest to find magical talismans for her primal rituals. Her nomadic journey, accompanied by her friends, is fraught with danger, adventure and sexual experimentation. The mood is eerie and full of symbolism, and the book is evocative of the best-selling novel *Clan of the Cave Bear*.

ISBN 0 352 33500 9

A SPORTING CHANCE
Susie Raymond
£5.99

Maggie is an avid supporter of her local ice hockey team, The Trojans, and when her manager mentions he has some spare tickets to their next away game, it doesn't take long to twist him around her little finger. Once at the match she wastes no time in getting intimately associated with the Trojans – especially Troy, their powerfully built star player. But their manager is not impressed with Maggie's antics; he's worried she's distracting them from their game. At first she finds his threats amusing, but then she realises she's being stalked.

ISBN 0 352 33501 7

If you would like a complete list of plot summaries of Black Lace titles, or would like to receive information on other publications available, please send a stamped addressed envelope to:

Black Lace, Thames Wharf Studios,
Rainville Road, London W6 9HA

BLACK LACE BOOKLIST

All books are priced £5.99 unless another price is given.

Black Lace books with a contemporary setting

THE NAME OF AN ANGEL £6.99	Laura Thornton ISBN 0 352 33205 0	☐
BONDED £4.99	Fleur Reynolds ISBN 0 352 33192 5	☐
CONTEST OF WILLS	Louisa Francis ISBN 0 352 33223 9	☐
FEMININE WILES £7.99	Karina Moore ISBN 0 352 33235 2	☐
DARK OBSESSION £7.99	Fredrica Alleyn ISBN 0 352 33281 6	☐
COOKING UP A STORM £7.99	Emma Holly ISBN 0 352 33258 1	☐
THE TOP OF HER GAME	Emma Holly ISBN 0 352 33337 5	☐
LIKE MOTHER, LIKE DAUGHTER	Georgina Brown ISBN 0 352 33422 3	☐
ASKING FOR TROUBLE	Kristina Lloyd ISBN 0 352 33362 6	☐
A DANGEROUS GAME	Lucinda Carrington ISBN 0 352 33432 0	☐
THE TIES THAT BIND	Tesni Morgan ISBN 0 352 33438 X	☐
IN THE DARK	Zoe le Verdier ISBN 0 352 33439 8	☐
BOUND BY CONTRACT	Helena Ravenscroft ISBN 0 352 33447 9	☐
VELVET GLOVE	Emma Holly ISBN 0 352 33448 7	☐
STRIPPED TO THE BONE	Jasmine Stone ISBN 0 352 33463 0	☐
DOCTOR'S ORDERS	Deanna Ashford ISBN 0 352 33453 3	☐
SHAMELESS	Stella Black ISBN 0 352 33485 1	☐

------------- ✂ -------------------------

Please send me the books I have ticked above.

Name   ....

Address   ....

                ....

                ....

           .... Post Code ....

Send to: Cash Sales, Black Lace Books, Thames Wharf Studios, Rainville Road, London W6 9HA.

US customers: for prices and details of how to order books for delivery by mail, call 1-800-805-1083.

Please enclose a cheque or postal order, made payable to **Virgin Publishing Ltd**, to the value of the books you have ordered plus postage and packing costs as follows:

UK and BFPO – £1.00 for the first book, 50p for each subsequent book.

Overseas (including Republic of Ireland) – £2.00 for the first book, £1.00 for each subsequent book.

If you would prefer to pay by VISA, ACCESS/MASTER-CARD, DINERS CLUB, AMEX or SWITCH, please write your card number and expiry date here:

....

Please allow up to 28 days for delivery.

Signature ....

------------- ✂ -------------------------